# DOORS

# DOORS

## KIM PRITEKEL

SAPPHIRE BOOKS

SALINAS, CALIFORNIA

of generative AI training and development of any language learning system.

To the extent that the image on the cover of this book depicts a person or persons, such a person is merely a model and is not intended to portray any character feature in this book.


This and other Sapphire Books titles can be found at
www.sapphirebooks.com

# Check out Kim's other books

*Standalones*
*1049 Club*
*After Shadow*
*Blinded*
*Connection*
*Damaged*
*Shadow Box*
*Swann Song*
*The Gift*
*The Plan*
*Wild*
*Zero Ward*
*Control*
*Unmasked Desire*

*Dance with Me Series*
*Curtain Call*
*Encore Performance*

*The Traveler Series*
*The Traveler - The Hunted*
*The Traveler - The Hunter*

*The Wynter Series*
*Finding Faith*
*Taking Liberty*
*Justice Won*
*Keeping Hope*
*Showing Mercy*

*The Destiny Series*
*She Who Would be King*
*Daughter or Ankou*

# Dedication

To all those who are finding themselves.

# *Prologue*

## Part I

### 1378

To Roishin's surprise, a man was waiting for her when she stepped through the door at the end of the passageway. He was dressed in the blue cloak with gold stitching she'd come to recognize as a symbol of those who belonged to the Order of Ankou. She'd never seen him before. She was also still a bit sketchy on what this order even was.

He wasn't as old as her grandfather, though she wasn't sure anyone was, but he was definitely on the older side. His hair was short, something that shocked Roishin like it had when she first glimpsed Enori's cropped hair, and a sea of gray threatened to take over the light brown it once had been. His deep, chocolate-brown eyes were kind, a roadmap of wrinkles around them and between his brows.

They looked like they were always furrowed, in constant concentration. She was amused by that. His simple outfit beneath the cloak didn't look like much more than baggy brown pants held onto a slender frame with a rope belt and a very simple light brown tunic shirt. The sandals upon his feet made his passage nearly silent as he led her through tunnel after tunnel.

Roishin was all eyes as she followed him. She had her bow and quiver slung over her back and shoulder. All of her worldly possessions outside of that were loaded into her chaneries, the bag pulled tight with a drawstring and hung over her other shoulder.

"What's your name?" she asked him after they'd gone several minutes and tunnels in silence.

"They call me The Mystic."

"Nice to meet you, Mystic," she said. "I'm Roishin."

He stopped suddenly, the girl nearly running right into him. He looked down at her, one bushy eyebrow raised. "I should hope so, or I've been leading the wrong person to Roishin's room."

She blinked up at him a few times. "Valid point, sir." She turned her head and realized they were standing in front of an arched doorway and he was indicating she should enter. A quick glance showed her it was a very small room which seemed to be carved out of the stone, almost like a cave that had a bit more structure and purpose in shape. She looked at him. "Mine?"

With a nod and small bow, he began to walk away.

"Wait, Mystic?" When he turned and looked at her, she said, "There's no door." She indicated the archway, waving her arms through the open space.

He raised that caterpillar of an eyebrow again and said, "Then I guess you'd best be learning how to not be seen, hmm?" With those cryptic words, he shuffled on.

She watched him go, no clue what he meant by that. Stepping inside the space, she looked around. There was a niche in the wall that looked just big enough for either a dead body or a sleeping person to fit in. She hoped it was the latter and not the former. A firepit was tucked into its own little nook at the opposite end of the cave, which was not much larger than a servant's room back home. A small, welcoming fire popped in the firepit, adding light and warmth.

In between the bed niche and firepit was a small table for one carved out of the stone, a solitary stool sitting nearby. There were some hooks jutting out of the wall, Roishin figured to hang something on, such as those marvelous cloaks everybody seemed to wear here. She hoped she got one, too. There were some little nooks in a few places in the stone that would work great to store things like the few books she'd brought.

"Welcome, Roishin."

Turning, she immediately smiled. Enori stood in the open archway. "Hello."

Surprisingly, Roishin felt really shy as she stood there, looking at the woman she'd always seen as her angel. It was no longer about visits or desperate utterances of *I hope to see you soon*. There she was, in the flesh. She was so beautiful, and Roishin was in *her* house now.

"May I?" Enori asked, indicating the space Roishin stood in. At Roishin's nod, Enori entered. She was in her usual white flowing gown, no cloak. Roishin could only hope to be half as beautiful and graceful as Enori was...like Elsie. That thought hurt her heart, so she pushed it away. There would be plenty of time to contemplate that one.

Roishin felt so small next to this woman. Not in size, as they were getting closer to the same height, but everything about Enori radiated power and knowledge and just...*everything*! Her mouth went dry as she tried to swallow, but she suddenly felt lost, so very out of her element.

"It's all right," Enori said, lightly running her fingertips over Roishin's cheek. "I know how you are feeling right now, Roishin, and I promise you, it gets better."

Roishin met her gaze. "Did you have to do this, too?" she asked quietly. "Leave your family?"

"In a matter of speaking." Enori took the bag from Roishin's shoulder, placing it on the table. "When I was ten years old," she began, removing the bow and hanging it on one of the hooks. "I was to be sacrificed." She smiled at the huge eyes the comment earned her.

"By Ankou?" Roishin whispered.

Enori shook her head, chuckling. "Oh no." The smile that brushed her lips was soft, filled with affection. "No, he saved me, actually." She glanced over at Roishin, who had plopped down on the stool, listening intently. "It was a small cult who had come to the shores of Brittany. They worshipped a great evil, Roishin. And, for this god, a sacrifice of virginal blood would give him strength." Her smile was sad as she hung up Roishin's quiver on another hook. She sent Roishin a meaningful look.

"Bahutha," Roishin whispered. At Enori's nod, she rested her chin in her open palm, elbow resting against the tabletop. "He was going to sacrifice you?"

Enori nodded. "In his name, yes. There was a group of us."

"Wow," Roishin breathed. "What happened?"

"A war happened," Enori said quietly. She walked over to where Roishin sat and brushed her cheek with the backs of her fingers. "I'll tell you more later. One thing I need to know is, have you begun your bleed yet?"

Roishin's eyebrows shot up. "A little personal, isn't it?"

Enori smiled, her hand falling away. "Yes, but we must know the moment it does."

"Aye," she said slowly. "I will let you know."

"Good. For now, you must rest."

Roishin glanced around her then up at the woman standing in front of her. "Um…"

Enori smiled, then nodded toward the door. Roishin looked over to see a young woman standing there with an armload of supplies. Roishin blinked. She *knew* the little brunette hadn't been there a second ago. She looked up again at Enori, eyebrows drawn.

With an unreadable smile, Enori touched her cheek again before she headed for the door.

"Wait!" Roishin called out, feeling almost panic at the thought of the only person she knew here leaving. "How will I let you know? How will I find you?"

Standing near the newcomer, Enori glanced at her over her shoulder. "You won't. I will find you." Nodding a greeting at the young woman waiting patiently, she turned out of the room and was gone.

Feeling utterly alone and deflated, Roishin turned her attention to the young woman, who looked to be maybe a year older than herself. She smiled shyly, no clue what she was supposed to do. Invite her in? Tell her to go away? Take the things she held from her and *then* tell her to go away?

"Can I enter?" the young woman finally asked.

"Um, sure." Roishin popped up from the stool, not entirely sure what else to do.

Her hair was longer, like Roishin's, and not near as dark in color, though still a darker brown than that of The Mystic. Her eyes were hazel, and she just looked like an all-around average girl of fourteen or fifteen that Roishin would have seen in one of the villages at home. She immediately went to the niche and carefully unloaded her armful.

"This is where you sleep," she said, glancing over at Roishin. Her words were Gaelic, but her accent was anything but. Roishin couldn't place it, actually. The girl turned back to her task, which seemed to be unrolling a bed pallet in the space. "You will be assigned a duty," she continued. "And you will be expected to arrive for your duty at the appointed time."

Roishin watched her. "Is that what you're doing?" she asked. "Is this part of your duties? And, what's your name?"

"I am Hannah," she said. "And yes." She made sure everything was perfect, then gathered the other items she'd brought and turned to where Roishin once again sat. "Here are the clothes you are to wear."

Roishin looked down at the folded pile in Hannah's arms. She noted they were similar to what The Mystic and Hannah wore, at least in color. Whereas he'd been wearing pants and a shirt, Hannah wore a dress of light brown. It was very simple, nothing ornate about it. Roishin groaned inwardly. Had her fight for the Surshan rule change for women been all for naught?

To her pleasant surprise, when she shook loose the top garment, it was a tunic shirt, much like her earlier host had worn. The second garment was plain brown trousers, just her size. Pleased, she looked up to the young woman, who lay a separate pile on the table.

"Undergarments," Hannah explained.

"Why are we all dressed similarly?" Roishin asked, fingering the other pile with mild curiosity.

"All of us dressed in these colors," Hannah said, tugging lightly at the skirt of her dress, "live here." She indicated the cave-like room around them. "These colors help us to learn."

"Learn? Learn what?"

"How to survive," Hannah said softly, then turned and left the room, Roishin watching her go.

Left alone, she looked down at the garments in her hands then glanced at the bed. Pushing to her feet, she set the clothes down atop the pile of undergarments and walked over to the sleeping niche. She had to admit, it looked cozy and comfortable. Turning back to the table, she looked at everything Hannah had brought.

She had never felt so alone in her entire life. And, it wasn't just a numbers game, as she liked to be physically alone. She felt *alone*. She wasn't entirely sure why she was there, why she'd felt so drawn to even be there. She thought of her parents, now very much regretting not seeing them one last time before she'd left in the early morning hours.

She thought she was being a big girl, off to start her new life all by herself. Now, she'd never felt more like a child in her life. Pursing her lips, she tried desperately to stave off the pricks of unshed emotion that threatened behind her eyes. Blinking rapidly to try to make it go away, she walked over to her bag.

Tugging the drawstring loose, she reached in and removed her daidí's dagger, which to her shock, Fallon had told her to keep. Knowing it had been with Fallon every single day since she'd been a bit younger than Roishin, she hugged the sheathed blade with the rose etched onto it to her chest like the rag doll Laigen had held on to for so many years.

It was something her daidí had touched, something she'd cherished, and something she'd given to her. Maybe it could at least bring her a little comfort.

# *Part II*

Dressed in the garments she'd been given, Roishin followed The Mystic down another dizzying round of corridors. She was trying to memorize the way, find a landmark of any kind to remember, but everything looked the same. Frustrated, she followed along.

She'd changed into the provided sleep shirt and had fallen asleep in the extremely comfortable little sleep niche. To her surprise, when she'd awoken, not only were all of the clothing she'd worn in removed, but more supplies and food had been left for her to find. She'd dressed and had been enjoying the sweetest fruit and most flavorful bacon she'd ever had when The Mystic had shown up to collect her.

"How will I know how to get back to my room?" she asked. "I'm so lost."

"Seek," he said quietly. "And ye shall find."

She stared at his back as they continued. "Do you ever speak in anything but riddles?"

"Should I?"

Roishin rolled her eyes. Finally, after two—or was it three?—more tunnels, they reached a set of double doors that were massive, taking up the entire tunnel. They stepped up to it, Roishin's head craning as she looked up to see just how tall the doors actually were.

"Do you like to read, Roishin?" he asked, one aged hand upon one of the doors.

She met his gaze and nodded, mouth still hanging

open, so impressed with the size. "Aye."

A smile spread across his gnarled features. With a turn of the handle, he pushed one of the doors open, the other swinging slowly open with it. Any thoughts she had about the impressive size of the doors fell flat out of her head when she saw what lay beyond them. It was an absolutely massive chamber, but that wasn't only what held her in awe.

Unending shelves, rows, and aisles of books and scrolls were tucked in everywhere. Catwalks spiderwebbed the space directly overhead to reach the incredibly high shelves. She'd never seen anything like it. In fact, it made her nauseous to even consider taking any of those stairs or ladders, or walking across the catwalks, which were ten, twenty, fifty feet above the ground.

"My. Gods," she whispered. "There aren't even this many books written." She looked over at The Mystic. "Right?"

The look on his face said it all. Clearly that was not correct.

She ventured over to the nearest aisle. What confused her was that there were some books that were colorful. The only books she'd ever seen were brown, as they were bound with leather in one form or other. Eyebrows drawn, she plucked a rather thick tome, pulling if from the shelf and looking at it,

The cover was colorful and slick as she ran her thumb over it. It was smooth, whereas the books she knew and owned had the title and author embossed into the leather. Looking to The Mystic, she asked, "Who's Stephen King? What is he king of?"

"I want you to find a starting point," he said, indicating the immense space around them. "Pick five books to take back to your room," he instructed.

"Choose ones that are in a language you can already read, and the same five in a language you do not."

She looked at him, blinking. "All right." She grinned. "I love to read. I guess I'll do this during my free time."

"Free time?"

"Well, yes," she said, hugging the thick book to her chest, wondering how on earth they'd gotten a fresco onto the cover. "Hannah told me I'd be assigned a duty." She shrugged. "So, what's my duty?"

The Mystic grabbed the book from her arms, then held it back out to her.

She took it back, confused. "So, while poor Hannah is to play maid servant, I get to sit around on my butt and read?" Her eyebrows fell. "That doesn't seem fair, Mystic."

"You and Hannah serve two very different purposes, Roishin," he said sagely. "And you're not reading for amusement." He tapped the book, eyeing her. "You're learning. You read every book in this chamber," he said, indicating the massive collection. "Most will confuse you, as you will read of things you've never heard of, seen, nor know the name for." He held up a gnarled finger. "You must take this task seriously. Am I understood?"

Looking back down at the book in her hands, which was written in French, she nodded. "Aye."

⁂

Roishin gasped, her eyes popping open only to squeeze shut as another round of pain twisted her insides and made her pretty sure they were going to fall out. The squeeze lasted for a moment before it relaxed, but only for a moment.

She cried out, curling her body into the fetal position as she rode out the pain in her lower stomach. As she did, the fire that was burning low in the firepit across the room roared to life briefly with a huge tongue of fire that licked the underside of the nook it was tucked into. Her eyes widened, momentarily distracted from the intense pain in her nether regions.

The distraction didn't last long as she gritted her teeth when another sharp pain sliced through her. Given a moment to breathe, Roishin pushed the covers off her and sat up, looking down at herself. She saw nothing, but when she lifted the skirt of her sleep gown, she saw it.

"Uh-oh…" Looking around her small room, she wasn't entirely sure what to do. She wasn't even positive if what she thought had happened, had happened. She growled as yet another round of pain gripped her, leaving her breathing hard. "Okay, Enori," she gasped. "Not sure if this is it, but—"

She cried out again as a particularly violent pain stabbed at her uterus. The room flared to life once again with another flash of the fire. Roishin glanced over, afraid it would catch her stack of books on the table on fire.

"Okay," she muttered with a gasp. "You really need to stop that." Her eyebrows fell when the flames eased back into the firepit, a more normal glow throwing shadows.

"It's powerful, isn't it?"

Eyes moving from the firepit to the source of the voice, Roishin wasn't sure whether to be relieved or embarrassed. Enori stood just outside the archway of her room. She was wearing one of the blue cloaks, her shoulder resting against the stone.

"Am I dying?" Roishin gasped. At Enori's raised

brow as she indicated the entryway, Roishin nodded.

"In a way." The priestess walked over to where Roishin sat, arms hugging her midsection. "The little girl inside you is bidding you farewell." Enori ran her fingers through dark, damp hair, as the pain had made Roishin break out in a sweat.

"Then forget that" Roishin grunted, eyes squeezing shut with another painful cramp. "This woman stuff can go away."

Enori chuckled softly. "It's worth it, I promise."

"Well," Roishin said, the cramp finally relaxing. She glanced up at the woman. "You wanted to know..." She indicated the blood on her night dress. "Now you know."

Enori smiled and held out her hand. "Come with me."

Roishin took her hand and allowed herself to be helped to her feet. She groaned. "Oh, that was not a wise move." She leaned against the woman who wrapped an arm around her.

"The first one is always the worst," Enori murmured, leaving a kiss on the side of her head. "Waking all that power inside you." She brushed Roishin's hair back from her face as she looked into her eyes. "Come with me," she said again.

Roishin nodded and took a deep breath.    She was going to be strong. Taken by the hand, she was led to the archway of her room and...

...stepped into the woods. She whirled around, seeing the castle guard twenty yards from her. With a gasp of panic, she began to run. He was loading a crossbow, and all she could think to do was try to outrun him while he was distracted, find a place to hide or at least take cover. Her knees were pumping high as she pushed her legs as fast and hard as she could.

Up ahead she saw a felled tree, the trunk massive. More determined than ever, she launched herself into the air to clear it. *CRACK!* She cried out in pain and surprise as white-hot pain spread throughout her entire right side. She cleared the fallen tree but crashed hard on the other side.

Her hand went to her side and came back bloody. She lay there stunned and in pain, but suddenly a vision of Livia came into her head—Livia lying there motionless, a crossbow bolt protruding from her back, much like the one protruding from Roishin's side. Fury, anger, and rage like she'd never known began to rush through her.

Lifting her head, she looked across the woodlands at him. The guard was reloading, and as she watched, she saw a black aura around him. It was like a shadow, just a bit larger than the man himself, hovering. Her anger turned into hatred.

"How dare you," she growled.

Still in pain, she sat up and crawled over to the fallen tree. It was incredibly painful to do so, but she felt as though she were being urged or drawn by someone or something. She looked to the huge trunk of the tree, which she could easily take refuge behind.

No. He needed to pay for what he'd done to Livia.

Pressing her hand to her bleeding side, she looked down at her palm, covered in fresh, shiny blood. Locking her eyes on him, she pressed her hand to the fallen tree, sliding her hand down along its rounded girth. A bloody handprint and smear were left behind.

"You will die today," she whispered as her eyes never left him. "I will crush you with my will." She looked to the fallen tree. "Go!"

As she watched, the massive trunk rocked, first

one way then back the other, only to rock back the first direction. With a groan of heft and flattened earth, limbs and twigs began to snap and crack as the trunk popped up out of the ditch it had been partially buried in due to the immense weight upon its fall.

Roishin's gaze moved up from the tree to the man who paused, eyes widening at what he was seeing. The tree gained speed as it rolled, crushing everything in its path, including smaller trees, and sending rocks spitting out back behind it. Roishin raised her hands as one flew right at her.

Rock batted away, she watched through spread fingers as the trunk gathered more and more speed and headed straight for the guard like a game of ninepins. With a scream, he turned to run, only to run headlong into a tree that was suddenly behind him, its roots visible as it literally seemed to have sidestepped into his path.

He fell flat on his back on the forest floor. He didn't even get another scream in when the trunk plowed over him, stopping as abruptly as it had begun moving. The sudden silence was near deafening.

Slowly getting to her feet, Roishin stared at the spot where the fallen tree had been, now nothing more than a deep divot in the forest floor. Rocks and critters were revealed where they had once taken shelter. Her wide, stunned gaze went to the tree that still stood when she heard a loud crack. Slowly, as if in a dream, the tree, no longer anchored by its roots, fell atop the felled trunk with a massive crash and shake of branches and leaves that rained down upon the forest floor.

She felt nauseous, and once again she saw Livia's body lying there in her mind. The tears began…

…hot and heavy. She buried her face in her hands

when she felt arms begin      to wrap around her. She pushed Enori away, glaring at her. "Why did you do that?" she demanded through her tears. "Why did you take me back there?"

Infinite patience and understanding in her cerulean gaze, Enori gave Roishin her space. "We had to see what you are capable of, Roishin," she said softly.

"By taking me back to the worst day of my life?" Roishin turned away from the priestess, a hand coming up to cover her mouth. The tears wouldn't stop, the trauma of that day—and then what she'd just done—hitting her squarely in the soul.

She cried for the loss of Livia, she cried for the loss of the life she knew back in Sursha. She cried for missing her parents, and she cried for missing Elsie. She cried at the loss of herself. She didn't try to fight it as strong arms once again went around her. Instead, she leaned into the only friend she had right now.

Enori held her tightly, murmuring soft words of comfort into her hair. "I know this is hard, but you are more powerful than you can even dream right now, Roishin." She urged Roishin to rest her head down on her shoulder. "Your powers are brought on by high emotion, pain, fear, all of it." She eased out of the hug just enough to look into Roishin's tear-streaked face. "I had to put you back into a situation where emotions were high." She used her hand to push some hair back from Roishin's face. "To see your raw power and your instincts to use it."

Using the sleeve of her sleep dress, Roishin dried her cheeks, even as tears silently continued to fall. "Why? I don't know how I did that."

Enori smiled. "Yes, which is why it is still raw." She tucked some long, dark strands behind an ear. "When it is time, I know what you will need to be trained on."

Roishin looked at her. "When it's time? Isn't that time now?"

Enori smiled. "Come," she said. "Let us get you a fresh sleeping gown and something to help with the pain."

# *Part III*

It had been six months since Roishin had left, and it was surprising just how much it had affected Elsie. She was in the young princess's bedchamber, as she'd been asked, doing a weekly cleaning.

The first morning she had entered the unoccupied room, it had been strange that there hadn't been a trail of clothing for her to follow, nor deep, forest-green eyes watching her from the bed as she'd done it. At one time the servant had thought Roishin was just a spoiled, privileged little sprite, but one morning she'd caught the look on her face as she'd watched Elsie perform her duty.

She'd recognized that look: a young girl figuring out the disconcerting fact that she enjoyed watching other females. It had been equally disconcerting for Elsie when she'd been of similar age back in Scotland. There had been a young village woman who had captivated her, and she'd watched her as surreptitiously as she could while doing her daily tasks to help her sick mother.

Elsie had heard tales of her own great-great-grandmother who had been executed by the Christians. One tale she'd heard was that the death sentence had been imposed because she had been a high priestess in the order of the Druids. Another tale was that she'd been executed because she'd been caught making love with another woman.

In Elsie's heart of hearts, she knew both

reasons were to blame. She spoke to her great-great-grandmother, Mariota, all the time, if even just in her own mind and heart. She liked to believe she heard her. And, Elsie believed, she'd inherited her own gifts from Mariota.

As for Roishin, as feisty and precocious as she could be, Elsie knew she was harmless. Initially, she'd felt that if she could help a young girl figure out who she was, then so be it. Initially, she'd thought young Roishin was an absolutely beautiful young girl, her eyes such a deep green and so soulful. Initially, she'd thought of her as just that—a young girl.

Over the last several months before Roishin had left, however, it was becoming obvious that she'd grow into an absolutely stunning woman. That transformation had been well and fully in swing before Roishin departed. Elsie, in turn, had been very confused by how she had started to react toward her lady.

Somehow, though just shy of thirteen, Roishin had seemed older than any of them. It was in those eyes, eyes that had chased Elsie into many a dream. In her dreams, however, they'd both been older, perhaps into their twenties. More than one night Elsie had awoken with a racing heart and aroused body.

She'd retained little memory of the actual dream content but knew it involved Roishin and things she'd never done or experienced in her waking moments.

She'd never been with another woman before, nor anyone else. And in fact, on that horrible day in the woods, when as a last resort she'd grabbed Roishin and kissed her to cut the pull from the evil in the sky, it had been her first kiss. Well, apparently, a first for them both. Everything in her screamed at her that day just how dire the situation was becoming, so she'd done what she needed to do, but it had affected her deeply.

Now, she was in Roishin's bedchamber for the week's cleaning. She took careful care of the space, eyeing everything to make sure all of the belongings left behind were untouched. She swept, dusted, polished the furniture, and checked the mattress to make sure no infestations were starting, which often happened in an unused room.

Early on, she'd wondered why Cateline had wanted her to do this, but as time passed and Roishin's absence grew heavier and heavier, she understood. Somehow, it was almost as if maintaining the room was also maintaining hope that someday she'd return.

She finished up what she was doing, as she'd been told to hurry back up to the family chambers upon finishing. She was to meet with Cateline in her private rooms. She was a bit nervous as to why but certainly would be there.

※ ※ ※ ※

Breakfast had long ago been served, eaten, and cleared up, and the royal family had dispersed to their various duties for the day. So, Elsie headed to the bedchamber of the prince and princess, one side of the double doors standing open.

"Milady?" she called out from the open doorway. When she heard the soft voice inside inviting her in, she entered.

Cateline was sitting at the desk in the portion of the huge chamber that was set up and used for adviser meetings and such. She glanced up as Elsie walked toward her. The warm, beautiful smile the servant received made Elsie smile in return. Cateline truly was one of the most beautiful and kind women she'd ever known.

That and her wife, of course. It had confused Elsie greatly why everyone was so certain that Fallon was a man. She'd known her true identity the first time she'd set eyes on her. No, Fallon's beauty was not typical, not like her wife's. Her features were stronger, and her height far exceeded any other woman, though not quite as tall as some men Elsie had seen.

But she certainly did have a bearing that warned a fool to keep his distance. Pushing those thoughts out of her head, Elsie lowered her eyes and bowed in deference to her princess. "Milady."

"Hello, sweet Elsie," Cateline said. "Please." She indicated the chairs before the desk. "Sit."

Doing as bade, Elsie perched on the edge, knees together and hands clasped in her lap. She sat quietly, waiting for instructions or whatever Cateline had to say.

"As you know," Cateline began, setting aside the parchment she'd been reading upon Elsie's arrival. "We will be leaving on the morrow for Laigen's wedding at the main castle."

Elsie nodded. "Aye."

"I'd like you to join us, Elsie," Cateline said. The smile that slowly spread across her lips was so lovely. "I want you to begin shadowing Fiona."

Surprised, Elsie did her best to hide her expression but wasn't entirely sure how successful she was. "Aye, milady. No doubt your lady-in-waiting will need extra help with the mother of the bride."

The princess laughed. "The kind of help I need with the knowledge that my eldest daughter is getting married is not the kind of help either of you can provide."

Elsie smiled. "Aye, milady."

"No, Fiona's service is up very soon, and she's

decided to leave the castle upon finishing her ten years in February." She pushed up from the desk and walked around it to sit in the second chair next to Elsie's. She took the young woman's hands into her warm ones. Elsie met her motherly gaze. "There is not a single other person in this country that I'd want to be by my side as my lady-in-waiting than you, Elsie." She lightly squeezed Elsie's hand. "Your dedication and loyalty to duty and our family is unlike anything I've ever seen."

Elsie could only stare at her, stunned. There were other servants who had been there far longer than her two and a half years, and they were far more seasoned than she at such an important job. Swallowing, Elsie tried to speak, but words failed her. Trying again, she succeeded.

"I accept, milady," she whispered.

Cateline got to her feet and pulled Elsie to hers. She took her in a warm hug, which Elsie allowed herself to relish. She was so rarely touched, and certainly not with the maternal affection that she craved. After a long moment, Cateline pulled away enough to look into Elsie's face.

"I'm so deeply pleased," she said softly. "I very much look forward to spending time with you, Elsie," she added, as a lady-in-waiting was so often with her mistress.

"As do I, milady," Elsie said, her own smile slowly spreading across her lips.

With another squeeze given, Cateline released her and walked back around to her desk. "I have something for you." She held something out to Elsie, and it was then that the servant realized there was a glow in the beautiful gray-blue eyes that she hadn't seen in many months. In fact, the princess seemed to be beaming with happiness.

Taking it, Elsie saw that it was a folded parchment, sealed and with her name scrolled across it. She glanced up at Cateline's face again before taking it, uncertain.

"She wrote us," Cateline said quietly, emotion making those three precious words thick.

Breath stolen from her, Elsie looked down at the parchment in her hands. She blinked rapidly as tears had suddenly arrived unbidden. Swallowing a few times, Elsie took a deep breath and looked into Cateline's eyes. "Is she all right?" she whispered.

Cateline nodded with a smile, tears in her own eyes. Elsie let out a long, slow breath. To her knowledge, only she, Cateline, and Fallon knew the truth in the castle. She didn't think Laigen or Garratt had been told, and little Isabeau, at nearly a year old, was certainly too young to understand or, sadly, even remember her older sister.

As far as she knew, Laigen and Garratt had been told that Roishin had been sent by the king to a private tutorship in France. No doubt an easy sell, as everyone knew of Roishin's brilliant mind and insatiable curiosity. Nobody for a moment believed she'd end up as a wife and mother somewhere. The young princess was far more likely to take over Livia's advisory role than anything else.

Therefore, Laigen and Garratt believed what they were told.

"Thank you, milady," Elsie said, cradling the missive against her chest. "May I be excused?"

"Of course."

Elsie popped up and hurried from the bedchamber. Her heart was racing, so relieved to know Roishin was all right! She didn't have a lot of time, but she scurried down to her own chamber and hurried inside, closing the door behind her. Leaning back against the cool wood, she looked down at the letter she held in her hands.

About to push away from the door to sit on her bed and read, she was startled—and irritated—when there were three firm knocks on her bedchamber door. She quickly tucked the note into a pocket in her dress and pulled open the door, expecting to find a fellow servant needing her for something.

Instead, a cloaked figure stood at her door, hood raised to shield the wearer's face. As she watched, two hands came up and pushed the hood back just enough to reveal her eyes. Gasping, Elsie grabbed one of the hands and tugged the person inside, closing the door with finality behind them.

The hug was instant and all encompassing. For many minutes, they just held each other, absorbed what had been missing for six months. The person she held was taller, taller than she was now, and her body, though covered by the bulky cloak, had begun to fill out. It was no longer the skinny, scrawny, all-limbs body of a growing girl.

Now, heading toward her fourteenth year, it was evident Roishin was leaving childhood behind. And, when the hug broke and the hood was pulled down, Elsie smiled. Though still freckle-faced and fond of lopsided grins, Roishin was growing up.

"What are you doing here?" Elsie managed finally, unable to believe what she was seeing.

Roishin shrugged out of the plain brown cloak and draped it across the end of Elsie's bed. All her very simple clothing were in tones of brown—baggy trousers and a tunic shirt which just barely hid the womanly curves she was getting. She blew out a breath and ran her hands through her long, dark hair before plopping down to sit next to her cloak. Elsie sat next to her, unable to keep her eyes off her. She was still utterly stunned at the surprise visit.

"The Mystic let me come for a little bit," she explained. "I can't stay long at all."

"Does your mamaí know you're here?"

Roishin nodded with a grin. "How do you think I knew to follow you?"

Elsie smiled and looked shyly away. "I guess it explains her good spirits this morning." She met Roishin's gaze again, unable to look away.

"Aye. I was so happy to see her." Roishin said nothing for a long moment, just seemed to take in as much of Elsie visually as she could. "So good to see you," she whispered, almost as if more to herself than the young woman of nearly seventeen who sat next to her.

Absently, Elsie reached over and took Roishin's hand in her own. Instantly, Roishin's fingers curled around hers. "Will you be going to Laigen's wedding?" she asked.

Roishin shook her head. "No. I can't stay away that long." She gave her a smirk. "The Mystic will have my hide."

"Who is that?" Elsie asked. She felt Roishin's thumb lightly caress the back of her hand.

"He's essentially my boss, I guess," the princess responded. "He's extremely witty and intelligent and extremely militant." She smiled.

"Your boss?" Elsie grinned. "I never in a million years thought somebody could actually tell you what to do."

"I know." Roishin sighed dramatically. "Trust me, not my favorite thing." They shared a smile. "Which," she added, so much affection in her beautiful green eyes. "Congratulations on *your* new boss."

Elsie burst into laughter, both at the words chosen but also the facts behind it. She hadn't had a lot of time to absorb the offer and the honor, but she looked down at her joined hands. "Thank you." She met that penetrating gaze again. "She told you?"

"She asked me if I thought you'd be willing to do it," Roishin said softly.

"And you told her yes?"

Roishin smirked. "Well," she drawled. "You're not having to pick up after this mess-maker anymore," she said, hitching a thumb at her own chest.

Elsie raised an eyebrow. "Truer words have not been spoken. My days have become downright boring."

Roishin's laughter was loud and joyous at that. Elsie couldn't help but chuckle along with her. "Well," the princess finally said. "If it makes you feel any better, I have to keep a tight ship where I am now." She indicated the room around them. "It's a space about this size."

"Must be so hard," Elsie said, not an ounce of sympathy in her voice.

Roishin shrugged as she looked around. "Honestly?" she said, meeting Elsie's gaze again. "I adore my parents, you know that. And I'm so grateful for all they've done for me. But none of this," she said, indicating the castle around them, "matters to me." Her smile was lovely. "I just want to see and protect those that I love." She looked deeply into Elsie's eyes. "Beyond that, I don't care about titles and money."

Elsie met her smile and lightly squeezed the fingers wrapped around her own. A return squeeze and Roishin pushed to her feet, then a sense of panic filled Elsie's heart for a moment. She also stood.

"I must go," Roishin said, though it was absolutely clear that she didn't want to.

Elsie nodded. "I understand," she barely managed as emotion threatened.

Roishin stepped up to her…so strange for Elsie to look up a bit into her eyes now. She allowed herself to be gathered into a tight hug, which she returned just as tightly. Her eyes fell closed as Roishin buried her face in her neck.

"When will I see you again?" she whispered into the hug.

"Not for quite some time," Roishin murmured. "I was given this Solstice gift, but The Mystic told me that would be all for a while."

Eslie nodded, unable to speak for several moments. Finally, she asked, "Are they good to you, Roishin?"

The princess nodded. "Aye. Just keep me very, very busy."

"Doing what?"

Roishin lifted her head from Elsie's shoulder and looked deeply into her eyes. "I explained it in my letter," she said softly    . She brought up a hand and gently brushed her fingertips over the side of Elsie's face. "I have to go."

Nodding, Elsie swallowed to keep from crying. She was shocked at how strongly she was feeling the abandonment wash over her. "Will you write again?"

Roishin nodded. "I will, I promise." She grinned. "Now I know where I can leave them. Do you know of the secret passageway off the family chamber? That leads to the hidden passage through the trunk?"

"I'll find it," Elsie said.

"I'll leave my letters there, on the top step leading up to the trunk." Roishin smiled at the utter bafflement on Elsie's face. "I haven't gone *that* mad." She caressed her cheek again. "Leave your responses there, too, and

I'll get them."

"Someday," Elsie said. "Will you explain all this to me?"

Nodding, Roishin leaned forward, pressing her lips to Elsie's. The kiss was so soft, Elsie responding. There was something different in this one than the previous kisses they had shared, even from the morning Roishin left. It wasn't just a press of lips, but the slight movement of lips—touching, caressing—before the softest last touch as Roishin moved away.

Elsie met her gaze, something passing between the two for a moment. She didn't understand it in her head, but her heart did. She stepped aside as Roishin moved past her to grab her cloak off the bed. She swung the garment around until it settled around her body.

Roishin studied her for a long moment, as if memorizing Elsie's face, her hair, and even her dress. With a smile, she reached out and lightly cupped her face before she brought the hood of her cloak up and into place.

"Want me to check to make sure nobody is coming?" Elsie asked softly. "So you won't be seen."

Roishin's smile could just barely be seen in the shadows of the hood. "I won't be seen." Lightly squeezing Elsie's hand, she turned and opened the door. One last look to Elsie, then she turned out into the hall and was gone.

# *Chapter One*

### *Four years later*

Roishin scanned the chamber she'd spent more hours than she cared to count in over the last four years. She was stunned that the three books in her hands were the final books left to read in the enormous library.

One was a book on cake-making recipes, one was yet another Bible—King James edition this time—and the third was a book by an author called Louis L'Amour. He seemed to have about thirteen thousand books published about the "Old West," and she'd read every single one of them, per instructions, in three different languages.

Tucking the books against her side, she headed to the double doors, nearly dropping them in startlement when one side opened. The Mystic stood there, looking at her. "Yes?" she drawled.

"Your final batch?" he asked, nodding toward the books she held.

"It is." She grinned at him. "When I finish these, will you finally tell me exactly *why* I've read every stinkin' book ever written?"

"Does the sea tell the sky why it rages today yet is calm tomorrow?"

Cocking her head to the side, she studied him. "Really? Well golly, Mystic, why don't we ask Poseidon? Or, maybe we can ask the Vikings their thoughts as they tried to sail the seven seas. Or," she added, eyebrows shooting up. "How about we ask all one thousand, five hundred and three that died on the Titanic in nineteen twelve for *their* thoughts!"

His smile was wider than any she'd seen in all the years. "That, young Roishin," he said, lightly tapping the center of her forehead with a finger,  "is  why you've been reading all these books."

She stared at him. "What? Why?" He breezed past her, saying nothing more. She felt really angry in that moment. "Mystic, I've spent the last four and a half years of my life away from my family, haven't even seen them in *four years*, and you won't tell me why I've been doing this?"

She watched as he ambled his way over to one of the myriad ladders and began to climb. She knew she wasn't going to get anything more, and frankly, she was sick of it. She was about to drop the three books she held where she stood.

"Finish what you started, Roishin," he said, never even glancing her way.

She growled low in her throat. She absolutely hated when he did that. Grumbling to herself, she turned and shoved out of the room. The door slowly closed behind her as she stepped out into the short corridor. She continued on her way, the destination of her own room in her mind.

Reaching the end of that tunnel, she passed through the door that shimmered just ahead of her. Stepping through, she only had one more turn, and that was directly into her room. With a heavy and irritated sigh, she slammed the three books down onto the table. She was tired. It wasn't just a matter of her eyes being tired or her brain being tired, so much information passing through it nonstop. Her *soul* was tired.

For a very long time, doing nothing but reading

had been incredible. She'd read about worlds far away, times in the distant future and the distant past. She'd read about every single culture ever created, even the crazy one that someday would be called America. She'd also mastered more languages than she could count on both hands.

If it had happened, was happening, or was going to happen, she'd read about it—and in what *language* it happened, no less. She still had no idea how on earth all those books had gotten here, though. Honestly, part of her wondered if they were the feverish imagination of The Mystic. Maybe his mysticism was creating an arsenal of insane literature, and she'd been appointed the *New York Times* reviewer of the fourteenth century.

She wanted answers. She wanted to know the whys.

She glanced over to the firepit and flipped it the bird, a flame whooshing to life before settling in at a nice, comfortable level of light and warmth. She walked to her bed niche and ducked her head before sitting on the edge of the bed pallet. Her head grazed the top of it now.

She'd grown a full six inches since she'd been in the Underground, what the inhabitants lovingly called the catacombs they all shared. It was a beehive of tunnels, chambers, rooms, and caves. To the unindoctrinated, it was like a Rubik's cube—she'd had to read the manual on those, too—where everything seemed to change no matter which way you'd gone.

What tunnel system took a person to one destination yesterday and a new one today? It was all about playing with the mind, of course. These tunnels had kept people safe for thousands of years. She'd had to learn very quickly how to create her own doors. When in a place like this, so filled with the energy of those like her, it wasn't hard.

Other than the endless supply of books for escape, however, she'd not been allowed to the outside world since her short visit home years before. So, she'd yet to learn about doors on the outside, save for the one she knew exited through the trunk in her family chamber at home.

Letting out a heavy sigh, she lifted long legs and whipped them over to stretch out on her bed pallet, her head resting upon the pillow. She tucked her hands behind her head and stared up at the underside of her little sleep cave, as she sometimes called it. If she ever slept in a regular bed in a regular room again, she'd feel incredibly utterly exposed and vulnerable.

A sound caught her attention, and she glanced over to the archway entrance to her room. "Don't do it, Laif," she murmured, noting the newcomer who carried her dinner. Sure enough, he lifted a foot to enter and promptly vanished. "Told you not to do it, Laif." She sighed.

A moment later, the young man reappeared, his dark hair hanging in his face and plastered to his head in wet strands. His tunic shirt clung to his narrow chest like a second skin. He spit some water out of his mouth, which made Roishin's grin widen.

"I'll, uh…" he said. "I'll go get you another." He lifted the dinner, now not more than a puddle of floating vegetables and soggy bread.

"Sounds good." She chuckled, watching him turn and walk away.

She'd had to learn the hard way, too. Were folks here polite? Sure. But was asking for permission to enter an absolute necessity? Definitely. Everyone had their own way of blocking off the entrance to their personal space. In her early days, Roishin had been zapped, flung backward, and even ended up on the entire other side of the tunnel system, forced to find her way back.

As for Roishin's choices, it depended on her mood. Poor young Laif had chosen bad manners during a time of discontent on her part.

She returned her attention back to the ceiling and contemplated. She'd read so much and had so little interaction with anyone other than The Mystic and the handful that came and went to bring her food or whatnot, that sometimes she felt like she was losing herself in the tunnels of her own mind.

And to make it all worse, she hadn't been able to keep her promise to Elsie. Once she'd crossed back over into the Underground, the door had been locked. Adding insult to injury, she hadn't seen Enori again, either. Absolutely no other options available, she'd been forced to just hunker down and do as she was told.

She remembered stories her daidí had told her about her days in the elite guard—the horrible conditions she'd endured or orders she'd had no choice but to follow. She'd made a commitment to her men, to her king, and to her country. So, Roishin had followed suit and, not sure if they were trying to see how far they could push her or if they could break her, she had dug in her own heels.

Now, she glanced over at her table and saw the final three books. The Bible, of course, was huge, the cookbook medium-sized, and the western an evening read. She was almost done. Then what?

She had little time to contemplate that as Laif returned. He looked rather sheepish with his sodden clothing and hair and fresh plate of food. "May I enter?" he asked.

"Sure." Roishin sat up and whipped her legs over the side of her sleep cave, booted feet hitting the ground. She'd worn sandals all these years, new ones appearing as she outgrew the last pair. For her seventeenth birthday, she'd been excited to receive a brand-new pair of boots, her preferred footwear.

The young man, who looked to be fifteen maybe, entered and gingerly set the loaded plate on the table next to the stacked books. He gave her a polite smile before heading for the exit.

"Oh," he said, turning before he left. "You're wanted in the library on the morrow after breakfast." With a small bow of his head, he hurried off.

Closing her eyes, Roishin counted to ten, then counted to ten again. Somebody was going to die if she got there only to find it had been replenished with twelve thousand new volumes overnight.

❧ ❧ ❧ ❧

All three books finished and her multiyear task complete, Roishin headed to the waterfall before breakfast. She wanted a swim and a bath. The waterfall was much like the one Fallon had taken her to many years before. Though that one had an open top as the rock had eroded away, this one was completely enclosed.

There was only one way in, the water seemingly roaring in from an unseen source, pooling invitingly at the bottom of the cavernous space. A stone ledge curved a third of the way around the huge pool. She wore her sleep dress and carried her clothing with her, as well as some plant-based soap. Though the soap was routinely provided, like her clothing and food and other essentials, she'd learned how to make it over the years and found pleasure in its simple creation.

She stopped short when she realized somebody was already in the water. Deep in the pool, closer to the waterfall portion, she saw a pale body dart beneath the surface before a pale head broke through. Hands came up and brushed back short blond hair. Roishin swallowed. She wasn't sure what to do.

Glancing to the stone ledge, Roishin saw a small pile of clothing, discerning among it a white gown. She was filled with mixed feelings in that moment: embarrassment for walking in on someone else's swim, but also anger at the specific woman in question.

"You don't have to go, Roishin."

Roishin's head whipped back to the figure, who was now facing her. Enori was treading water, the paleness of her naked skin a shimmering pale blob beneath the water.

"Come," she said, waving Roishin over with a hand before continuing to tread water. "Have your bath and your swim." She gave her a winning smile. "Plenty of room."

Yes, there was. There was enough room for twenty people to comfortably bathe, but Roishin felt shy. In four years, she'd not seen a single female over the age of fourteen. And, with some of the books she'd read over the years, she'd learned a new term: lesbian.

As she made her way farther into the chamber, she kept her eyes away from the figure in the water. Why was it that when she finally saw a grown woman, not only was she the most beautiful creature Roishin had ever seen, but she was also *naked*? It was Enori, she kept telling herself. Enori, not just any random woman.

She stopped and sat to pull off her boots, which no doubt looked ridiculous with her sleep dress, but she was there to read for eternity, apparently, not be a fashion plate. Boots removed, she got to her feet again and whipped off her sleeping gown and undergarments. She could feel Enori's eyes on her, and that made her even more nervous.

With little fanfare, she walked to the edge of the deep end of the pool and dove in. The cool water felt amazing on her heated skin as she shot like an arrow through the depths. Her fingers grazed the bottom before she arched her way back up, exploding through the surface with a gasp for air.

She brushed back her long hair from her face and spit out some water. Using her fingers to wipe at her eyes, she glanced over to see Enori twenty or so feet away. "Where have you been?" she asked.

"Where I've been needed," Enori said easily.

Roishin had to look away for a moment. How was it that she was even more beautiful? Painfully so. Swallowing, she forced herself to look back over to her. "And you didn't think *I* needed you?" she asked, trying to keep her anger and hurt in place to distract her.

The smile that crossed full lips was so sweet. "I knew you didn't, Roishin," she said impossibly softly, yet somehow loud enough to be heard over the roaring water from the falls. "I knew you were safe, taken care of. I made sure of that." She swam over to Roishin, stopping a handful of feet away and shaking her head. "My goodness," she said. "You're all grown up! So beautiful."

Roishin looked away shyly. "I'll be eighteen in June."

"Five short months away."

Roishin nodded. "So, why are you here now, then? For another lost soul?" She couldn't keep the bitterness out of her voice. For so many years, especially early on, she'd needed Enori, needed her comfort and her strength. "Another kid taken from their family?"

Enori shook her head. "No," she drawled. "I am here for you."

"Laif told me I was supposed to go to the library again today," Roishin said, telling herself to not notice the swells of Enori's breasts just below the water.

She felt like an absolute cad. The poor woman was trying to have a relaxing swim and Roishin's eyes and mind kept wandering to where they had absolutely no business going. She turned away and headed back to the ledge to grab her soap, which she'd left within reach.

"He is correct," Enori said. "That is what I told him to tell you."

Hearing movement behind her, Roishin glanced over her shoulder to see Enori also headed to the ledge. She watched as she placed her hands upon the stone and heaved her body out of the water. Roishin could only stare as the absolute perfection that was Enori emerged. She left wet footprints on the stone as she walked over to her clothing.

Grabbing a large piece of fabric that had been folded next to her cloak and gown, Enori turned and faced Roishin, who quickly cast her eyes away, but not before she saw the smaller framed woman in all her glory.

Her breasts were proportionate to her petite size, and the full, light pink nipples were rigid and beads of water dripped off them. A slender torso flared into womanly hips and beautiful legs. She felt her face flush with embarrassment. It was like she'd been spying on her sister or something, and that felt awful even as she was fascinated.

There was a soft chuckle, and then, "You can

look now."

Roishin cleared her throat, feeling so ashamed. Glancing over, she saw that Enori had dried herself off with the material and had tugged her gown over her head. A small little smirk of amusement quirked her lips as she ran her fingers through short, wavy blond hair to comb it.

"When you are finished here and have eaten," Enori said, her mirth disappearing as her tone was friendly once more. "You and I will go to the library and get a few books from The Mystic."

Roishin's dark eyebrows drew. "But I've read everything there."

"You have," Enori agreed with a nod, pulling her cloak—blue with gold stitching—around her shoulders. "But there are a few you will need for…" She looked away, as though trying to come up with the words. "On-the-job training, as it were." She gave her a beautiful smile. She gathered the damp fabric she'd used to dry herself, then turned and left the cavern.

# *Chapter Two*

Dressed and fully recovered from what she'd seen mere moments ago—though no doubt it would come back to her during quiet times—Roishin arrived at the library. Admittedly, she felt a bit better that Enori would be there, but she was still nervous. Clearly something was changing, her time in the Underground perhaps over. Did that mean she was going home?

As she stood there, watching Enori talking quietly to The Mystic, something occurred to Roishin. Her brow furrowed as she contemplated. Her thoughts were interrupted when suddenly she was brought into the conversation.

"Huh?" Startled out of her contemplation, she looked from Enori to The Mystic and back.

She wasn't entirely sure which one had said her name—it had just registered somewhere in her mind that it had been said. Not surprisingly, The Mystic looked at her with disapproval, and Enori was studying her with a bit of knowing amusement in her beautiful eyes. Roishin looked away from her gaze right quick.

Clearing her throat, she said, "My apologies. What?"

"These will be taken with you," he said, holding out three books to her. His gaze was more intense than she'd ever seen it. "Study them."

Looking down at the tomes held out to her, Roishin recognized two from the previous year and one from three years ago. Taking them, she nodded.

"Aye." It was obvious he and Enori were engaged in discussions that didn't pertain to Roishin, so she focused on the books.

One was about the assassination of Abraham Lincoln, one was on nineteenth-century fashion, and one was on the history of women on the stage across time. Tucking the books at her side, an automatic position adopted over four years of doing this, she looked back to the other two.

"I agree," Enori was saying. She glanced to Roishin, who met her gaze. She gave her a small smile before saying with finality, "Thank you so much, Mystic. Ready?" She arched her eyebrows at Roishin.

Nodding, though having no idea what she was supposed to be "ready" for, she turned to the man who had annoyed her, driven her crazy, inspired her, and given her the greatest gift of knowledge over the last four years. She lowered her eyes as she bowed in deferential respect. Looking up again, the two shared a moment of mutual understanding of a special bond that had grown over the years.

With a small bow of his own, The Mystic turned and left the two women alone as he shuffled out of the great chamber. Feeling *very* shy after her shocking morning, Roishin glanced over at Enori, waiting for instruction. She couldn't hold Enori's gaze and had to look away. She felt a hand rest on her shoulder. Swallowing, she looked over at her.

The look on Enori's face was kind, filled with understanding. Reaching up, she gently tucked long strands behind Roishin's ear. "You've grown up so much, Roishin," she said. "No longer a child." She smiled. "You're tall, like Fallon," she whispered as if talking to herself.

Roishin nodded, her shyness now that of a young

woman who felt out of her depth. "Aye."

It was so strange to be looking down at the priestess, as she now had a few inches on her. Even still, looking at the woman who had for so many years been her angel, and honestly still was, she felt unworthy. Yes, though a young woman of seventeen, Roishin still felt like a child.

She had lost so many years of true life experience, only living vicariously through those in the endless books, scrolls, and manuals she'd consumed. Now, she had no idea how to make the transition between the girl who had first entered the tunnels and the woman who was apparently leaving them.

"Roishin," Enori said, her voice soft. She waited until she had Roishin's gaze upon her. "There was purpose for this." She took one of the young woman's hands in her own. "I assure you. You will understand."

Roishin voiced her earlier thought. "Was I hidden away here? Until the danger was over for my family?"

Enori's entire being softened, her head shaking. "No. You weren't hidden away at all. For you, young Roishin, the danger will never be over. We're just teaching you how to combat it."

"Here?" Roishin asked, her voice filled with the anger she felt. "Locked away in a prison of tunnels and perpetual books?"

Enori quirked a challenging eyebrow. "Are you not grateful?" she asked, arms crossing over her chest. "The time invested in you, to bring you to the great one you were born to be?"

There was absolutely no way Roishin could compete with the fire in those penetrating eyes, especially when she had no answers as she had no idea what the questions even were. Her head hanging, she chewed on her bottom lip. "I am grateful. What now?"

Enori used two fingers under her chin to bring her head up. "Now," she said. "We go to your room and collect your things, and then I have a very special surprise for you."

"What?" Roishin asked as they turned and headed out of the chamber.

Enori playfully bumped her shoulder with her own. "Would not be a surprise if I told you."

Roishin smiled. "Ture enough."

They stepped through the massive doors, Roishin turning around to get one last look at what had become her second home. No idea what was next, she wasn't sure if she'd see it again. Enori waited patiently for her in the tunnel beyond before the pair began to walk again. Not even thinking, Roishin created a door as she had so many times before.

It shimmered into existence, Roishin stepping through followed by Enori, who sent her an approving look once they stepped into Roishin's room. Though it had been second nature for her to do it, she admittedly felt proud to show off what she'd learned and become quite skilled at.

"Come in," she invited, crossing the threshold into the small space she'd inhabited for four and a half years. Looking around, Roishin thought of what would go with her. Turning to the woman who stood quietly by, she asked, "What do I need to take?"

Enori walked past her and removed the bow and quiver off the nails, two items which had never been removed since Enori herself had hung them there. She spared a glance over to Roishin, who watched before Enori moved on to grab the chaneries from the other hook, laying it next to the quiver.

She flat-out ignored the neat piles of clothing and pair of sandals. Instead, she grabbed Fallon's dagger that lay within easy reach in one of the shelving nooks, placing it on the stone table before she grabbed Roishin's brown cloak, which hung by its deep hood. Walking over to the young woman, she wrapped it around her shoulders, standing in Roishin's personal space as she fastened the cloak at her throat with the ties.

"I want you to find your own identity, Roishin," she said, her gaze focused on her fingers as they tied the heavy garment. She spared a glance up into deep green eyes. "It is imperative."

Roishin nodded. "I will try." She glanced down, watching nimble fingers work. "I'm sorry I walked in on you earlier."

Enori flicked her eyes up to meet Roishin's. "Why?"

"Because you were bathing."

Enori shrugged a shoulder. "The human body isn't to be ashamed of, Roishin." Finishing, she adjusted the garment into better placement over Roishin's shoulders. "We all have one, and it is beautiful and a work of art. It is the ultimate design for mobility, power, and pleasure." She smiled, hands resting on Roishin's shoulders. "We are all beautiful. Do not forget that." She leaned up and left a kiss on Roishin's cheek. "Come."

Roishin placed the dagger into her bag and shrugged the strip over one shoulder, the bow and quiver the other. She followed Enori, watching as the ageless woman reached a hand out toward the firepit. The smallest gesture and the flame eased down to nothing more than a thin wisp of smoke, plunging the space into darkness.

They headed into the tunnel beyond Roishin's room then stepped through the door Enori created.

Startled, Roishin looked around to find them back in the waterfall cave. Despite Enori's words and obvious fact that she wasn't bothered by what had happened, Roishin felt a warm blush suffuse her from her toes to the tips of her hair at the memory. A work of art, indeed.

Those thoughts were tossed right out of her mind when she followed Enori to natural steps in the stone that led up to the waterfall. Her eyes widened in shock when they got close to the falls, as she had no idea it was possible to step behind the roaring crash of water. But, sure enough, they stepped into little private nook.

Enori walked to the farthest corner then stopped, turning to face Roishin. She took her in a warm hug, tight and comforting. Roishin returned it, relishing the closeness which she'd missed for so long.

"See you soon," the priestess said into her ear.

"How long?" Roishin asked, almost feeling panicked as if she were being thrown into another round of unknown territory.

Enori pulled back from the hug, her hand resting upon the side of Roishin's face. She smiled. "You will know when it is time." She stepped away and indicated the wall before them.

Initially confused, Roishin looked back to the woman who stood a foot away, then looked back to the wall. It took a moment, but then she saw the familiar shimmer of the stone. With one final look to her angel, she stepped to the wall. The strange, almost lightheaded feeling she had grown used to filled her as she stepped through it and…

…into her daidí's waterfall. Gasping, she stepped down from the edge of the pounding waterfall. When she saw Fallon jump off the flat rock and begin running over to her, Roishin cried out in relief and bolted toward her. She was caught up in strong arms and, despite the fact they were nearly the same height now, lifted off her feet as she was swung around.

She was crying as she held on. Yes, Enori, the best surprise ever! When she was put back on her feet, Fallon, too, was crying. She held her by the shoulders as she looked her daughter over with a mother's eye.

"You're all grown up," she said, her voice thick with emotion before taking Roishin back into a painfully tight hug.

Roishin's eyes closed, feeling safe and at peace for the first time in more than four years. "Daidí," she murmured, closing her eyes as she inhaled the familiar scent of leather and just...*Daidí*.

Fallon kissed her cheek loudly before pulling away, grinning at her. "My gods," she whispered. "Let me look at you." She shook her head. "Where did my little Roishin go?"

Roishin laughed through her tears, finding it so strange to be looking at her nearly eye to eye. Fallon still had an inch or so on her. "How'd you know to be here?" she asked. "Or were you just here?"

Fallon shook her head, slapping Roishin on the back as she led the way to the exit, which Roishin remembered would take them to the forest beyond. "No, Enori told me in her letter to be here to get you." She glanced over at her. "She's been writing to us regularly, letting us know how you were, what was happening with you."

"She has?" Roishin asked, shocked.

"Aye," Fallon said with a nod. "Explained that your studies couldn't be interrupted with the outside world to write yourself." She looked at her daughter, almost as if she couldn't get enough. "I missed you so much," she whispered.

Roishin was taken into another hug, this one calm and to reconnect, not to nearly strangle her from excitement. She smiled into it, really able to just… breathe. She absolutely could not wait to get home and do the same with her mamaí. And she wondered if Elsie was still at the castle. Not a day had passed without the thought of her either marching through her day or into her dreams.

Once they both ducked through the small crevice in the wall, Roishin looked down at the small stream that she'd been picked up and lifted over the last time she'd been there. She met Fallon's eyes, the two grinning before she easily hopped over it, the warrior following. Fallon's sharp whistle rent the air when she brought two fingers to her mouth.

Roishin was excited, expecting to see Toirneach trotting to his master, but the horse who made its way over to them was decidedly not the midnight-colored war horse. She looked to Fallon for explanation. The sadness in her violet eyes told the story.

"Oh, Daidí," she murmured. "I'm so sorry."

"He was a good horse," Fallon said, walking up to the brown-and-white beast who stopped once he'd cleared the trees. "This is Stoirm." She patted the stallion's thick neck. Glancing to Roishin, she said, "I'm going to take you to see Daideó before we head home." The look in Fallon's eyes brooked no argument.

Nodding, Roishin simply said, "Aye."

⁂

It felt so good to be at her grandfather's castle, the king's castle. It also felt good to see so many familiar faces. She'd spent many a summer running through these halls with Laigen and some of the servant children. Her grandfather had been kind and absolutely tolerant of the parade of running, giggling children that stampeded the corridors.

They reached the bedchamber that was Roishin's. She could almost cry at the familiarity of it. She likely *would* cry when they got home. Sitting atop the bed was folded clothing, and a new pair of boots sat on the floor next to the bed.

"We got notice a little while ago that you'd be returning for a bit," Fallon said. "So, I hope you like these. I had them made for you."

The two entered the bedchamber and Roishin took the folded shirt. It wasn't much different from the tunic shirt she had on, though made from a more billowing material that was certainly less scratchy than the fabric she wore now. Especially against her breasts. She rubbed it against her face, nearly purring.

She grinned at Fallon's chuckle. "Thank you so much, Daidí. I love it." Tossing the shirt aside, she was surprised to see the folded trousers were leather, like Fallon's.

"Enori told me you were nearly my size now," Fallon explained. "So, I had these made just a bit smaller." She looked a bit shy as she shrugged. "These will keep you warm and hold up much better." She reached out and lightly tugged at the baggy trousers Roishin had worn for more than four years.

Beyond excited, Roishin dropped the trousers and hugged Fallon again. "Thank you." She was squeezed tightly in return.

꧁꧂

Dressed in her new clothes and boots and her hair

brushed and braided, Roishin felt like a new person. She'd been utterly delighted to see that a sheath had been sewn into the inside of her right boot, a perfect size for the rose blade. Fallon had showed her how to ease it in and out without slicing herself open in the process. She knew it would be something she needed to practice. A lot.

Now, she was entering the bedchamber of the great King of Sursha. She wasn't prepared for what she'd see. The mighty King Carthac, with his powerful build and loud, boisterous laugh, was not who lay in his bed now. The man with snow-white hair was nearly unfamiliar to her, his thin frame dressed in a sleep shirt and his sunken eyes closed in slumber.

She looked to Fallon for explanation, who gave her a sad smile. "I think he's been waiting," she said softly.

"For what?"

Fallon brought up her hand and lightly touched Roishin's cheek. "For you."

Roishin had to stand there for a moment to let the words sink in before she could even breathe, let alone take another step. She swallowed hard, then took a deep, steadying breath. Nodding, she forced her emotions down as she needed to stay strong. Sparing a glance to the warrior, she walked across the huge chamber of the king to the bed.

When she reached it, she looked down at the shrunken, bearded figure that lay beneath the covers. She couldn't get over how small he was, shoulders once broad and powerful now slender and bony. The one hand that lay outside of the covers was still large, but gnarled and fragile looking. She took that hand with gentle fingers, glad to find it still warm.

"Daideó?" she said, her voice soft. "It's me,

Roishin."

Slowly, dark eyes opened. They were unfocused, but a slow smile spread across the thin, dry lips. "Roishin," he whispered. He blinked a couple times, eyes growing a bit more focused as he took her in. They widened. "My gods," he whispered. "You look exactly like Fallon did at your age." He studied her, drinking in her face and her hair. "How is this so?"

She smiled, tears welling in her eyes. "Magic," was all she could think to say, as she, too, had seen the eerie resemblance, especially once she'd dressed and braided her hair. It was uncanny and had left her speechless for several moments.

The king chuckled and nodded. "I have no doubt." He looked deeply into her eyes. "I love you, child," he whispered, voice weak.

"I love you, too, Daideó." She lowered her head and left a kiss on the fingers of the frail, dry hand she held.

# Chapter Three

Her lady ready for the day, Elsie began to pick up the mess from the morning rush. They were at King Carthac's castle, the entire household holding their breath. She had liked the king very much the dozen or so times she'd met him in her more than six years serving the royal family.

It was her fourth year acting as Cateline's lady-in-waiting, and the two were like a well-oiled machine. Well, three, technically. Being one of the few in the castle who knew the truth about Fallon, she helped her out as well. She was primarily there for the princess, of course, but she enjoyed doing what she could for the so-called prince when asked.

They treated her exceptionally well, far more like a daughter in many ways than a servant. She smiled at that thought as she shook out her lady's night dress. She wasn't sure how long they'd be staying on the eastern part of the island, so she'd have to figure out a good routine for them. They'd left in a hurry once word arrived about the king's dire condition.

Elsie was startled nearly out of her shoes when a loud cry erupted outside the closed door of the queen's chambers where Cateline and Fallon were staying. At first, she expected it was a howl of heartbreak, expecting the worst. But after a moment, she realized it was a shrill exclamation of utter joy. More exclamations and tears followed.

She stood there, sleeping gown still in her hands as she stared at the closed door. She knew it wasn't her place to go see what was happening, even as she could hear excited voices and the sounds of lots and lots of happy tears. Caring as much about the family—*her* family—as she did, she couldn't help but smile, too.

She knew soon enough she'd be let in on what had happened, so she turned back to her task. She was nearly startled out of her shoes yet again when the double doors to the bedchamber burst open, an elated Cateline dragging another person in tow. All Elsie could do was stare. She was positively struck dumb.

If she didn't know better, she would think she was looking at what Fallon must have looked like in her late teens. Her height, her hair, her naturally powerful bearing—though with this one it wasn't about her muscles, but her energy. When she looked closer, however, she also saw Cateline's features—favoring Fallon more, yes, but the princess was in there all the same, her natural beauty and more delicate features apparent in this young person.

But it was the eyes, those deep, deep green eyes she knew so well, that cemented the identity. "Roishin," she whispered.

Four years' worth of confusion and hurt were pushed aside for a moment by not only the appearance of Roishin at the castle, but the *appearance* of Roishin. She was stunning. Long ago Elsie had to accept that she had been nothing more to a young Roishin figuring herself out than a young woman in the village had been to Elsie.

Difference was, Elsie and the village woman had never even spoken, let alone shared a few kisses and promises. But alas, the young girl in Roishin had made promises that a maturing Roishin apparently had no desire to keep. It hurt, but she'd had no choice but to let it go. So, seeing her there now, looking back at her as a young woman and not a girl, Elsie had no idea what to do or say.

For a moment, it was like the air was sucked out of the room. Roishin walked over to her, her gaze never leaving Elsie's, who was having a difficult time keeping eye contact. She felt shy, she felt confused, and she felt completely overwhelmed by Roishin's presence. She fidgeted absently with Cateline's sleep dress.

Without a word, Roishin gently took the garment from her and tossed it to the made bed before she enfolded Elsie into a tight hug. Elsie was stiff for a moment, her feelings and emotions confusing her response, but also the fact that Cateline and Fallon were in the room with them. Would it look bad if she hugged her back? Would they be angry?

A quick glance over at them showed they were speaking quietly to each other and not paying the pair a bit of mind. After a moment, she decided to risk returning the hug. She heard a sigh from Roishin, sounding relieved, when she did. Elsie's eyes fell closed, allowing herself for just a moment to enjoy the warmth and closeness.

⁂

"Is that what you think that is?" Elsie asked, grinning.

She was sitting on a stone bench in the rose garden that Her Highness had had constructed on the property, and she was utterly charmed by the five-year-old who sat in her lap. It was spring and the flowers were beginning to bloom, as well as the tiny red-and-black creature that crawled around on Elsie's palm.

"Then what's this called?" the little one asked, dark blue eyes focused intently.

"Bug of Our Lady," Elsie explained.

Eyebrows furrowed, Isabeau looked up at her. "What kind of name is that?"

Elsie smiled, charmed. "Well, some believe this bug was sent to protect crops." She omitted the part about those beliefs being that Heaven had sent this bug, and it was named after the Virgin Mary. As the family did not follow the Christian faith, she knew the girl wouldn't understand that part or have any reference point for it.

"So, it's a warrior bug?" she asked, little mouth hanging open in surprise as her focus returned to the bug.

"It could very well be." Elsie met her surprised gaze.

"Like Daidí and Garratt?"

"Just like that."

Suddenly, the little bug's wings spread, and it flew away. That was when Elsie noticed somebody was walking their way. She glanced over, her stomach flipping a bit when she saw that it was Roishin. The family had all gathered in the king's chamber, so Elsie had taken Isabeau to keep her entertained, as Cateline wanted to limit what the little girl saw during this difficult time.

"Isabeau," she said softly to get the girl's attention. "Look who it is." The youngest child of the royal family looked to Roishin, then back to Elsie with wide, slightly frightened eyes. "That's your sister, Roishin." Though she had no memory of her, Elsie knew Isabeau had been talked to extensively about her absent sister.

Elsie glanced over again when the steps slowed. She saw that Roishin's eyes were wide,    her beautiful face awash with wonder. Never taking her eyes off Roishin, Elsie leaned in a bit and whispered to the girl.

"Go say hello."

Put on her little feet, Isabeau stood there, a finger in her mouth as she looked up at the approaching figure. Roishin stopped a few feet away and squatted down. The softest, most beautiful smile graced her lips.

"Hello, Isabeau," she said softly. "I'm your big sister, Roishin."

The little girl stared at her. With one more questioning glance back to Elsie, she took a tentative step forward. "Hello."

Roishin has a beautiful smile, Elsie thought as she watched this most precious reunion. She wondered if Isabeau would ever know just how special her sister was. Would she know what Roishin did for her?

"Why are you wearing these?" the girl asked, only taking her finger out of her mouth long enough to point at the brown leather trousers Roishin wore.

"I don't like dresses," Roishin said easily.

"I don't, either."

A wonderful burst of laughter escaped Roishin's lips. "Aye," she said with a nod. "You *are* my little sister." She plopped down on her leather-clad butt right there in the middle of the pathway. "Can I give you a hug?" After a small moment of hesitation, Isabeau nodded. Roishin smiled at her and took her in her arms, holding her tightly to her.

Elsie felt as though she were interrupting their special moment, so she pushed to her feet. She stopped when Roishin's gaze caught her own over the little girl's shoulder, Isabeau laying her head on Roishin's.

"Don't go," Roishin said softly up to her.

Elsie met her gaze and held it before she nodded and retook her seat. It was a bit chilly, so she wrapped her cloak more firmly around her body, watching as Roishin held Isabeau to her with one arm while using the other and her legs to stand. The girl giggled as she held on to her sister like a baby monkey would its mother.

Elsie chuckled. It looked like Roishin was nearly being strangled by the girl, but she didn't complain one bit. Instead, she carried her over to the stone bench, teasingly bouncing the giggling girl with silly accompanying sounds the entire way.

Though she didn't want to be, Elsie was charmed. She glanced over at her unexpected companion. The two met eyes for a moment before Roishin helped Isabeau get settled in her lap. "How's he doing?" Elsie asked.

Roishin shrugged. "He wanted some time alone with my parents," she said, meeting Elsie's gaze again. She smiled over the girl's head. "So, I came looking for you."

Elsie looked away, feeling shy. She hugged herself beneath her cloak. She had so many questions but wasn't entirely sure they were hers to ask. Finally, she said, "You didn't write."

Roishin met her gaze full on, not looking away or seeming ashamed in her expression. "I know, and I am so sorry. I actually *did* write," she explained. "I figured I'd be able to get letters through the same way I did when I wrote to you that initial time. But when I got back, I wasn't allowed any access to the outside world."

The sadness and pain in Roshin's expressive eyes made Elsie want to believe she was telling the truth. "Why?"

Roishin was quiet as she returned her attention to Isabeau for a moment, who was playing with the ties of Roishin's own cloak. She smiled at the girl before running a hand down the long, brown waves that reached to the girl's upper back. Finally, she spoke.

"I honestly don't know." She sounded troubled. "I have so many questions when I go back." She smirked. "*If* I go back."

"Do you have a choice?" Elsie asked.

Roishin let out a heavy sigh and met Elsie's gaze. "Honestly, I don't know. I'm done in the Underground, but I don't know what's next."

"Can we walk?" Isabeau blurted, looking from one to the other.

Roishin and Elsie shared a quick glance, then stood. Isabeau seemed delighted to have the two women on either side of her, little hands tucked into theirs as they began to stroll the paths.

"I can't believe how she's taken to you so quickly," Elsie marveled.

"Well," Roishin drawled. "I am fairly delightful."

Elsie smiled but said nothing. She stole glances at the princess, still stunned all over again. She was surprised at the differences in her, not only the physical changes, but also the spirit of the young woman herself. She had certainly matured, but there was a stillness to her that hadn't been there before. It was like a quieting of the soul, and she wondered what had brought that on. She was pulled out of her musings when Roishin spoke.

"I guess perhaps you finally got your stroll around the rose garden, hmm?" She gave her a lopsided grin. "No roses yet, though."

Elsie smiled. "No, not yet." She looked over the flower beds, many still barren, but that would change in the coming weeks.

"Aha!" Roishin released Isabeau's hand for a second before she trotted off to a flower bed on the other side of the large fountain at the intersection of the pathways. She bent over, most of her body hidden due to the water fixture in the way. A moment later, she stood and jogged back to the pair. She held a small bouquet of beautiful primrose in her hands. "For you," she said, handing the majority of it to Elsie, a little smile on her lips. "And," she added, bending at the waist to hand the little girl a single flower. "For you."

"Thank you, Roishin," Elsie said, unable to help the smile that crept to her lips.

"Thank you, Roishin!" Isabeau exclaimed, grinning big at her older sister who looked adoringly down at her. She giggled when Roishin tweaked her nose.

"How do you like working with my mamaí?" Roishin asked as the three continued their stroll, she holding Isabeau's flower for her so the little one could hold Roishin's much larger hand.

Elsie couldn't keep the smile from her lips. "I love it," she said. "Her Highness is such an amazing woman." She glanced over at Roishin. "You know?"

Roishin nodded. "I do." She let out a long, heavy sigh. "I was pretty sure she was going to squeeze my head right off my shoulders this morning when she saw me."

Elsie chuckled. "I know she's missed you terribly." She looked down at her free hand, which held the flowers. "We all have."

"I missed you, too," Roishin said quietly.

Elsie cleared her throat, suddenly feeling a bit emotional. She looked away, out into the sunny spring day. "What did they have you do? Were you with Enori?"

Roishin shook her head. "No. I hadn't seen her since I got there, basically." She shrugged. "Showed up this morning and showed me how to get home. Said I'd know when it was time to go again."

"More reading?" Elsie teased, not even sure if that's what Roishin had continued to do.

Roishin quirked an eyebrow as she met her gaze. "I will run away. I'm telling you right now, I will run. Away." She shook her head, looking down at Isabeau when she got her attention to ask her something about one of the flowers they were passing. Roishin easily and patiently answered her question before looking back to Elsie. "That is literally all I did for all those years."

"Why?" Elsie asked, truly enjoying watching the interaction between the sisters. Though not related by blood or even time together, it was clear an instant bond had formed. She wondered if somehow it was because Roishin had saved her life. Did Isabeau know that at a soul level somehow?

"No idea." She grinned over at Elsie. "I truly don't. That's all I did." She looked up into the sky, closing those beautiful green eyes as she inhaled the fresh air around them. "I so missed this," she murmured.

"You're so pale," Elsie said. "Is that why?" At Roishin's nod, she added, "That must have been so hard. You're so used to running around and being outside with your bow or off reading by yourself." She smirked. "Ironically."

"You knew I used to go hide outside somewhere and read?" Roishin asked, surprised amusement in her voice.

Elsie nodded. *Am I blushing?* She looked away and quietly cleared her throat. "Cateline always wanted me to find out where you were," she explained. That had been true—in the beginning. She smiled and made herself meet Roishin's amused gaze. "I think she wanted to make sure you hadn't run off with the minstrels, or something."

"Well, if you catch me reading another solitary

book while I'm home," Roishin muttered. "I give you absolute permission to take it and throw it into the closest fireplace."

❧❧❧❧

Later that night, Elsie lay in bed in her room just off the Queen's chambers. It was so strange being so close to the royal couple. Yes, the walls were about three feet thick, and they and Isabeau—who slept in their bed while in the king's castle—had their privacy, but it just felt strange.

One thing she liked a great deal about the setup at Caisleán Thíar was that she not only had her own small bedchamber, but the entire family chamber was available to her after the family retired, should she wish to spend time there.

She'd been given full permission, and more than one night had found her reading or knitting in one of the chairs by the fireplace. She also had her own garderobe in the evening. It was so nice not to have to share with the entire servant staff on the second floor as she'd had to in her previous position.

One hand was tucked under her head, the other resting upon her blanket-covered body. Staring up at the ceiling, she wasn't seeing the shadows dancing from the fire in the small fireplace. She wasn't hearing the howling spring wind outside the huge stone structure.

Her mind was squarely on the conversation she'd had with Fallon and Cateline, soon to be crowned king and queen of Sursha. King Carthac was still alive, but the castle physician predicted he wouldn't survive beyond the morrow. Coronation plans had been put in place a few years ago but actually put into motion days ago.

Fallon would have little time to grieve before she would take the throne. Elsie knew that she was devastated by what was happening. More than once she'd inadvertently walked in on a teary-eyed Fallon or Cateline holding her. So, here it was, an era coming to an end. Carthac had been one of—if not *the*—greatest kings Sursha had ever known in its history.

Elsie knew in her heart of hearts that Fallon and Cateline would continue the greatness, if not even surpass it. At almost forty-three, Fallon was young enough to have a long reign but old enough to be wise and experienced in life and the politics of the country and the world.

Cateline was already the heart of the country, what with all the work she'd begun nearly twenty years before when she'd first married Fallon's late brother, Fergus. All of her programs were designed to feed and clothe the poor, or otherwise provide assistance to the less fortunate during those rough times. Elsie had never seen anything like it from a government, only neighbor helping neighbor back in Scotland.

All this thought of course brought her back to the conversation that night. With Fallon's ascension to the throne imminent, Garratt, the heir apparent, would be taking over Caisleán Thíar once he finished up military service...and he would need a wife.

# *Chapter Four*

Looking surreptitiously around, Elsie sensed the mixed sentiments from those gathered in the great cathedral. The old guard of the country seemed to be somewhat divided in their feelings about Fallon being coronated as their new king. Their love and devotion to the family in general was strong, but for many of them, Carthac had been the only king they had ever known.

Despite how much Fallon was respected and revered as a warrior, and then as the prince and heir apparent, Fallon just wasn't Carthac. And, with a flourishing kingdom, no doubt they were worried what the new reign would mean.

Then there was the majority of the population, which was younger and had grown up right along with Fallon. For them, she was their hero, their brother-in-arms or protector. Many shed tears of joy or had smiles on their faces as Fallon took the throne.

The ceremony happening around her dripped with tradition, honor, and the heavy weight of an entire country—an entire people—transferred from Carthac's broad shoulders to Fallon's very capable ones.

For her part, Elsie was nearly in tears with pride seeing Fallon sitting up there, adorned with all the garb and honors of her new station including the large golden crown of the king. She knew Fallon had been ready for this her entire life. With Cateline, a born queen, by her side, the couple would take this island nation into the next generation with love, honor, and prosperity.

Her gaze scanned over to where the royal children were seated, Laigen and Garratt both present for this historic event. But Elsie's gaze went directly to Roishin. The castle seamstresses had jumped to action to create a gown for her. Certainly nothing she'd had before would fit, let alone be appropriate for such a momentous occasion.

She looked stunning, even though Elsie knew she was hating having to sit there in that dress. Elsie smiled at that thought. However, the young woman's fierce, independent nature was also on display, her hair brushed down with warrior braids, a nod to her deep Celtic roots, her pride in Fallon's warrior past, and her own unique and bright fire.

As though she felt herself being watched, Roishin's head lifted from where it had been bowed, her verdant eyes scanning faces until she found Elsie's. Their gazes met and held for a long moment before, with a small smile, Roishin turned back forward.

❧ ❧ ❧ ❧

Standing in the line with the other servants along the wall in case they were needed, Elsie watched as the grand gala commenced in the great hall. The who's who of Sursha was there, nobility all vying for position with the new king and queen. There were also many guests from other allied and not-so-allied nations who had come to congratulate the new king—and no doubt sniff around for weaknesses or vulnerabilities to exploit in the new reign.

Elsie had also heard tell that some had come looking at Roishin and Garratt, both eligible heirs of marrying age. Though she'd been approached by Fallon and Cateline regarding Garratt, Elsie wasn't sure what she thought of the idea. Her...*situation*—if there even was one—with Roishin was complicated at best, impossible at worst .

Though Fallon and Cateline had managed to pull off one of the greatest farces of all time, Roishin and her situation was quite different. Fallon had been raised as a male her entire life and seen as such by the world. Regardless of what any one person might think or believe individually, it was generally accepted that Fallon was the youngest son of Carthac and Roishin of Sursha. Said son had married a woman, Cateline. Man and woman make a pair. Woman and woman make a prison cell, or far worse. Just ask Elsie's great-great-grandmother.

She was pulled out of her dark thoughts when Garratt approached her. He was about Fallon's height, if not a bit taller, but had shoulder-length dark blond hair and bright blue eyes much like Laigen's. He had broad shoulders and a powerful build. He was a very handsome man, she admitted, especially when dressed in his military finery.

His smile was welcoming, dimples flashing at her. "Good eve, Elsie."

"Good eve, milord," she replied with a small bow of deference to his station.

"You look lovely," he said, gaze traveling over her dress and face with appreciation.

"Thank you, milord," she said softly.

He clicked his boots together in dramatic fashion and bowed, giving her a boyish smile in the process. "Will you be joining us tomorrow?"

"Aye," she said. Many of the servants would be escorted back to the castle of the former prince and princess to begin getting things ready for the transition to the king's residence.

His smile grew. "Wonderful." He looked out over the large gathering, a goblet of something in hand. "What do you think of today's festivities?" he asked, looking back at her.

"I think it's a wonderful and deserved celebration of the king and queen, milord." Though it was the appropriate response, she meant it.

He nodded, sipping from his drink. Elsie felt a bit nervous. Garratt had never given her any personal attention that didn't have to do with a request or question appropriate to her position as a servant. Certainly he'd looked at her before, though simply as a young man who spotted a pretty girl and nothing more.

But now, at age twenty-five and his parents upon the throne, everything had changed for him. No longer could his life be that as a mostly transient soldier on the battlefield, but a man who must now grow into his own as the heir to the throne.

For him to now seek her out and be speaking to her outside her station, she wondered if Fallon and Cateline had spoken to him as well. Perhaps he had been the one to put the bug in their ear regarding her as a possible match for him?

She didn't know Garratt well at all, having only swapped perhaps two dozen words with him during the entire six years she'd been at the castle. He'd always seemed nice, if not a bit brooding, though she'd always taken that for the nature of a warrior, not that she knew many personally. Her father, of course, had been one, and she remembered a similar bent to his nature.

Had marriage and children ever been in Elsie's mind? Not necessarily. But, now that things had changed so dramatically for her and she was well into the second half of her ten-year requirement of service, she needed to begin considering her future and what she wanted for herself.

"There you are!"

Elsie's head whipped to her right to see Roishin walking over to them. She quickly had to avert her eyes because the young woman was just so unbelievably beautiful. She worried her admiration would be written all over her face if she continued to look. Clearing her throat and schooling her expression, she looked up again.

"Hey," Garratt said to his sister. "Yes, here I am."

"Daidí is looking for you," Roishin said, nodding in the general direction where the king stood with several others. "Discussions are being had for tomorrow's travels." She grinned, lightly punching him in the arm. "And you, you lucky guy, get to be in charge of it all."

"You're coming with us, right?" he asked her.

Roishin nodded. "Aye."

Garratt nodded in acknowledgment before turning back to Elsie. He gave her a charming grin before taking one of her hands in his. He brought it to his lips for a light pass over the backs of her fingers. She gave him a polite curtsy before taking her hand back as it was released. A quick glance to Roishin showed that she had glanced away, looking decidedly… uncomfortable? Unhappy?

Without another look at Elsie, the siblings headed off to speak to Fallon.

※ ※ ※ ※

Elsie nodded, adding to her list as she and

Cateline sat down together to discuss what needed to be done—or begun—once Elsie reached Caisleán Thíar. She looked over the items she'd already written down, and the list was extensive. She understood it was simply a guidepost for her to get started and assign the other servants tasks.

Looking up at the woman sitting across from her, she asked, "Anything else, Your Highness?"

"May I?" the queen asked, tapping the parchment. When it was gently pushed over to her, Cateline turned it around and read what had been written down. She reached for the quill, which was handed to her. Jotting a couple more items down, Cateline handed both quill and parchment back to Elsie with a smile. "Thank you so much, Elsie."

"Of course." She placed the quill back with the inkwell and lightly blew on the parchment before carefully folding it to tuck away in the pockets of her dress. She felt eyes on her.

"Have you given any thought to our proposal?" Cateline asked softly.

Tucking her bottom lip underneath her top teeth, Elsie was quiet for a moment, trying to decide how to respond. She knew the question would be coming and had yet to figure out how to answer it. Finally, she said, "I would think you'd want a princess or at least a noblewoman from another kingdom for him."

"I wasn't going to tell you this," Cateline said, a smile in her eyes. "But we were waiting until Fallon took the throne. We will never forget what you did for our Roishin before she left, Elsie." She reached across the table and covered the younger woman's hand with her own. "You saved her life, and you helped in a situation that, honestly, I still don't fully understand."

Elsie gave her a shy smile. "Neither do I."

"Exactly. So, regardless of what you do, Fallon is going to bestow a title upon you. Our deepest gratitude."

Elsie could only stare at her, stunned speechless.

"This will ensure your personal safety and that you'll be taken care of," Cateline explained. "And, as for Garratt, he will be king one day. We want to ensure he has a solid marriage with a woman who can be a partner to him. A woman who loves this country as much as he does to keep the balance." She smiled. "Like Fallon and me."

Elsie felt incredibly nervous at the idea of marriage to a man, and she wasn't entirely sure why. Swallowing, she asked, "When would this have to happen?"

"Well," Cateline said gently. "Garratt still has a year left before he can finish his service in the elite guard. After that, we'd want the marriage to move forward. Until then, it would be an engagement."

Elsie looked up when her hand was lightly squeezed to get her attention.

"I was your age when I was told I'd be married," Cateline said. "I was absolutely terrified." Her smile grew. "Granted, I had good reason with Fergus. Fallon and I had no idea we were intended for each other." She studied Elsie for a long moment before she continued, voice low. "Elsie, there are many types of marriages."

Surprised by the quiet comment, Elsie gave Cateline her full attention. The look in the queen's beautiful gray-blue eyes told her to listen carefully to what she was saying.

"What Fallon and I have is very rare. We have a deep, profound passion for each other and are partners in every way. But," she added, holding up a finger. "There are marriages of convenience certainly, marriages to simply knit two nations together. And there are marriages of friendship, mutual respect, and mutual love of a country."

Elsie had the very distinct feeling that this last type was what was being proposed. It was insurance to make sure Garratt had the support to be a good king—namely, the support of a wife who held some of the cards dealt by Fallon and Cateline before passing the torch. This gave her an entirely different perspective on many things, and a great deal to think about.

"Would children be required?" she asked softly, feeling a bit nauseated at the question. It wasn't being a mother that concerned her. In fact, her time with Isabeau over the last almost five years had been moments of great joy for her. It was the…process…of conception that left her cold.

A small smile graced Cateline's lips. If Elsie didn't know better, she would think there was something behind that smile, but she wasn't sure what. "Oui," she said, thumb gently rubbing the back of the hand she still held. "A moment in time to serve generations."

"Would you have done it?" Elsie asked, unsure.

Cateline's eyebrows shot up. "I would have, yes." She smirked. "I tried, but Fergus just never showed up."

Elsie gasped at the playful little twinkle in Cateline's eyes. "You never…" Her hand came up and she covered her mouth with her free hand. A small laugh escaped with the huge grin that spread across the queen's face. "So, Fallon…"

Cateline nodded. "She's been the only one for me," she said softly. "In every way."

"How—" Elsie stopped herself, not even sure what she was trying to ask.

Cateline chuckled, squeezing her hand one more

time before releasing her. "Someday," she said. "I'll tell you." She sat back in her chair. "If you don't want this, Elsie, that is your right. We will not push you or force you. We believe you'd be a perfect match for Garratt in your strength, your temperament, and your intelligence. You are beautiful and exceptionally good with Isabeau and anyone who is privileged enough to be around you."

Elsie lowered her eyes, feeling incredibly honored that a woman she looked up to so much and admired felt those things about her. "Thank you," she whispered.

"Our family already loves you," Cateline added quietly. "And I believe you already love our family."

Elsie's eyes flicked up to meet hers again, but she couldn't hold that gaze. Instead, she simply nodded and said, "Aye."

⁂

It had been a long ride home, though relatively uneventful. She'd hoped to ride in the same carriage as Roishin to be able to talk and catch up after so many years, but alas that had not happened. Elsie had been placed in the carriage with the other servants who were headed back, and Roishin rode with Laigen and Reinaldo.

The couple would be heading back to Spain soon, and the harbor was much closer to Caisleán Thíar than the king's castle. Fallon and Cateline would remain there for a bit longer in order to get some things wrapped up before heading back home for the final packing and transition. It would be a big move; nearly nineteen years of a life built in that castle would have to be dismantled and rebuilt on the other side of the country.

It was late, and Elsie was tired. It had been a whirlwind of weeks, and certainly one of emotions. She'd yet to really and fully allow herself to just *feel*. The death of the king, the coronation of Fallon, and the return of Roishin, for however long she was back, was a lot to deal with, and she knew tomorrow she'd have to hit the ground running.

There was a lot to do and not a terribly long time to get it done. She so much wanted to prove herself to Cateline and Fallon, as this was a huge responsibility that had been placed upon her shoulders. For now, she sat alone in the family chamber of the castle she'd lived and served in for more than six years.

Elsie figured the same setup would be put in place in the new castle. She knew Fallon and Cateline would slit their own wrists before no longer sharing a bedchamber. She smiled at that thought as she curled up in one of the chairs by the huge fireplace. Another servant had been kind enough to make sure it was nice and warm before they'd even arrived back at the castle.

It had been rainy and stormy all day, skies gray and pregnant. The evening now was cold. As she stared into the flames, she had the strangest craving. It was actually something she hadn't experienced but once since her mother died: to be held. The night of Livia's death, when she and Cateline had sat in this very room, Cateline had held her after those horrendous events.

That had been so long ago, Livia nearly five years in her grave. Now, sitting there curled up, Elsie's mind was buzzing. Thoughts bounced around from what needed to be done, to the conversation she'd had with the queen two days before, to what needed to be done, to Roishin, to what needed to be done, and back to Cateline again. Nonstop, it went.

She looked around, taking in the large chamber. This was the princess's chamber, where Cateline traditionally would have slept. Should she take them up on their proposal, it would be her chamber. She had absolutely no intention of sharing a bedchamber with Garratt—or any husband, for that matter.

What would it be like having such a place all to herself? To come in here at night, have a huge bed all to herself, the boudoir and garderobe all to herself. To have a lady-in-waiting of her very own. Who would she be? What could she do to make her life better, as Cateline had done for her?

The other side of that coin was, what would she have to do for Garratt? What sort of wife would he want or demand? Would he be able to come into this very chamber and claim his marriage bed rights whenever he wanted? She glanced over to where the table was now, where she'd served and watched the family eat their meals for years.

Apparently, that had been where the bed was before the chamber had been transformed. She studied that area, imagining herself in that bed. She had to force herself to imagine Garratt in the bed with her, doing things to her that she honestly didn't want to think about. But, she reasoned, children were a must. It was part of the entire point, to continue the line.

Could she do it?

# *Chapter Five*

It just seemed so incredibly huge. Roishin lay awake, waiting for something to pop out of the shadows. This is ridiculous, she thought. She was no longer a child, but she felt uneasy all the same.

Sitting up in the bed she'd used since the age of two, she braced on her hands and looked around. She knew there was absolutely no way she was going to get sleep. Her mind was too busy and frankly, she felt too uneasy in such a huge space. Funny thing was, she'd never thought of her bedchamber as large before.

Next to her parents' chamber, it was downright dainty. But compared to what she'd had for more than four years, it may as well have been a bed plopped down in the middle of the Grand Canyon she'd read about. Growling in irritation, she shoved the blankets back and climbed out of bed. How had she slept at her grandfather's castle and then at the nobleman's estate they'd stayed at overnight on their journey back home?

"Ridiculous," she muttered.

Still in her sleep dress, she pulled on her boots, then grabbed her cloak. If nothing else, maybe walking the castle for a bit would help make her sleepy. She absolutely did not want to admit it to herself, but she felt that maybe there was another component to her insomnia. Maybe. Just *maybe* it was the knowledge that there would not be a certain blonde servant in her bedchamber to wake up to and watch.

"No," she muttered, adjusting the cloak in place

before tying it at her throat. "Ridiculous."

Walking to the closed bedchamber door, she grabbed the handle, but before she turned it, she focused and concentrated. She did not want to be seen, but to be left alone. In the Underground, one of the first things you had to learn was to disappear. Seeing another person or an animal was often about that person or animal actually *wanting* to be seen, then projecting that desire.

The energy produced was perceived by another person or animal, and thus connection was made. Seeing or perceiving was done much less with the eyes than with the brain and detection of energy. A truly successful hunter or warrior, such as Fallon, had the innate ability to still their energy and disappear even as they stood fully visible.

In the Underground, the only way to achieve privacy was to learn this principle or expand upon a natural gift. That was why there were no doors or curtains on the rooms. You want privacy? Figure it out and claim it.

Pulling her hood into place, Roishin opened the door and stepped out into the quiet hall. She looked around to see if anyone was in the vicinity, and there was not. Feeling comfortable, she chewed on her bottom lip as she determined where she wanted to go. Before her mind could catch up, her feet had already decided.

Her boots didn't make a sound on the stone stairs as she headed to the third floor. It took a moment for her to realize where she was heading, or that she'd even chosen a definitive direction. Once she reached the landing, she was passed by a young servant who hurried past her with an armful of cut logs.

He buzzed by her, no clue she was there. She

watched him go, turning into the family chamber where she saw the flickering light from the fireplace. Clearly he was there to ensure it kept burning. Roishin's gaze went past those double doors and to those at the end of the hall. They were closed, but she knew that chamber was empty.

Her heart hurt at that. Her parents were on the other side of the country, and she already missed them despite the fact she'd been able to spend so much time with them before the coronation. She had no idea when Enori would call her back, and she hoped very much that Fallon and Cateline were back here before that.

She could have stayed with them, but something told her to come back to Caisleán Thíar. Perhaps to see it one more time? She hoped it wouldn't be another four years before she was given time to return home, but no doubt whenever it was, it would be at the king's residence.

Pushing those thoughts out of her mind, she stepped into the family chamber. The servant boy was kneeling in front of the massive fireplace, feeding the fire the logs he'd brought up. He was oblivious to her presence. She immediately noted Elsie curled up in one of the two chairs. She was in a sleep dress but not asleep, her hair down and brushed to a golden shine.

She's beautiful, Roishin thought as she stood back and watched, unable to take her eyes off her. Elsie looked to be deep in thought, not really even paying much mind to the boy, though she did thank him as he scurried out, task complete. He shut the doors behind him at her request.

Now she was veritably trapped with Elsie, as she'd have to open the door to leave. She might be out of mind thus out of sight, but she, ironically, couldn't walk through the doors. Roishin moved over to the couch and quietly sat down. She'd been sitting there for a moment when suddenly Elsie gasped softly, lifting her head from where it had rested against her closed hand.

She turned in her chair, looking around the room. "Is someone there?" she asked softly.

Stunned, Roishin could only stare at her. Elsie's eyes scanned right over her, unseeing, but the look on her face made it quite clear she felt something, or someone. When she began to look uncomfortable, just this side of nervous, Roishin reached up and brushed her hood back.

"Here."

Gasping loudly this time, Elsie's eyes were huge as she looked at her. Hand to heart, she looked downright terrified for a moment. "Roishin?"

Giving her an apologetic smile, Roishin nodded. "Sorry. I was just going to roam around the castle for a bit to try and get tired." She shrugged. "Ended up in here."

"You scared me to death!"

"I'm really sorry," Roishin said, contrite. "I honestly didn't mean to."

Uncurling herself, Elsie pushed to her feet. She stood by the chair for a long moment, her hand resting on its back as she seemed to be caught in indecision. Roishin was rendered speechless. As the beautiful young woman stood before the fire, her sleep dress was made transparent by the flames behind her. She could see the outline of her beautiful body, the shadows of shapely legs and womanly hips.

As she turned slightly, the rounded side of one breast was visible for just a moment before she stepped away from the fireplace and walked over to the couch. Gazing down at Roishin, she looked unsure.

"Is it really you?"

At first Roishin was confused by the question, but then, remembering the horrible events before Roishin had left, she gave her a small smile. "Yup." She noticed something attached to the white sleep dress just above Elsie's left breast. "You're wearing it," she said softly, smiling broadly as her gaze flicked back up to meet that of the young woman who still stood over her. "I guess I *did* ask you to keep it safe for me." She hoped that would be enough to make Elsie feel comfortable that it was, in fact, Roishin and not the return of the evil bastard.

Elsie looked down at the gold triskelion attached to her garment, then looked shyly away as she sat down next to Roishin. "Yes, well," she murmured, looking down at her hands, which rested in her lap. "It seemed the safest place."

Roishin reached across the foot of space between them and covered Elsie's hand with her own. She smiled when Elsie looked back at her. "I'm glad." She was also glad when her smile was returned. "What are you doing here?" she asked, indicating the family chamber.

"I couldn't sleep," Elsie said, a little chuckle following her words. "Even though I'm exhausted." She met Roishin's gaze as she rested her head against the back of the couch.

Nodding, Roishin said, "I understand. Me, too, which is why I went wandering." She gave Elsie a side-eye. "This is going to sound pathetic, and I'm okay with that, but it feels so lonely down there." She indicated the floor below the one they currently inhabited. She smirked. "Here I am like a five-year-old wanting to be with people but not really sure how to go about it."

"I'm sorry, Roishin," Elsie said, turning her hand

over beneath the larger one covering hers, Roishin's fingers wrapping around it.

"Would you be terribly put off if I slept on the couch in here?" Roishin asked, indicating where they sat. She gave her an impish grin and a shrug.

Elsie met her gaze and studied her face for a long time. No, she wasn't just studying her face, it felt like she was studying Roishin's very *soul*. Finally, she said, "You don't want to be alone. Do you." A statement.

Roishin looked away. Oh, the child she felt like in that moment. She couldn't garner the courage to look over at the other woman let alone respond, though from the tone of her voice, it didn't seem like Elsie needed one. Clearing her throat, she simply shrugged.

"What did they do to you?" Elsie whispered. When Roishin didn't immediately answer, she pushed to her feet and gently tugged on Roishin's hand.

Looking up at her, Roishin saw that Elsie was patiently waiting for her to stand. She did, unsure why. Taking a better hold of her hand, Elsie led the way toward the small room just off the family chamber, that of the lady-in-waiting. A roaring fire was already burning in that small fireplace.

They both knew the young boy would make one more round to make sure all fires were out in unoccupied rooms before he went to bed, so they didn't worry about leaving the fireplace in the family chamber.

Once inside, Elsie dropped her hand and turned to her. She made short work of the ties of Roishin's cloak, easing the garment off her shoulders before she walked over to the wall near the door, which she closed, and hung it up on a hook.

"It'll be a bit tight," she said, walking over to the bed pushed against the wall. She pushed the covers back and climbed in, scooting all the way over.

Surprised at this turn of events, Roishin walked and climbed in. Elsie leaned up and pulled the covers over them both before she lay down on her side, arm tucked up under her head.

Roishin mirrored her position, lying on her left side. She looked into the eyes that looked back at her. They were guarded, though she thought she saw so much of her own need for comfort in their sapphire depths.

"Is it strange for you to be back here?" Elsie asked.

"In some ways, yes," Roishin responded. "In others, it's home. Will always be home. Well." She smirked. "Until my parents move into the other castle, I guess."

Elsie smiled. "Yes, but even there, you grew up in those rooms and it'll still be your family."

"Are you going, too?" Roishin asked, knowing that a number of servants would remain here at Caisleán Thíar to care for the castle until the next occupants moved in, which would no doubt be her brother and his wife, whoever that may be.

Elsie studied her for a long time, her expression growing troubled. "I...For a while, for certain."

Roishin raised her eyebrows in question. "Where are you going?" When there was no answer, Roishin felt her heart skip a beat. "Elsie?"

Eyes closing for a moment, Elsie finally blew out a long, slow breath. "Your parents have approached me about..." She swallowed. "About..."

Gasping, Roishin instantly felt tears come to her eyes, her stomach roiling. She threw the covers off herself and was about to fall out of the bed when Elsie grabbed her hand.

"Please don't go," Elsie cried, the emotion making her words thick. "Please, Roishin!"

Her own tears sliding down her cheeks, Roishin looked back at her. She felt sick, like she could throw up. She shook her head. "No. You can't."

"Please," Elsie whispered, pulling on Roishin's hand.

Collapsing onto the mattress on her back, Roishin could hardly breathe. Elsie hadn't protested anything, so she figured she was right. "Gods, no," she whispered, covering her weeping eyes with her hand. "Not Garratt." The sobs came in earnest then.

Also crying, Elsie moved over to her side, her body pressed to Roishin's side. "Look at me," she said through her tears. "Please, look at me."

Roishin's hand fell away, though it took her a moment before she could open her eyes. When she did, she looked up into tormented and tear-filled eyes. "Are they making you do this?"

Elsie shook her head. "No. I haven't even said yes yet." She arched her head so all her hair fell to one side as she looked down at her, resting on her side with upper body raised on a forearm. She brought her hand up and brushed Roishin's hair away from her face, thumb gently wiping at the tears on her cheek.

"Are you going to?"

"I don't know," Elsie murmured.

Roishin closed her eyes for a moment, then met her eyes again. "Do you love him?" When Elsie shook her head again, she asked, "Then, why?"

Elsie sighed heavily. "Roishin," she began softly, her fingers caressing the heated skin of Roishin's cheek and jaw. "You were gone for four years. Four," she repeated with raised eyebrows for emphasis. "You're leaving again, and who knows how long for. Another four years? Ten? Forever?"

Roishin closed her eyes again as her heart began to ache. She knew Elsie was right, but she hurt so badly. Taking a deep, steadying breath, she opened her eyes again. "I can't watch that. I can't watch you with him." She looked away, more tears beginning to leak out of the corners of her eyes. "How could they do that?" she whispered, turning her head away.

"I think Cateline knows," Elsie said, urging Roishin back to look at her. When Roishin looked at her again, she continued, her fingers never leaving Roishin's face. "She told me that they essentially want a wife for Garratt that can balance him out as king, which eventually he will be, Roishin." She shook her head. "This isn't about love, and your mother made it very clear that's not the intention."

That made Roishin feel better, until something horrible popped into her mind. "You'd have to..." She swallowed, not sure she could say it. "With him."

Elsie's eyes fell closed as she nodded. "There would have to be children."

"Do you want to do that?" Roishin whispered through her tears   . "With him?" she barely managed.

Elsie immediately shook her head. "No."

Roishin studied the tears that slid down Elsie's cheeks. She could see the truth in her face and hear it in that one word. She brought her own hand up, using her fingertips to brush away Elsie's tears.

Looking into her eyes, she saw her own feelings and her own heart reflected back at her. She also saw the knowledge that it was pretty much hopeless for them to be together in any sort of real relationship, even if it weren't for Enori, The Mystic, and whatever else was next. They were both women, and everybody knew it.

Maybe this is for the best, she thought, even as her heart broke to think it. Elsie deserved a future, one beyond being a castle servant, or even a lady-in-waiting to the queen. And if that future included becoming queen herself, who was Roishin to stand in her way?

The hand that rested on Elsie's cheek slid into her hair as she gently urged her head down. Roishin's eyes closed at the first touch of soft lips against her own. She sighed when Elsie lowered her upper body a bit, her breast resting lightly against Roishin's. She was getting lost in the softness of lips and the warmth of Elsie's body pressed against her side.

Elsie's hand moved from Roishin's cheek to the side of her neck, thumb running along her jaw as their lips caressed and moved against each other. It was a deeper physical connection than any before it, and only in that moment did Roishin feel her world right itself. Only in that moment did she no longer feel so alone or lost.

One thing Roishin had read about in her endless books was something that had immediately brought Elsie to her mind, thoughts that had caused infinite blushing at the time. This moment, right now, might be her only chance to live the fantasies she had conjured. She very lightly brushed her tongue against Elsie's bottom lip, making her gasp softly in surprise.

The kiss paused for only a brief moment before Elsie did the same thing, making Roishin sigh in pleasure. She did it again, though this time on the underside of Elsie's top lip, asking for permission. Both sighed a little moan at the first light stroke of tongue against tongue.

Elsie lowered herself even more until she was partially lying atop Roishin, whose hand moved out of thick blond hair and down along her shoulder to her back. The skin was so warm through the material of her sleeping gown. The two inexperienced young women soon found their rhythm, the kiss deeply sensual.

Roishin felt things she'd never felt before, her body so sensitized it was admittedly becoming overwhelming. Finally, she placed her hand on the side of Elsie's face as she slowed the kiss and eased back into the pillow.

Elsie raised her head, breathing hard. She looked down into Roishin's eyes for a long time, as if memorizing her face. Finally, she smiled, brushing the backs of her fingers against Roishin's cheek and moving off her, though not far. She snuggled up against Roishin, resting her head against her shoulder.

Roishin wrapped an arm around her, then pulled the covers back up over them as they fell into sleep.

## *Chapter Six*

Eyes blinking a few times before they remained open, Roishin came into wakefulness. She was alone in the small bed and, upon lifting her head, discovered she was alone in the small chamber as well. To her surprise, the sun was already coming up. She honestly couldn't remember the last time she'd slept this late.

Sitting up, she rubbed at her face with her hands before letting them drop to her blanket-covered lap. She'd slept better last night than she had…ever. She felt rested, even as her heart was heavy. Everything came back to her like water from an icy lake thrown at her, leaving her just as speechless as the night before.

Her hands found her face again as she sat there, taking several deep breaths to try to calm and center herself. She needed to get up, and honestly, she needed to leave. Whether she went back with Enori or she just left, she couldn't stay anymore, not if staying meant she would have to see her brother courting Elsie. Maybe she could go to Spain with Laigen and her husband and start over there.

Blowing out a breath, she tugged the covers off and pushed up from the bed. One thing that had been enlightening in the Underground was that she'd learned how to clean up after herself. She quickly made Elsie's bed to perfection before tugging her boots and cloak on and heading out.

Servants hustled and bustled about to perform their morning tasks, not one paying Roishin a lick of attention as she made her way down to the second floor and her bedchamber. She made sure nobody would notice the door open, then tucked herself inside. Leaning back against the closed door, she shut her eyes.

Taking several deep breaths, she tried to calm her emotions. She wanted to cry, and she wanted to scream, so much emotion coursing through her. Maybe she'd head out into the woods later. Pushing away from the door, she brushed her hood down and nearly jumped out of her skin.

Hand to heart, she glared. "You scared the hell out of me, Enori!"

A little smile quirked full lips. "Probably a good thing," the priestess said, remaining where she sat in one of the chairs. She wore her white gown and blue cloak, one leg crossed elegantly over the other. The gorgeous blonde looked for all the world like she was a queen upon her throne.

Anger instantly filled Roishin, everything coming down on her at once. "Why are you here?" she growled. "I don't want to see you."

"No?" Enori challenged with a raised eyebrow.

"No." Roishin glared at her as she walked farther into the room. She was a tempest of feelings, so many dive-bombing her heart like evil little hawks taking turns picking off a family of field mice.

"And why is that?" Enori asked, her voice never losing its soft, calm timbre.

"Because!" Roishin exclaimed, whirling on her, cloak fanning out like a cape. "You did this!" She pointed a finger at her. "You took me away from my family for more than *four years*! I don't even know my family anymore. My little sister is now a little kid. She was a baby when I left, Enori. A goddamn baby!"

She grew even angrier as tears came, hot and

bitter. She angrily swiped at them with the sleeve of her sleep shirt. Sniffling, she looked down at her feet.

"And now, I've lost Elsie." Her eyes fell closed when she heard the other woman push up from her chair. With a *whoosh*, a fire appeared in the fireplace before Enori walked up behind Roishin, who felt so defeated.

"Did you ever have her?" she asked quietly.

Roishin gasped, turning on her. "What kind of question is that?" she said, truly hurt.

"It is a serious question." Enori held her gaze before it fell to her fingers as they began to undo the ties to Roishin's cloak.

Roishin felt the warmth of the fire and coolness of the woman before her. The look in Enori's unusual eyes wasn't cruel indifference, it was more like aloof practicality. "Why are you here?" Roishin asked, her voice thick with emotion. "I don't want to go."

Enori's gaze flicked up to meet hers as she continued her task. "Would I be removing your cloak if I were taking you away at this moment?"

Roishin rolled her eyes. She wanted to growl at that damn practical logic again. "Then why are you here?"

"I have come to realize that I did not do right by you," Enori said.

After one final look into Roishin's eyes, she moved around behind her, her touch never leaving Roishin as her hand trailed along her back in her short journey. She eased the heavy material off Roishin's shoulders, the light touches sending little shivers through the taller woman.

"I was so ready to get you started in the work that I did not talk to you, explain things to you," she continued softly, moving away from the younger woman for a moment as she tossed the cloak to Roishin's bed several feet away.

"What work?" Roishin asked bitterly. "Reading forever?"

"I know it felt that way," Enori murmured, once again stepping up behind her protégé. She placed her hands on Roishin's hips, using the leverage to gently urge her to turn a bit to her right. "Look into the flames," she said, the pair now directly in front of the fireplace six feet away. "Watch the fire as I tell you a story."

Roishin nodded dumbly, feeling almost drugged by the soft, soothing voice near her ear and the hypnotic dance of the flames before her eyes.

"First," Enori said. "What do you know of your parentage?" Her hands remained on Roishin's hips, their bodies not quite touching.

"I was in an orphanage," Roishin said softly. "Parents dead."

"Is that what you were told?"

Roishin thought about it, then shook her head. "No. I guess I just assumed that since that's how Laigen and Garratt, and even Livia, came into my parents' lives."

"Do you wonder why you look so much like Fallon and Cateline?" she asked, fingers beginning to run through long, dark hair.

Roishin's eyes fell closed. "Yes," she whispered. Her body was so confused. It couldn't decide if it wanted to go to sleep or be deeply aroused by the closeness and touches of this gorgeous woman.

"The older you've gotten, the more you look like them," Enori murmured. "It is remarkable."

"How?" Roishin barely managed to not moan in pleasure as her hair was played with. She swallowed.

"How is it possible?"

"Because you are of their essence," Enori said. Her fingers left dark hair and rested on broad shoulders. "You have Fallon's size and strength," she continued, hands slowly smoothing down over Roishin's shoulders and down her arms. "Yet, you have Cateline's feisty, questioning nature." A soft laugh lightly swept across Roishin's neck, sending a shiver through her. "You also have her freckles." Soft fingertips roamed down Roishin's cheek, then ran a featherlight touch over her lips. "And her beautiful mouth."

Roishin's heart was racing, and she gasped softly at the unexpected touches on her face. She could hardly breathe.

"You were created from their love," Enori whispered into her ear.

"Why?" Roishin managed. "How?" She was grateful when Enori's hands returned to her shoulders.

"Because Ankou needed to right a wrong," she explained. "Your grandmother, the woman who shared your name and your eyes, was meant to rule Brittany and help to right wrongs upon the earth with her gifts." She leaned in again. "Your gifts." She moved away a bit, Roishin exhaling relief. "Except yours run deeper. Your grandmother was born of a normal human and someone born of the gifts of the Order."

"Was I?" Roishin asked, trying desperately to absorb what she was being told even as her body was infused with warmth and sensations she had no idea what to do with.

"Your mothers are both gifted," Enori said. "Fallon was born of the blood of Roishin, and Cateline carries her soul." She rested her chin upon Roishin's shoulder, her words soft breaths of air against the side of Roishin's cheek. "But you," she continued. "You have three parents."

In the flames, Roishin saw a woman lying on a bed, her legs spread and her face twisted in agony as a baby was pushed from her womb. As a woman eased the baby out the rest of the way, the woman went limp, sightless eyes staring into eternity. The baby was not moving, nor was it making a sound.

A cloaked figure stepped up to the woman holding the lifeless infant, and skeletal hands reached for it, slowly running its bony fingers over the tiny body until an identical but transparent version was cradled in the figure's arms. It turned and vanished, leaving an unmoving mother and child.

Another newborn lay upon a blanket spread out over a large stone slab, not moving, not even breathing. The cloaked figure appeared, easing its precious bundle down over the baby, the transparent energy vanishing within its tiny body. With a gasp, the baby began to cry, little fingers flexing and unflexing and a leg kicking out.

The baby was swaddled in the blanket it lay upon, then another cloaked figure took it in their arms, hurrying away from the stone slab. The scene disappeared with the quick surge of the flames.

"The blood of Ankou flows through your veins, Roishin," Enori murmured. "His true daughter."

Tears slowly began to stream down Roishin's cheeks as she stepped away from Enori. Sniffling, she looked at her. "What am I supposed to do with all this?"

"What you were literally born to do."

"Which is what?" Roishin exclaimed, using the sleeve of her sleep dress again to wipe at her eyes. While some things, like how she looked like both her mothers, made sense now, so much was even more confusing and unclear. "Isn't Ankou the God of Death?"

Enori nodded. "He collects the dead, yes." Her smile was so loving, so filled with awe as she spoke her next words. "But you...you are the bringer of life, Roishin. Together, you and Ankou are opposite sides of the same coin and will work together to fix what was wronged." She walked over to Roishin, taking her hands in gentle ones. "Like you did with Isabeau." She shook her head. "Her parents were not supposed to die, nor was she. You could not save them, but you saved her." She squeezed Roishin's hands to emphasize her next point. "On instinct, you followed your heart, followed the blood, and now Isabeau is connected to you forever."

Sniffling, Roishin met her gaze. "Is that why I feel so connected to her? Even though I haven't seen her since she was a baby?"

Enori's smile was beautiful. "Yes." She gave Roishin's hands one more squeeze before releasing them. "She will be very important to you, Roishin." She gently brushed dark hair out of a tear streak, tucking the strands behind an ear. "As for Elsie," she said, her voice gentle but matter-of-fact. "She will never be able to join you in the life you must live."

"What if I don't go with you?" Roishin challenged. "What if I stay here?"

Enori shrugged, noncommittal. "Your blood will call you home," she said. "But even if it did not, what would you do?" She raised a dark blond eyebrow in question. "Be together in the shadows? Sneak to not be seen, hmm?" For a very brief moment, pain flashed through her brilliant eyes, then it was gone. "They kill women like Elsie," she said. "And you will not be able to protect her." She dropped her hands from Roishin and turned away.

Roishin studied her for a long moment. Though

that look had been brief, the pain had exuded from Enori like heat from a fire. "You've experienced that," she said softly. "Haven't you?"

Enori turned to look at her, her expression guarded, almost hard. The exquisite beauty that was her face was almost like a statue, crafted lovingly by a master sculptor with features chiseled to perfection. But, like a statue, it was only to look at and not to touch.

"I will not tell you not to love her, as the heart does as it chooses. But," she added, voice firm. "I will warn you to do it from afar, Roishin. For her sake," she finished softly, "And yours."

Roishin was quiet for a long time. She hugged herself and turned back to the flames, mulling over everything she'd just been told. Despite the improbable nature of the claims, she felt in her soul Enori was telling her the truth.

"Now what?" she asked, not looking at the other woman who stood not ten feet from her.

"Now," Enori said, walking over and standing beside her. "Now you put to use all that knowledge you've consumed over four years."

"Four and a *half*," Roishin grumbled. She glanced over to see Enori giving her a small smile, which Roishin grudgingly returned.

"What is six months when you have eternity?" Enori asked.

"Will I ever die?"

"No. Not unless another god kills you."

"Like, Bahutha?" she asked quietly, almost afraid to say the name aloud.

"Yes. Like Bahutha."

Roishin nodded, no idea how to feel about any of this. "Are you a god?"

Enori shook her head. "No." She let out a long,

slow sigh, sounding tired. "After Ankou saved me when I was ten, I was taken into the Underground."

Roishin's eyebrows shot up. "Really?"

Enori met her gaze and nodded. "I served those down there for several years."

"Served? How? Who?" Roishin was intrigued, now, considering what she'd just gone through.

Enori shrugged. "Brought food, cleaned, whatever was needed for the members of the Order of Ankou. Finally, when I was fourteen, I joined." She smiled, seemingly at some memory. "It was a wonderful day to finally have a family. A purpose."

"You didn't? Before you were to be sacrificed?"

"No. I didn't know my parents, but I came to understand that, much like your grandmother, they were born of the Order. Gifts passed down through the blood." She hugged herself, sparing a glance to Roishin. "At fourteen, I took the vow to Ankou and was trained, much like you will be. Taught how to use my gifts and given more. Finally, after ten years, I was blessed by him and ordained the Head Priestess."

"Who you are now."

Enori nodded. "Who I am now."

"But," Roishin said slowly. "You don't age. Why? Are you immortal?"

Enori's smile was cryptic. "I am blessed." She met and held her gaze. "Once I reached my full power and strength, I stayed forever at that point." Roishin couldn't look away from the intensity in Enori's eyes in that moment. "As will you."

Roishin turned back to the fire. "Do my parents know any of this?"

"Some."

"Elsie," Roishin said. "She has gifts." She looked over at Enori again. "Doesn't she?"

Enori nodded. "Like me, like Fallon, and you," she added. "Elsie comes from a line of gifted blood. Her ancestors were Druids."

Roishin absorbed that for a moment. "Is that why you took her with you to take care of trapping Bahutha?"

Enori nodded. "Her mother taught her much about spells. I wanted an extra layer over that body Bahutha was trapped inside."

Roishin couldn't keep the smile of pride off her lips. "She did good?"

"She did very well, yes. Elsie is connected to her blood and very gifted, Roishin." She smiled. "It will serve her well in her life. Already has. She sees people, sees their truth."

"How do I stop loving her, Enori?" Roishin whispered.

"You won't," the priestess said softly. "You will love her, but with the understanding that you cannot keep her."

# Chapter Seven

Really?" Elsie asked, delighted as she glanced over at Millie, the castle cook but also a personal friend of the royal couple and Elsie. Her smile remained on her lips as she washed her midday meal dishes. "I worried you might decide to stay here."

Millie chuckled. "I think Fallon would have my head."

"I don't know," Elsie countered. "I think Cateline is pretty fond of your bread. She may be the culprit you'd have to worry about."

"Ture, true," the cook said with a dramatic sigh, rolling out dough for said bread. "Guess I'm not retiring anytime soon."

The two shared a laugh. "Well, thanks for lunch, Millie," Elsie said, still chuckling. "Back to work for me."

"When are they returning?" Millie asked, smacking the large ball of dough a few times before heaving it up and turning it over with a grunt before starting the process all over again.

"Not sure." She gave the older woman a smile. "See you for supper."

Her dishes washed, dried, and put away, Elsie headed out of the kitchen and through the great room to the stairs. Her mind was filled with all she had left to do that day, a list she'd desperately been trying to keep straight. Even with the written list she and Cateline had created, she was struggling.

Waking up that morning, still snuggled up

with Roishin, she'd been a mess. The previous night had come back to her, with all the beautiful moments together before sleep. She'd never kissed anyone like that before. She'd never heard of such a thing, such a deep and intimate kiss.

How wonderful! Did only women do that together? She'd never heard anyone talk about it and honestly couldn't even imagine such a thing with a man. This, of course, brought back thoughts of Garratt. Elsie looked around as she mounted the stairs. She could feel the emotion beginning to build again behind her eyes, and it just wouldn't do to have the queen's lady-in-waiting seen about to cry.

One of the hardest things about this was she had nobody to talk to. After her mother had begun to really get sick, Elsie had lost her one and only confidante in life. They'd been close, she and her mother. Her father had always been off fighting somewhere, and even when he was home, he didn't believe a father's relationship with his wife or daughter extended much beyond barking out orders.

She slowed as she reached the second floor, her gaze immediately going left. Roishin's bedchamber was down that way. She hadn't seen her all day since she'd left her own bed that morning, leaving the princess to sleep.

When she'd awoken, she'd just studied the face of the young woman who had returned, replacing the child who had left. She chewed on her bottom lip for a moment, considering if she should go see if Roishin was there. She was about to make her choice when she heard quick footfalls behind her.

Looking back, she saw Garratt trotting his way up to her. "There you are," he said with a smile. "Been looking for you, Elsie."

She turned to face him once he reached the landing. "Milord," she said, bowing her head. "How can I help you?"

"Well, I was going to ask you to join me for a midday meal, but Millie said you'd already dined. So," he said, eyes bright. "How about a stroll instead?"

Though wanting to decline for so many reasons, Elsie knew that wasn't really an option. This was, after all, the prince of Sursha and heir apparent. She gave him a small smile. "For a bit, aye."

His smile widened as he held his arm out to her, which she took. He led the way back downstairs and through the maze of hallways and corridors until they left one at a time through the small, narrow door that led to the kitchen gardens beyond. It was a shortcut to the outside.

"Rose gardens?" he asked, indicating the gorgeous acres past the rows of spring vegetables.

Elsie gave him a short nod, again taking his offered arm. Her stomach roiled as they headed there. It was a place she'd hoped to stroll with Roishin, as they'd discussed briefly before Roishin had left years ago. When, so young and so naïve, they'd all but promised themselves to the other.

If only they'd known what lay ahead, just how much time would lapse, and what would change. And the pain of last night. She tucked her lips in for a moment as she tried to fend off the emotion that was insistent on coming. Again.

"Aww, dear Elsie," Garratt said softly. "Here."

She looked at him, noting he held out a handkerchief. She was confused for a moment but then mortified to realize that a tear had escaped and was slowly trailing down her cheek. She took it with a quiet, "Thank you."

"I remember as a boy thinking my grandfather, who just so happened to be the king, would never die." He gave her an understanding smile. "He was so big, so powerful. Big, booming voice," he added, deepening his own voice in emphasis on his last point.

Elsie smiled, grateful for the topic and easy unspoken explanation—or excuse—for her upset. "He was always so nice to me," she said, using the kerchief to delicately dab at her eyes, willing the emotion to cease. "I'm truly sorry to you and your family, milord. A great loss."

He nodded. "It is. But," he added brightly. "I know my father will make an exceptional king."

"Aye!" she said enthusiastically. At least they could agree on that. "Sursha is a very lucky country for their new king and queen, milord."

"Which," he said, sounding a bit nervous as he spared her a quick glance, "brings me to why I wanted to speak to you today."

Elsie's stomach nearly revolted. She swallowed, hard. Saying nothing, she allowed herself to be led along the meandering pathways in the rose garden, yet to fully come to life. She desperately wanted to be upstairs working. She'd walk over hot coals in bare feet to escape this situation.

"Listen, Elsie," he said, voice taking on a very different tone. "I know my mamaí adores you, and Daidí does as well. You're honorable, chaste, respected, and very loyal to our family. I know you're close to Roishin, also." He chuckled. "As much as anyone can be close to her. A strange one, that kid."

Her immediate impulse was to protect and defend Roishin, but she stopped herself from doing so. She understood Roishin very well, but it was understandable how others might see her: aloof, obstinate, stubborn, or idealistic.

Yes, some of those things were very true when she was younger, but now Elsie saw all of that for what it was—Roishin innately knew things the rest of them didn't. No doubt it was frustrating for the young girl, who had no idea how she knew these things but just *did*, to have to deal with all the pushback and rolled eyes.

She smiled inwardly at that. It was nice to understand and be in the know, as it were. Even though she knew there were layers to the young woman that went deeper than even Roishin understood, Elsie knew two things for certain: Roishin was an exceptional person, and she craved her. She—

"Don't you agree?"

Ripped out of her thoughts of far more pleasant things, Elsie glanced over at him. *Uh-oh.* "Milord?"

"I asked if you agree," he repeated.

She knew she needed to be very careful here. She needed to focus on him, not his sister. "Please forgive me, milord," she said sweetly, hoping to appeal to the man and not the prince. "My brain is a little foggy with everything happening so quickly." She gave him a beseeching smile.

It worked, as she saw his features soften and he covered her hand at the crook of his arm with his free hand for just a second of affectionate understanding. "Of course," he said. "This probably isn't the best time for me to be bringing all this up, but I'll be heading out again in two days, so…"

She nodded, her stomach in knots as she hoped she hadn't played her cards too well. He kept his hand resting upon hers, an entirely possessive indication. She closed her eyes briefly as they continued to stroll. Swallowing, she waited for him to speak.

"I was saying that I know it's expected of me to leave military service once my tenure is finished in a year or so," he explained. "I'll be taking over Caisleán Thíar when I return, my duties changing to that of prince and heir." He gave her a broad smile, though she could see the nervousness in his normally confident, assured manner.

She swallowed again, wishing she hadn't eaten as much of the midday meal as she had. It was threatening a comeback. "Aye, milord," she managed.

Garratt stopped their stroll, urging her to sit with him upon one of the many stone benches that were strategically placed around the large outdoor space. "I know my mother spoke to you about this, so I figure I may as well toss in my two pence." He took a long breath, then met her guarded gaze. "Elsie, I think you're absolutely beautiful, and I love your quiet nature." He smiled. "Always so much going on behind those eyes of yours. You intrigue me, and I'd like to formally court you."

She stared at him, wide-eyed. She hadn't expected him to fully ask.

He plowed on, not seeming to notice she was turning green at the gills. "You see, I was so grateful that my parents were giving credence to my own thoughts on this and not just plopping some princess in front of me from the other side of the world." The smile he bestowed upon her was genuine and boyishly charming. "I've been watching you for a few years now," he admitted shyly. "I've found myself all too often getting lost in your beautiful blue eyes."

Elsie was stunned to hear this from him, as she had no idea he even knew her name most days, let alone the color of her eyes. She hadn't minded his indifference over the years. Rather, she had been grateful for it.

"I will do everything in my power to make you happy, Elsie," he promised earnestly. "I will give you many children and a safe home to raise them in." His voice was dreamy, as though he, too, wanted these things and wasn't just saying what he felt she'd want to hear. "We can be a family."

In that moment, she knew she was in real trouble. She could see it in his eyes—Garratt had real affection for her that he hoped would turn to love. He wanted what his parents had, a deeply loving and passionate union. She didn't think Cateline had lied to her or had tried to manipulate her into this union with talk of what amounted to a ruling partnership with occasional bouts of fornication to reproduce.

She wondered if the queen had misjudged her son and his intent. Elsie knew in her heart she couldn't give him what he wanted. Looking down at her hands in her lap, she took several steadying breaths. Finally, she looked over at him.

"Would you give me time to consider, milord?" she asked softly, hoping she wouldn't anger him. She knew she had to be careful, as soon enough he would wield real power, and were he to be a vengeful sort, she could lose what little she had. "With everything happening and the grief over losing the king, I feel my head is so overwhelmed."

He took one of her hands and brought it to his lips. Leaving a small kiss there, he nodded. "Aye. As long as you promise to tuck this proposal in with all the other things cluttering your brain."

Relieved, she was able to give him a genuine smile. "I promise."

Yet again, nighttime found Elsie curled up in the family chamber. The day had been a blur once she'd escaped Garratt. He'd left her be to fulfill her duties, and she'd been grateful. The one person she had wanted to see, however, had been absent all day. She worried that perhaps Roishin had left without saying goodbye.

Her heart was heavy, as was her mind. What would she do about Garratt? She didn't honestly feel she was in any real position to say no. She knew—hoped—her place would be secured as long as Fallon or Cateline lived, but what then? And, what about when she aged out of her duties as the queen's lady-in-waiting?

A position mostly relegated    to young women, it was a rare thing to see a woman the age of a grandmother performing such duties. What of Elsie's future prospects as she grew older? To the kitchens with her, no doubt. If she refused the union, what happened when Garratt came into power and still held a grudge? And what if—

Elsie's dark thoughts were interrupted when she raised her head from where her chin rested upon her knees. She looked around the firelit chamber, feeling she wasn't alone. As with the previous night, she knew Roishin was near. Her smile was slow to spread across her lips when suddenly, as though she'd been there all along but unnoticed, Roishin appeared reclining on the couch. Her cloak was in place, hood pushed away from her beautiful face.

Looking into her eyes, Elsie could see that she, too, was troubled. Without a word, she uncurled herself from the chair and walked over to the couch. She held out a hand. Roishin looked up, meeting her gaze for just a moment before she took it, allowing herself to be pulled to her feet. Together, they walked to Elsie's bedchamber.

Once inside, Elsie closed the door and turned to Roishin. She looked into her eyes briefly as she began to untie her cloak.

"I have to leave, Elsie," Roishin said softly,

Elsie nodded, something she'd known deep down. "But not tonight."

Once the cloak was untied, she hung it up on the hook near the door just as she had the night before. Turning back to Roishin, who was still dressed from her day, Elsie had no idea what to do. All she did know was that she needed Roishin. She needed to feel like her true self, with her true wants, if just once. She feared she knew in her bones what decision she'd ultimately have to make.

Roishin's lips were as soft as she remembered, her touch just as gentle as Roishin's hands rested at her waist. She sighed at the first touch of a soft tongue against her own. Her hand moved from the side of Roishin's face to bury in her thick, dark hair. Roishin's hands moved from her waist down to her hips, gently urging their bodies closer.

Elsie sighed into the kiss, able to feel the warm length of Roishin against her. She marveled at the feel of Roishin's breasts pressed against her. She gasped into the kiss when those hands moved to cup her behind through her sleep dress. She was on fire, and she knew that only Roishin could put the fire out.

As the kiss continued, deep and growing very passionate, Elsie needed to touch her. Her hands moved away from her hair and eased down her back to the hem of her tunic shirt. With just the smallest moment's hesitation, her hands slipped underneath the material to the warm skin of Roishin's back.

They both sighed at that, one never touching the naked skin of another woman, the other never being touched by one. That realization eased their fire for a moment as the kiss broke. Roishin looked into Elsie's eyes as if asking, *Are you absolutely sure?* In response, Elsie eased her hands back down her back, only to lift the garment up and over Roishin's head and toss it to the floor.

Roishin now topless, Elsie looked at what was bared before her. *Exquisite* was the only word that came to mind. Absolutely exquisite. She took in Roishin's breasts, full and beautiful, with dark rose nipples that were already rigid.

She ran her hands over the rounded sides of them, in awe of their softness. She brushed her thumbs over the hard tips, looking into Roishin's face to see her lips fall slightly open and her beautiful green eyes hooded. She took her lips into another kiss as her fingers lightly explored, this kiss slow and exploratory, just like her fingers lightly touching, caressing, and tugging.

As they kissed, Roishin's own hands went on the move. She took fistfuls of the skirt of Elsie's sleeping gown, slowly gathering it up until the entire lower half of Elsie's body was revealed. She broke the kiss long enough to pull the garment up and off.

Elsie's hands went to Roishin's trousers. She unlaced them as their kiss began again. She thought she'd feel shame, or at least nervous being naked in front of someone for the first time, but she wasn't. This was Roishin, the person she now believed she'd loved since the moment she'd met her.

She sighed when she eased her hands into the loosened waistline of Roishin's leathers, hands covering the warm skin of Roishin's bare behind. Roishin sighed into the kiss. Her fingers came up and slowly ran along the smooth skin of Elsie's sides. It was heaven.

Moving out of the kiss, Roishin's gaze fell to her fingers, watching their progress. She gave Elsie a sexy little grin as her fingers moved up toward the sides of Elsie's breasts.

"That night that you showed me the triskelion your mother had given you," she said, voice soft and reverent as her fingertips caressed the undersides of Elsie's heavy breasts. Light pink nipples were painfully hard with Elsie's arousal. "You undid a couple buttons of your dress to show me where it was attached to your chemise."

Elsie smiled, nodding. "Aye. I remember."

"I nearly died that night," Roishin said, grinning as she met her gaze. She brushed her fingertips lovingly over the tops of the breasts that were revealed now. "First time I'd ever seen any part of a woman's breasts."

Elsie smiled, her breath catching a bit as those fingers got closer to sensitive nipples. "Did I unwittingly convert you that night?" she teased.

Roishin's grin was wicked. "Let me show you just how much," she whispered.

# *Chapter Eight*

**H**er trousers and boots removed, Roishin watched as Elsie climbed beneath the covers before she followed. Very surprised at the turn of events for the night, she was going to allow herself to experience it, experience what she'd wanted for so long. Further, this would probably be their only chance.

After her stunning discussion with Enori in the morning and then the heartbreak of watching Elsie with Garratt in the rose gardens in the afternoon, she knew by that night it was time to leave, this time for good. She'd see her parents when she could, but she needed to move on. *Had* to move on. She had to let Elsie find her future, too.

For now, she scooted over to Elsie, who accepted her with open arms. She moved to lie atop her, both moaning into the kiss as their naked bodies were flush for the first time. Elsie was so warm, so soft, and felt so amazingly good. She didn't know what she was doing, so she went with pure instinct.

Fingers explored her shoulders and down her back. She'd never been touched this intimately before. She loved it and wondered how she'd live without it. She braced herself on a forearm, allowing her other hand free to wander.

As her mouth left Elsie's to explore her neck, she cupped one of her breasts. She'd caught herself so many times looking at those very body parts, as well as Elsie's beautiful backside. A young girl's fantasies turned into a young woman's delight. The little whimpers and sighs that escaped Elsi's lips urged her on.

She kissed, licked, and nipped her way down a soft throat before moving to the breast that beckoned her. Her mouth watered to taste the flesh, to know what it was like to run her tongue over the hard nipple. A surprised gasp sent a surge of arousal through Roishin once she had the nipple in her mouth, Elsie's back arching as if to offer herself to her.

Fingers buried in Roishin's hair, Elsie whispered her name, so much need in that one word. Roishin took ample time on the first breast before moving to the other. Her body was cradled between Elsie's legs, and she could feel her hips moving up into her in a slow, sensuous wave with her arousal.

Of its own accord, Roishin's body pressed back against the incredible amount of wetness. At Elsie's little gasp, Roishin lifted her mouth from the nipple she'd been caressing and looked into Elsie's face. Her eyes were closed, lips open, an absolute portrait of pleasure and need.

She wanted those lips again. Moving back up Elsie's body, she initiated a slow, sensuous kiss, resting her hips between Elsie's spread thighs. They both gasped, eyes opening at the lance of pleasure that seared them at the contact of their most private places. Looking down at Elsie's hooded gaze, Roishin pressed again, causing the same effect.

Spreading her legs a bit more to open herself to the wet heat between Elsie's legs, Roishin braced herself on her hands as she began to slowly move her hips. She knew from some of the books she'd read that this was sometimes how a man had sex with a woman, but she never thought it could also be how two women had sex.

But in that moment, as she slowly moved with

and against the woman beneath her, it felt for all the world like she was inside of Elsie and Elsie was inside of her. Elsie pulled her knees up closer to her body while spreading her legs a bit more. It was the most incredible feeling to be on top of her like that, gently thrusting her most sacred place against and into Elsie's.

They kissed from time to time but mostly just looked at each other. Looking into the sapphire depths of Elsie's eyes, Roishin knew she was looking into her soul. She also knew that no matter what happened, they'd always be connected in a way that Garratt could never dream of touching.

Elsie's eyes fell closed and her grip on Roishin's back tightened. Her breathing was growing heavier, whimpers higher pitched and almost constant now. Roishin felt her own body beginning to prepare itself, a massive buildup of pressure between her legs. She forced herself to stay with the slow, steady thrusts, even as she wanted to grind against Elsie.

Finally, an eruption of pleasure stole her breath as it exploded, pulling a loud cry from her throat with it. Half a heartbeat later, Elsie also cried out, clinging to Roishin and seemingly desperate to catch her breath even as her breasts heaved. Roishin was pulled down into a crushing hug, Elsie's entire body wrapping her in a tight cocoon of just the two of them.

Roishin held her, face buried in Elsie's warm neck as her tears came to wet the soft skin. Elsie caressed her back with one hand and her hair with the other, comforting her. After long moments, she lifted her head to look down into Elsie's own tear-streaked face. She cupped it with her hands, leaving a soft kiss on lips made salty from their combined tears.

"I love you," Roishin whispered against them.

"And I love you," Elsie responded. "I always

will."

Roishin lifted her head, looking down into her face again. She smiled and nodded. "Always."

❧ ❧ ❧ ❧

Bodies entwined, Roishin opened her eyes. She felt Elsie's deep, even breathing against her upper chest as she slept. A glance at the small domed fireplace showed her that it had burned down to mere embers. She lay there, trying to decide what to do. She needed to leave—that much she knew.

Snorting internally, she thought about Enori's words to her at the waterfall before Roishin stepped through the door. *You will know when it is time.* That day, she thought maybe she'd feel when Enori was on her way to get her, or that some major storm outside would clue her in.

Now, she knew it was time. She considered the warm body she held, soft blond hair tucked up under her chin. In her heart, Roishin knew Elsie didn't love Garratt, knew she wasn't a woman who loved a man as they were supposed to. She was like Roishin, Fallon, and Cateline. She loved other women, was attracted to them.

Why was this? Wasn't life hard enough as it was? She hoped over time Elsie could find happiness, if not in the passions of the man she was married to, then perhaps in her children and her duties to her adopted country, which she did love. They could both look back on their night together and draw some pleasure from that, some happiness. They would remember the night they were both able to understand true passion and what making love really meant.

She held Elsie a bit tighter, eyes closing as she

buried her face in her hair. She inhaled her scent, memorizing it. Memorizing the texture and feel of the cool blond tresses that she'd once wondered about. She'd memorize the feeling and softness of Elsie's skin, so smooth, so warm, so beautiful.

Hoping she was deep enough in sleep, Roishin gently resettled Elsie's body on the mattress instead of partially on top of Roishin. She froze when Elsie moaned a bit in her sleep. Soon enough, however, she settled down and her breathing once again became deep and even.

Roishin placed a kiss on the back of her shoulder before slowly easing herself out of bed. She never took her eyes off the other woman, looking for any sign that she was waking. Once fully out of bed, Roishin quietly dressed and shrugged into her cloak.

Gathering Elsie's night dress off the floor, she pressed the garment to her face, inhaling and cuddling it to her. Finally, she folded it lovingly and placed it atop the small trunk that sat in the corner of the room beneath the arrow slit window. Making sure Elsie was tucked in and would stay warm, she carefully leaned over the sleeping woman until she could place one last kiss on her lips.

"I love you," she whispered, then left the room.

※ ※ ※

Back in her own bedchamber, Roishin used the garderobe then unmade her bed to look as if she'd been there all night. No reason to throw any doubts on her whereabouts. She gathered up the new clothing she'd made—three pairs of leather pants and four shirts—and stuffed them into her bag. She also eased the rose blade into her boot before deciding it was finally time to go.

Looking around her bedchamber, she knew this was likely the last time she'd see it. She noticed her bow and quiver hanging on the wall, brought back with her from the Underground. Once so incredibly important to her, even if she hadn't used it in a few months or even years, just knowing it was there, just seeing it, had given her comfort.

Now, she felt nothing. Somehow she knew that what she would be doing had nothing to do with archery. Turning away from it, she looked to the door of the bedchamber. Her intention was to head upstairs to the trunk and back to the Underground, as she had no other idea how to find Enori.

But, no. She wanted to say goodbye to her parents. She had no idea how long she'd be gone this time, and she wasn't going to do what she'd done last time. It hadn't been fair to any of them. Taking a step toward the door, she stopped again.

She could easily see the queen's chambers in the main castle. She saw every detail, but then she saw the bed where her parents and Isabeau slept. No, redirect. She saw the hallway beyond. She concentrated on the long, maroon-and-gold rug that ran the length of that hallway to help dampen the cold and the noise.

There. Near the large, ornate chair that sat against the wall near the king's chambers. Yes, she could sit there and wait for them to stir.

Before her, the air began to shimmer, then it stopped. Roishin's head hurt, and she was short of breath. She blinked several times before she began to focus again, concentrating on that chair.

*Seek and ye shall find.*

A space the size of a dinner plate at chest level began to shimmer. It held steady. Roishin focused on it. In her mind's eye she saw hands easing the spot open, wider and wider, taller and taller, until it was the size of a door. Her heart was racing, and it was taking a tremendous amount of energy to hold it, so she quickly hurried through it…

…and nearly skidded into the wall. She just barely caught herself with a hand, hissing when it landed directly on a wall sconce heated by the flame within the protective glass. Pulling her hand away, she waved it close to her body the way a child waved away an owie. Looking around, it took her a moment to get her bearings. She wasn't on the fourth floor, but on the third.

A little confused at that but quite proud of herself that she was in the king's residence at all, she hurried past the line of closed doors to the stairs. Reaching the landing, she saw the floor was quiet, as expected. She looked down the length of the hallway to see that the chair no longer was outside the king's chambers.

*Guess that's important to know.* She headed down that way, passing the door to the lady-in-waiting's chamber. It made her feel sick, as that would be where Elsie lived until… Well, until. She forced herself to look away so she wouldn't burst into tears.

Walking past the queen's chambers, the doors closed and parents tucked inside, she headed to her grandfather's old rooms, where her parents would eventually move. The door was ajar, so she pushed it open a bit more and stepped inside. The chambers were huge, and she remembered as a child they'd been so intimidating to her.

Though the castle where she'd grown up had been more than adequate for their needs and safety, the king's residence was not quite twice as large, but almost. So many unused rooms that had been a child's delight when they'd stayed there. She smiled, thinking that when Laigen and Reinaldo had children, it would be the same for them. Or for Elsie's.

Unshouldering her bag strap, she let the heavy object fall to the floor as she looked around. It was dark in there, the only light coming from the moon outside. It didn't matter, as she knew every detail, every corner, and every piece of furniture. These places, these structures, and this country would always be her home—that much she knew.

But then, why were things beginning to feel so strange to her? She felt a shift happening inside of her, and she didn't understand it.

"Roishin?"

Startled, she looked to see a figure entering the room carrying a candle in candleholder. She smiled. "Hello, Mamaí. I hope I didn't wake you."

"No." Cateline used the flame from her candle to light a couple more scattered about the room. "I had a dream you were here." She smiled at her daughter as she walked over to her, candle set down on a table. "It was so real, I had to come check."

Roishin's eyes closed as she was held by the woman that she loved above all others. She rested her head on the shorter woman's shoulder, so glad to be held like a babe again. She smiled when soft fingers combed through her hair.

"You're leaving us," Cateline said simply.

Roishin nodded, not opening her eyes. "Oui." When talking to her mother, they always went back and forth between Gaelic and French, and had since she was a child.

"I fear we are losing you," Cateline whispered, emotion tinging her words.

Roishin shook her head, lifting it to look into the face of her mother, her actual, true mother. Now knowing that truth…oh, how she saw it! She smiled, bringing up a hand to lightly touch the light smattering of freckles across Cateline's cheek. "I got your freckles," she said softly. She took in the entirety of her mother's beautiful face. "And I think I got your nose, too."

"She told you?" At Roishin's nod, the queen's smile was brilliant. "You have no idea how happy it made Fallon and me. We love all our children," she said with conviction. "But to know you are truly ours is such a gift." She reached up and cupped her daughter's face.

"When did she tell you?" Roishin asked, not sure whether to be surprised, happy, or hurt.

"When you were twelve." Cateline took Roishin by the hand and led her to the couch. She sat, urging her daughter to cuddle up with her. "You've gotten so big," she said into dark hair as Roishin's head rested upon her shoulder. "So much like Fallon."

"Why didn't you tell me?"

"We felt it was best for Enori to," she said easily, resting her cheek against Roishin's head. "She understands all of this better than we ever could." She left a kiss there before returning her cheek. "I love you so much, my Roishin."

"I love you, too, Mamaí. I'm sorry I left without saying a final goodbye last time," she murmured, feeling sleepy as gentle fingers once again ran through her hair.

"At least you didn't this time, hmm?" They sat in silence for a long moment. "When will we see you again?"

"I don't know. I have no idea where I'm going next. Mamaí?"

"Hmm?"

"Please look out for Elsie. No matter what she chooses to do, though I think I know what she'll do, please…" She lifted her head, looking into her mother's face. "Make sure she's okay."

Cateline tucked dark strands behind Roishin's ear. "You love her?" she asked gently. At Roishin's nod, she smiled. "We're doing all we can to keep her safe, mon amour." She kissed her forehead, Roishin's eyes closing at the affectionate touch. "We will keep her with us, I promise you."

Roishin nodded. "Thank you."

Cateline looked deeply into her eyes. "You look so tired," she said, a mother's concern in her voice. "In your soul, tired."

"I am." Roishin gave her a sad smile. "I feel so lost, Mamaí."

Cateline nodded. "You will find your place, my Roishin. You feel lost because you have yet to find it. You were always so different from the rest of us." She chuckled. "Sometimes I'd look at you and think I was looking into the eyes of a two-thousand-year-old man. You will do great things," she said.

Roishin's eyes fell closed again as she once again rested against her mother. "I hope so," she murmured.

# Chapter Nine

Roishin gasped as she breached the surface, sputtering and flailing about like a dying trout. Finally, she got her bearings and dragged her bag behind her as she swam to the rocks surrounding the pool at the foot of the waterfall. When she got closer she looked up, shocked to see Enori reclining on the flat rock that Roishin and Fallon had sat on that day so long ago.

She flopped her saturated bag on the area surrounding the pool, accidentally splashing the priestess in the process. Roishin gave a sheepish look at the raised eyebrow she received.

"Sorry."

Enori said nothing, simply got to her feet and leaned over, offering a hand to her. Roishin took it and allowed herself to be helped out of the water. On solid ground, she looked down at herself, then to Enori through her sodden hair, which hung in her face.

"Going to live?" Enori teased, slapping Roishin on the back when she began to cough as she spit up more water. She smiled at the glare she got.

"Funny." Roishin brushed her hair out of her face and took several deep breaths. Well, tried to but ended up in another coughing fit. Finally, her lungs were clear and she tried the deep breath thing again.

"Seriously, are you all right?" Enori asked. At Roishin's nod, Enori picked up the bag that was just barely on land, moving it away from the water's edge. "All right then," she said, hand on hip. "How did you end up here? There is no door to this place except from the Underground."

Roishin looked at her, surprised by the tone of her voice. It was hard, almost accusatory. "Um," she murmured, then considered lying and telling her she'd done the Underground circuit from the trunk to get here but realized that made no sense. "I created one."

Enori stared at her. For the first time in the years Roishin had known her through their limited interactions, she'd never seen the priestess look stunned, even a bit scared. Roishin watched her, feeling mighty nervous.

"Did I do something wrong?" She smirked, trying to lighten the heavy energy. "Other than landing in the water?"

Enori took a full thirty seconds to respond, seeming to take time to center herself. "Um," she said at length, looking away and clearing her throat. "I am assuming you are ready to go?" She spared Roishin a glance over her shoulder.

Roishin met her gaze and held it for a moment, trying to read anything in her eyes to indicate what she'd done wrong. Seeing nothing but incredibly guarded, cool cerulean eyes looking back at her, she nodded.

Enori grabbed her bag again, holding the straps in both her hands as she studied Roishin. Finally, she held it out to her. "Let us go."

Roishin took the bag and nodded as she shouldered it. She turned to head toward the waterfall, where she knew a door back to the Underground was located. She stopped when there was a touch to her arm.

"Not that way," Enori said.

Confused, Roishin glanced to the waterfall and

then back to her mentor before following when Enori turned away from the water and began to walk toward the dense vegetation that covered one entire side of the inner cave wall. They walked, and they walked, and they walked. Roishin was baffled, as they should have run into the wall rather quickly as they crossed the cave.

Gasping, she realized there *was* no wall. Turning back to look over her shoulder, she still saw the waterfall and the confines of that eroded cave, but it was as if she was observing the scene through slightly smudged glass. She looked over at Enori, who was grinning at her.

"Welcome," she said.

"Where are we?"

"Duras."

"What is that?" Roishin asked, looking around.

The area that the waterfall was nestled in was nothing like the rest of Sursha, which was filled with green rolling hills from the constant rains, rocky shores on the beachfronts, and wooded land and trees in the highlands. Instead, the waterfall area was more like a jungle with vines and vegetation with large, dark green leaves and deep, rich soil.

Mouth hanging open and eyes wide, she took in her new surroundings as they continued. She heard the chatter and calls from birds she'd never heard before, their bright, colorful feathers seen briefly through the massive tree canopy overhead. She started when she saw a little dark figure jump from one tree to another before vanishing again.

Enori looked amused at her wonder. "Monkeys," she explained.

"Like, *Curious George*?" Roishin asked, stunned.

Enori nodded, chuckling. "Yes."

They walked for several more minutes until the mass of trees, vines, lush vegetation, and brightly colored flowers began to thin out. Then, as if stepping over a boundary, they were no longer in the jungle but in a valley surrounded by farmland as far as the eye could see. Roishin looked back along the path they had traveled, and once again it was like looking through smudged glass at the jungle behind. She shook her head as she turned back around to assess the new landscape.

Farmhouses dotted the countryside, as well as large red barns and windmills spinning lazily upon the soft breeze. The skies above were blue with fat white clouds floating around. They walked along an old dirt road, one of the farmhouses off to the right a hundred yards or so. She saw children chasing each other around a woman who was hanging wet laundry on a clothesline. A dog, all tail wags and excited barks, chased after the kids.

She was amused watching the dog's antics until she felt a tug on her sleeve. Looking that way, she saw that Enori was heading down a small dirt path that led to what appeared to be a deep, dense thicket of trees. It was completely out of place next to the beautiful, peaceful valley she was just walking through. But then again, how exactly did a valley with rolling hills and farmland belong near a jungle? Roishin's mind spun with confusion and fascination.

The bright, warm sunny day became cool in the dense forest, more like what Roishin was used to. Woodland creatures scurried here and there. She could smell the comforting stench of chimney smoke in the air as well as feel the immense temperature and pressure change in the air that denoted imminent snowfall.

The deeper into the woods they went, the colder

it got, and the ground, which started with a thin glazing of snow, was soon covered by several inches of the fluffy white stuff. Small log cabins dotted the forest in partially cleared spots, the small structures sporting chimneys that released the smoke from the fireplaces within.

They passed a few folks out and about, one man splitting logs, another carrying firewood into his cabin from a neat stack outside. Neither gave the two women an ounce of attention, just carried on with their duties. She glanced over at Enori to see she had a small smile upon her lips and amusement in her eyes.

Finally, like the other environments, the snow eventually waned and the trees grew farther and farther apart until they were crossing yet another boundary, this one almost like a line had been drawn in the proverbial sand. They stepped out of the trees, and Roishin's eyes widened even more and her mouth fell open in awe.

Before her was a massive round structure, easily the height of a four-story building with a slight dome at the top. There were no windows, and the bottom level was made up of large archways all around the circumference. It was a strange design, but what made the building remarkable was that she couldn't even fathom what it was made of.

There was no brick, no stone, and even no wood. The entire thing was made up of billions of shards of glass that all created their own tiny prisms that sparkled like the night sky and its endless stars. It was dazzling, almost dizzying. What caught her eye next was the sky directly above the building. It was a constantly moving mass of clouds in varying shades of gray, slowly turning and swirling.

From the clouds, a stream of what looked like

red smoke floated down to the top of the dome, streaks of crimson glistening off the prism-like structure like little red ribbons of lightning flickering through the arches and up the sides and across the dome.

When finally she was able to clap her mouth shut and look away from the spectacle, she noted the building was encircled by a maze of knee-high hedges in circular patterns, reminding her a bit of the triskelion. Along the tops of the deep green hedges were flowers of every color, every type, from every season.

"What is this place?"

"This is the Crystal Palace," Enori said. "But," she added, grabbing Roishin's hand. "You'll see that later. For now, let's get you settled."

She headed down one of the pathways of the maze that spread out like the spokes of a wheel with the Crystal Palace at its hub. It looked as though the hedge maze went on forever, but suddenly, the air in front of them began to shimmer in that familiar way just before they stepped through…

…and walked into a small village of stone cottages. Some were one story, others two. They were simple but beautiful in their simplicity. At the center of the village was a well, the crank spooled tight with rope and a bucket sitting upon the ledge of the well, the slack end of the rope tied to its handle. It looked to be a very peaceful place, something similar to what Roishin had seen in Surshan villages many times.

"Roishin."

She'd been so lost in her examination of the village and the well that she hadn't noticed Enori walk right past her and into a nearby house. She hurried over to her, again taking a look at the familiar sights as Enori held the front door open.

"Come," Enori said, amusement in her tone as Roishin entered.

Stairs to the second floor lined the right side wall just inside the door. To the left was a cozy living space with a large stone fireplace that took up the entire wall, a hearth running along its length.

Comfortable-looking furniture was set up for one to enjoy the warmth of the fire and read—Gods no, Roishin thought. Anything but reading—or knit or enjoy a good conversation. A simple yet adequate kitchen lay beyond a wood plank table with bench seating on either side. The floors were wide-plank wood, but the walls were covered with a smooth white substance, which made her brow furrow in confusion.

"Who lives here?" Roishin looked to Enori, who was watching her. "What is this?" she asked, trailing her fingertips over the cool, white surface.

"I do," Enori said. "It's called plaster. Come," she said again, heading upstairs.

The statement stopped Roishin in her tracks for a moment. It just seemed that Enori appeared or disappeared into the ether at will, and Roishin had never given consideration to the possibility that she might have a house, or a kitchen table, or stairs to an upper floor. But, kitchen table, stairs, and an upper floor she had. Like the lower floor, it was simple yet beautiful in that simplicity.

There were two bedrooms, and the first was small and practical, with a nice-sized window, which was so new to Roishin. She was used to the slim beam of sunlight that was allowed in through an arrow slit. How wonderful, she thought. It also contained a tall wooden piece of furniture that had knobs on the front going all the way down like buttons on a garment.

Confused, she looked to Enori, who showed her

that each knob was attached to a little compartment that slid out. She glanced over at Roishin. "It is called a dresser."

Roishin's eyebrows shot up. "I read about these!"

Enori had that same small, somewhat amused smile upon her lips. "Your belongings go in here," she said, lightly tugging on the strap that was hitched over Roishin's shoulder. "One type of clothing goes in one drawer, which is what these are called," she added, lightly patting the open drawer she'd pulled out a bit.

"It's like a really tall trunk," Roishin murmured, astounded.

"It is," Enori agreed. "Just a bit easier to find things." She pushed the empty drawer closed and tapped the top of the dresser, which reached Enori's shoulders. "You can place things here that you use often. A shelf, if you will."

Roishin nodded, understanding that concept well enough. "So, am I staying here?"

Enori nodded, easing the strap off Roishin's shoulder to set the bag down on the bed, which was covered by a quilt. It was then that Roishin realized that not only was her bag completely dry, but so was she. She filed that one away for later, as her brain was about to explode.

"You will stay with me during this next training phase," Enori explained. "We will be working closely together, so it makes more sense for you to be here."

Feeling a bit nervous but understanding the logic, Roishin nodded. "All right."

"Come." Enori walked to the door and farther down the hall.

Roishin glanced into the second bedroom as they passed it. It was similar to the first but clearly already in use, with various items atop the dresser and the famous blue cloak hanging from a hook on the door.

"This," she said, turning to make sure Roishin was paying attention. "Is what is called an open door." Her smile was downright saucy. "Meaning, no intent of destination is necessary, and you will not end up nearly drowning."

Roishin rubbed the back of her heated neck as she gave her a sheepish grin. "Yeah, um…"

Smirking, Enori stepped through the doorway and to what lay beyond, which from the hall looked like a dark nook. Roishin followed and was stunned to find herself in a very small cave-like structure with an open top, much like the waterfall cave back home. This one, however, had a narrow waterfall, perhaps only three feet wide.

Looking up, she saw that it just seemed to magically appear, like the waterfall in the Underground. No real visible source, it just *was*. The water fell to a stone floor, a narrow chasm off to the side that the water flowed into so the space didn't flood. There was also a buildup of stone that created a bit of a natural stool. Roishin realized it had a hole in the flat seat portion.

Enori answered her question before she asked it. "All of your bodily needs will be taken care of here. I loathe baths," she said with a small laugh. "I think I got spoiled with the waterfall of the Underground for all those years." Enori pointed to a nook in the stone to the right of the waterfall and added, "Any soaps you need are there." She gave Roishin a beautiful smile. "You are welcome to all I have."

Roishin looked around, not exactly feeling overwhelmed—even though it was a lot—but more anxious to learn, to understand. She met Enori's gaze. "Thank you for all this." She grinned. "I have no idea why I'm here or what I'm doing, but I'll do the best I can."

Enori's entire countenance softened. She took both of Roishin's hands in her own. "Roishin, there is only one of you in all the world. I know in here," she said, placing a hand on Roishin's upper chest over her heart, "you are ancient. But," she continued, moving her hand to lightly tap on Roishin's forehead with her finger. "In here, you are still young with much to learn and understand."

Roishin gave her a shy grin. "Truer words were never spoken."

Enori smiled. "Ankou would never have wanted me to bring you here if he did not think you could do this. And" she said softly, once again holding Roishin's hands in both of her own. "*I* would never have agreed to bring you here if I did not think you could do this."

Roishin looked down at their hands for a moment and felt Enori's belief in her to her core. She took a deep breath and finally met those calm, understanding eyes. "Thank you."

"Come," Enori said. "Let's get you settled."

❦❦❦❦

Later that night, Roishin lay in the most comfortable bed she'd ever encountered. She stared up at the ceiling, finding it so strange that the room was so well lit by the moon outside. There was no fireplace in the bedroom, no flickering light, heat, or smells of smoke to accompany her. She'd never experienced that before.

The clean, fresh air was something new to her. There were no smells of manure or unwashed bodies. Just…fresh. She realized that was its own scent. She'd actually had to ask Enori what it was that she was smelling. She smiled, thinking about her hostess. Enori had been so incredibly kind and patient with her.

She'd answered every single question Roishin had asked. Heck, they'd spent about two hours just discussing the plaster covering the walls, the point of it, how it was made and applied. Now, lying there in somewhat familiar surroundings in an altogether unfamiliar place, she knew in her gut that things in her life had changed radically the moment she'd stepped into that jungle.

She had absolutely no clue what lay before her, but she felt she was ready. At least, she hoped she was.

# Chapter Ten

Roishin just stood there. And then she stood there some more, and maybe a little bit more. The water felt so good running down over her naked body. It was actually warm water, which she couldn't wrap her mind around, considering there wasn't a fire up there heating it as it fell.

Though she could have stood under the falls all day, she decided she should probably be productive. She smoothed her hair back from her face and then used the proffered soaps to wash it and her body. As she did, she couldn't help her mind returning to Elsie. She closed her eyes tightly, trying desperately to keep her emotions in check.

But as her hands ran over her own breasts in the basics of body cleansing, she felt Elsie's soft, curious touch. She saw her face again, felt her warmth and her kiss. And then, she remembered Elsie's silent and unwitting goodbye as she'd slept on, as well as how leaving that way had made her feel.

"Stop it!" she hissed at herself, angrily swiping at a tear that managed to escape. She closed her eyes and took a deep, centering breath. "It's for the best," she reminded herself. "It has to be this way."

Raising her face to the spray, she allowed the water to wash away the tears. She couldn't afford those thoughts or those feelings now—there was simply too much to learn and focus on. She quickly finished up her bathing and stepped out of the spray of the waterfall. She eyed it, amazed at its existence, before she grabbed the folded cloth Enori had left for her to dry herself.

Dressed and carrying her sleep dress and damp cloth with her, she made her way back to the shimmering door to Enori's house. In her bedroom, she hung the cloth on the hook and folded her sleep dress to place in her new drawer.

She had to admit, she liked these dresser things. Trunks were great as they were mobile, but it was a pain to have to dig through to find things. With the dresser, she just opened a drawer and there it was! She smiled at her thoughts, hipping the drawer closed before grabbing the brush from on top of the dresser to brush out her mop as she looked out the window.

It looked like a beautiful fall day. The large trees that peppered the village, though mainly along the perimeter, were painted in autumn colors. She wanted to run out there and flop down in the rainbow of leaves that littered the bases of the trees. But, alas, she needed to get downstairs.

Finishing with her hair, she headed out, dressed in her leather pants, basic tunic shirt, and boots. As she made her way to the stairs, she ran her fingers along the plaster-covered walls once again, still so bemused by it.

Her boots thudded dully on the wood stairs, something else she'd never seen before. Living in Caisleán Thíar her entire life, she was used to stone being the main building material in all things. Even in the Underground, that was the rule of the day. Though the outside of Enori's cottage was stone, the inside was such a mixture of materials that it was a veritable playground for the eye and fingers.

Reaching the bottom step, she saw that a fire popped and crackled in the fireplace, emitting its warmth throughout the entire first floor. She saw that

Enori was curled up on what looked like a very small couch, though far more stuffed than the somewhat uncomfortable furnishings she was used to back home.

She was reading, her bare feet and legs curled up next to her on the cushion. She wore a gown of white, as per usual, however this one was far simpler, not as flowing. From what she could see, it reminded Roishin of a chemise. The neckline was lower and wider, revealing the delicate structure of her throat, collarbones, and shoulders.

Her arms were bare all the way up to the shoulders, which was something Roishin never saw on any woman except for when her mother donned the lighter weight summer sleep dress she would wear from time to time. And, of course, when she had seen Elsie naked.

Forcing herself to look away and shut down that train of thought, Roishin stepped up to the piece of furniture, not entirely sure what she was supposed to do. Enori looked up from the book she held in her hands and smiled.

"Good morrow," she said.

"Good morrow," Roishin responded.

She noticed a relaxed lightness to Enori that she'd never seen before. The priestess was consistently calm and downright aloof, but there was always an underlying feeling that she was there for a purpose, a mission. Now, she just seemed to be relaxing in her home and enjoying whatever she was reading.

"Did you sleep well?" Enori placed a ribbon between the pages before closing the book and setting it aside.

"Very well." Roishin gave her a sheepish grin. "I think I slept like the dead last night."

Enori's smile was unreadable. "I am sure you

did." Uncurling herself, she rose to her feet. She lightly tugged on the hem of Roishin's shirt to indicate she should follow. "A good breakfast for you, then we go."

Roishin could see the upper part of her back and the column of her neck laid bare by the gown, tendrils of the short, wavy blond hair curling at the nape. The dress she wore was fitted around her torso but flared slightly at womanly hips, which swayed ever so gently with each step, making the skirt of the dress move with them. It was mesmerizing.

Very guiltily, she looked away once they reached the table. Her attention refocused when she heard Enori's soft voice wash over her.

"Fruit," she said, indicating a wooden bowl filled with colorful, delicious-looking options. "Apples, pears, bananas, papayas, and cherries." Her finger hovered each one as she named it. She met Roishin's wide gaze. "Some of these you know," she explained, indicating the apples and cherries. "Some, you do not." She smiled. "And," she continued, waving her hand toward little cubes of pure white in a little wooden dish by themselves, sitting in a small amount of liquid. "Coconut in a bit of sugarcane water."

Roishin took it all in, her mouth beginning to water. "What is coconut?"

Enori reached down and plucked a cube from the bowl with her fingers. Head slightly tilted to the side, she held it up to Roishin's mouth. Taking it gently with her teeth, Roishin brought the fruit into her mouth, curious. She tasted sweetness from the sugar water mixed with that of the coconut, flavors she'd never had before.

"Good?" Enori asked softly. At Roishin's nod, Enori said, "And, a bit of home."

Opening her eyes from the pleasure of the new

tastes as she continued to chew, Roishin saw Enori pull the covering off a wooden plate. Sliced upon it was what she'd had for breakfast her entire life. "Millie's bread!"

Enori tapped a small clay container next to it. "And her sweet butter."

"Did you…" Roishin couldn't even speak, tears stinging the backs of her eyes from both the sudden feeling of homesickness and the fact that she was deeply touched by the gesture.

Enori nodded. "We had to keep you so isolated before. I want you to know that now, this is not the case. There will be a lot of new in your life," she said, indicating the fruit and their surroundings. "But you are not a prisoner."

Not sure what to say for a moment, Roishin swallowed the bite in her mouth before she walked the few steps to Enori and initiated a hug. She wasn't sure if Enori would allow it, but she smiled when she was wrapped in the other woman's embrace.

"Thank you, Enori." The hug continued for many moments, Roishin realizing she needed it.

Enori held her, gentle fingers running through still damp hair. "Of course," she murmured in response. Finally, Enori gave her a hearty squeeze and released her. "Sit."

Feeling energized and strangely happy, Roishin sat on one side of the table, Enori sitting across from her. "Did you eat already?" she asked, noting Enori rested an elbow on the table and her chin in an open palm.

"I did." Even so, Enori snagged a cherry and tucked it between full lips before giving Roishin a little smile.

Roishin smirked and shook her head. "I've never

seen this side of you before."

"What side?" Enori asked.

Roishin shrugged as she took an apple, something she recognized and knew how to eat. "I don't know. Just kind of…" She took a bite as she considered. "So light and free, I guess," she managed around the bite of fruit. "This is so good," she nearly moaned. "So sweet."

Enori's smile was immediate, making her even more beautiful. It was nearly painful to look at her. There was just something about her that Roishin tried to put a finger on. It was otherworldly, somehow, like she was almost too beautiful to be of the earth. As she sat there, that incredible look of joy upon her face, it struck Roishin even more keenly.

"You just seem free, I guess," she said again. "Relaxed." She smirked. "Maybe even, dare I say, playful?" She nodded at the bowl of fruit with more cherries.

Enori raised an eyebrow, never taking her gaze off Roishin as she plucked another of the deep red fruit. She popped it into her mouth, using straight white teeth to bite it in two. Roishin burst into laughter.

"No P-word, got it." She looked at the fruit. "Speaking of a P-word," she murmured, picking up a piece of what Enori had called papaya. "Pretty sure you wouldn't go to all this trouble just to *poison* me now, so…"

The look on Enori's face was downright wicked as she eyed her.

"O-okay, you're making me really nervous today." Roshin chuckled.

"Fine," Enori said. She grabbed one of the orangish-peach-colored slices and lifted it for Roishin to see, then brought it to her own mouth. She raised her eyebrows as if to say, *See?*

Roishin smirked and brought her own slice to her nose, sniffing before she took a tiny bite. She was surprised to hear a loud burst of laughter from across the table, Enori clearly very amused. Quirking a brow of her own, Roishin took a big bite, then another, and finally a third until the entire slice was in her mouth.

"Uh?" she grunted, cheeks bulging.

Enori gave a deep belly laugh. "I will have no need to poison you, Roishin. I think you will manage to choke on your own."

"Or drown," Roishin muttered around the food she was swallowing as she chewed more of it.

"Or drown."

"It's a wonder I made it to seventeen."

❧❧❧❧

"So," Roishin said, turning in a slow circle as they walked. "We're back in the farmland area." She glanced over to her companion. "How are there all these areas? This, the woods, your village…"

"Do not forget the mountains," Enori added, nodding off toward the left.

"Oh!" Wide-eyed, Roishin looked to her. "Can we go there?"

"Of course. But first," Enori said with a smirk. "We have business."

"All right, all right," she muttered good-naturedly.

"Duras is a crossroads," Enori explained. "It is where those like you and I live, and where we can access the doors. It is a mirror to the world you and I were born in." She glanced over at Roishin. "All this, mountains, farmland, valley, jungle…whatever you can imagine, it is here."

"Wow. And do you have to live in the mirror of where you were born?" Roishin asked, thinking that Enori's village looked a lot like what she imagined Enori's homeland of Brittany must have. "Is where you live not like Brittany?"

"No," Enori said, her voice very soft, a note of sadness to it. She took a deep breath before slowly letting it out. "Where I live is similar, to a point, to a place where I once knew a great deal of happiness for a time."

Roishin was surprised by the words, and even more so by the deep well of sadness she saw in Enori's expression before it was expertly guarded once more. "I'm sorry, Enori."

"Thank you. So," she said, sounding like she was forcing a happier tone. "Once you are finished with your training, you will be able to choose where you want to live here." She indicated the world around them.

"I can have my own house, or whatever?"

"You can."

Something occurred to her. "Yesterday, when we were walking through all this, nobody even seemed to notice us. Why?"

Enori shrugged. "People are here for all sorts of reasons, Roishin. For some, their peace is in seeing what they want to see. They are here for a specific reason, and nothing beyond that matters to them."

"So, in your village, if you wanted to, you could only see your house and your life, and nobody else would exist?"

"Yes."

Roishin kind of liked the thought of that. Her whole life, she'd always felt intruded upon. From family to servants, there was so much obligation at times. "I can see the benefit in that," she muttered. They turned off down a long path that led to a two-story farmhouse at the end. There was a large front porch with two chairs set on curved rails that she'd learned were called rocking chairs.

The house reminded her a lot of those described in some books she'd read. "Why are we here?"

"I am going to introduce you to the team that will be helping me train you."

With that, the nerves really began to hit her. Roishin was just beginning to feel comfortable around Enori. Now, to throw even more people into the mix, she wanted to throw up. She took a very deep breath, trying to settle her nerves—and her breakfast.

They stepped onto the porch from the few steps leading up to it, stopping at a wood-framed screen door, something Roishin had never seen. She was fascinated by the screen material, running her fingertips over it. When she felt eyes on her, she glanced over to see Enori watching her. With a sheepish look, Roishin stepped aside.

"Sorry."

Enori pulled open the door and stepped inside the house, Roishin following. She was immediately thrust into a world filled with things she'd only ever read about in books.

Atop the oval wood table was some delicate white lace. If the items were what she'd read about, that was a doily and that was a coffee table. She smiled, pleased at her recollection of the details. Elsewhere in the room, she recognized what had been described as a recliner, the wooden handle off to the side.

"Wow." She walked over to the large, overstuffed chair and was about to pull the handle when she heard somebody clear their throat. Glancing up, she saw

Enori again watching her, a look of slight disapproval mixed with amusement on her face. "Sorry," Roishin muttered again and walked over to stand next to her. She clasped her hands behind her back, so they'd behave.

The front room area looked like a living space, with the couch and recliner and another chair. Deeper in the house she saw portions of rooms—just the barest hint of a dining table in one, possibly a kitchen in the other. A set of stairs split the living space with another room, unseen. She looked up the stairs, which ended at a wall, then into a hallway blocked by another wall.

"How many will be on the team?" Roishin asked to distract her from taking a self-guided tour. Her curiosity was killing her.

"There will be four, all told," Enori said. "Myself and three others."

Roishin nodded. She was bouncing on the balls of her feet, anxious energy really beginning to course through her. "I'm so nervous," she whispered, sending an apologetic look over to Enori.

"Do not be," her mentor replied, that sweet smile on her lips. "I promise, it will be okay."

The screen door opened and Roishin turned to see a man enter. He looked to be in his twenties, perhaps thirties. His light brown hair was shaggy and fell over his eyes. He was dressed simply in a button-down shirt and baggy trousers held up by two straps she thought might be suspenders, yet again bringing to life the descriptions she'd read in books. If she didn't know better, she'd think he'd stepped out of *The Adventures of Huckleberry Finn*.

"Roishin," he said, a strange accent clipping his words that she had never heard before.

She nodded. "Aye."

"John," he said.

"He is from America," Enori said quietly.

Roishin's eyes nearly bugged out of her head. "Are you from Maine, like Stephen King?" she asked, excited.

John threw his head back and laughed, nice and hard. Grinning, he shook his head. "Nah. Missouri."

"Misery?"

Again, that hearty laughter. "Some might say. Sure nice to meet you, finally. Been hearing about you forever now from this one." He nodded to Enori. He held out his hand, which Roishin took. "Sure fine to meet you, Roishin." He held her gaze with deep brown eyes. "Mighty fine."

She smiled shyly. "You too, John."

"Roishin," Enori said softly. When she turned to look at her, Enori nodded to the stairs behind Roishin. "Someone wants to say hello."

Roishin turned fully to see who it was. Her breath caught and tears formed to her eyes. She pressed her hand to her mouth, only able to stare at the woman before her. She couldn't move, couldn't think, could hardly breathe. The love she saw in those dark eyes nearly brought her to her knees. The soft, soothing word she knew so well brought on the sobs.

"Fanciulla." She heard the word whispered into her ear as she was taken into a tight embrace and held as she cried. "Ti amo, Roishin," the woman said softly.

"I love you too, Livia."

# *Chapter Eleven*

After many long moments, Livia pulled back, looking into Roishin's tear-filled eyes. "Roishin," she whispered, so much love in that one word.

"I'm so sorry," Roishin cried. "I'm so sorry."

"No, no." Livia smiled as she brushed long, dark hair from a heated, tear-streaked face.

"I tried, I swear," Roishin said through waning sobs. "I tried to save you, bring you back." She began crying all over again.

Livia brought her into her embrace again, gently swaying with her in her arms like she'd done so many times when Roishin was a child. "Shh."

It took several minutes, but finally Roishin began to calm. Not letting her go, she asked, "How are you here?"

"I told you," Enori said, stepping into Roishin's line of sight over Livia's shoulder. "Duras is a crossroads."

Livia pulled out of the hug and smiled. "She's right." She cupped Roishin's face and left two noisy kisses, one on either cheek. "Come with me," she said, taking Roishin's hand. "Let's go talk."

Roishin was still using her sleeve to wipe at her cheeks as she was led to the front porch and the very rocking chairs she'd noticed not ten minutes before. Roishin couldn't keep her eyes off the woman who had been her beloved aunt, her beloved Livia. The woman, who should be thirty-four now, looked exactly as she did the day she died. There was a glow about her, a happiness that Roishin had never seen before in those dark eyes.

Livia reached across the short expanse and took Roishin's hand in hers. "You are so beautiful, piccolo," she said with that big, beautiful smile that Roishin loved so much. "All grown up. Well," she hedged. "Almost."

Roishin grinned, feeling like she could run all the way to the moon and back. "I don't understand this. Am I dead, too? Is that why I'm here?"

"No." Livia rubbed her thumb over the back of the hand she held. "Duras is a reflection of the other world, where we were all born," she explained. "And the dead are a reflection of the living, Roishin. Do you understand?"

"So," Roishin said slowly, tasting her thoughts on her tongue before she spoke them. "The living and the dead live as one here?"

"The other world is about life, love, laughter, and family. No?" At Roishin's nod, she continued. "Here, it is the same. But I am not dead here," she said, hand splayed across her chest. "And you are not alive here. Duras is a perfect reflection of that life from the other world, without the boundaries of life and death." She indicated the land around them. "Or, the boundaries of woods and farm, snow and sun."

Roishin could only stare, stunned. "Can I take you with me, then?" she asked, almost in a whisper. "Through the door?"

"In that world, Roishin, the dead is a reflection of the living," she said again.

Confused, Roishin shook her head. "I don't understand."

"You will, I promise." She squeezed Roishin's hand and gave her a brilliant smile. "I'm on your team!"

"Really?" Roishin nearly yelled in happiness. At Livia's nod, she let out a long, deep breath, almost as if she could finally let go of the most traumatic event of her young life. "I'm sorry, Livia," she said again, looking out into the yard. "So sorry."

"Roishin, look at me." When Roishin finally did, her eyes once again welling, Livia said, "That day, I was set free."

"Free?" Roishin said, wiping at her eyes. "Livia, you died."

Livia used their joined hands to point off into a field fifty yards away where a man and a boy of perhaps five years were kneeling in the crops. It looked as though the man were explaining something to the boy.

"That man," Livia said. "He is my husband, Gerald. And that boy is our son, Mattia." She looked back to Roishin. "I was set free of all my fear to be happy, to love, and most importantly, to *be* loved" She smiled, the most beautiful, pure smile Roishin had ever seen on her face. "I have what I always wanted, Roishin."

"What's that?" Roishin whispered, tears slowly sliding down her cheeks.

"A family of my own." She brought Roishin's hand to her lips, leaving a kiss there before she cradled the hand lovingly against her chest. "That dream was taken from me in the other world. Here..." She indicated the beautiful house, the porch they sat on, and the two figures in the field. "I have all my dreams." Her smile grew. "And now, all the more. I have my other family, too." She squeezed Roishin's hand.

⁂

"What?" Roishin asked, feeling eyes on her. Sure

enough, Enori was watching her from the small chair she'd been curled up in that morning. Roishin had plopped down on the larger version.

Enori shook her head, a smile on her lips. "I am just sitting here wondering when your face is going to break from your smile."

A loud bark of laughter left Roishin's lips. "Any minute now."

"Good surprise?"

"Yeah. Best ever." Roishin rested her head back against the cushion and stared up at the ceiling for a moment before looking back to Enori. "Are Gerald and Mattia dead also?"

Enori nodded.

"Are all    those that die here?" Roishin asked, indicating the village and Duras around them.

"No." Enori slid her feet out of her sandals and curled her legs up beside her. "Some choose to return for another life." The look in her eyes grew sad. "Some souls are destroyed by the intention of those that kill them. I speak particularly of a religious cult, order, or mystic."

"Like, if you'd been sacrificed at ten?" Roishin asked slowly.

"That is one example, yes."

Roishin thought about that for a moment. "That's terrifying."

"Yes. It is. And other souls, ones who are murdered but whose souls are not destroyed by their killers, can be enslaved."

The air in the room grew heavy, so Roishin decided to change the subject. "Over dinner you mentioned that I'd be heading out tomorrow with you and Livia." At Enori's nod, Roishin asked, "Out, where?"

"Out through the doors," Enori said.

Roishin chewed on her bottom lip, thinking. "When I've gone from one place to another, even to the waterfall here to bathe, I've used doors. Right?" At Enori's nod, she continued. "Then, I'm familiar with those, but from the talks today with John and Livia, it sounds like there are other kinds of doors." She met Enori's gaze. "Am I wrong?"

Enori pushed to her feet. "Come."

Roishin also stood, following Enori up the stairs to her bedroom. Placed atop the neatly made bed was a stack of three very familiar books and one of the blue cloaks with gold stitching.

"I requested these to be dropped off while we were gone," Enori explained. She handed the three books to Roishin with a smile. "You forgot these."

"Oh," Roishin blew out, giving Enori a sheepish grin. "Yes, I'm sorry." They were the three books given to her by The Mystic before she'd left the Underground.

"This one," Enori said, indicating the one on the history of women on the stage across time. "You need to study tonight."

Nodding, Roishin ran her fingertips over the smooth cover of the book. "How will I know what to study?"

Enori moved to step up behind her, front nearly brushing against Roishin's back. She reached both hands around Roishin and took the book off the pile that Roishin still held with both of her hands. She rested her chin upon Roishin's shoulder as she began to randomly flip through the pages.

"You see these markings?" she said, her words brushing across Roishin's ear, sending a little shiver through her. She used a finger to tap a light X placed next to several paragraphs. "This is what you'll look for." She closed the book and placed it back on the pile. "Know it, Roishin," she murmured, hands resting on the younger woman's hips briefly before backing away.

It took Roishin several moments to be able to think straight. Finally, she was able to shake off the effects of Enori—which she wasn't always sure were intended. Blowing out a slow breath, she nodded.

"I can do that," she finally managed.

"Good." Enori picked up the blue cloak, eyeing Roishin for a moment as if considering something. She seemed to come to some decision in her head and held up the garment. "You have mastered the brown cloak." Her tone was kind, yet she was clearly very focused on what she had to say. "This one, however," she said, hugging the cloak to her chest with one arm while stroking it lovingly with the other hand. "Is a very, very different animal, Roishin."

Roishin looked down at it, curious. "Why so?"

Enori looked up from the garment to meet Roishin's eyes. "Tomorrow," she said softly. "Tonight, get some rest." She walked to Roishin's bedroom and hung the blue cloak on the hook on the door. She turned to Roishin in the hallway. "Study that," she said again, pointing to the book on top of the pile in Roishin's hands. With a sweet smile, she added, "Good night."

"Good night, Enori."

❧❧❧❧

The next morning, Roishin continued going through every single notated paragraph again and again. She studied, nearly memorizing the marked text, not entirely sure what she needed to know or why. She'd showered, as Enori called it, and was sitting on the bed putting her boots on when Enori appeared in the open doorway of her bedroom.

She was back in one of her flowing white gowns. The relaxed, easy-to-smile woman Roishin had come to know the last two days was gone. Back was the woman with piercing eyes and a cool, aloof demeanor. She looked Roishin over, making her feel extremely nervous.

"Did I do something wrong?" Roishin asked, pausing in her task.

Without a word, Enori stepped away but returned a moment later. She carried a leather strip in her hand. "Turn a bit," she said. "So your back is to me."

Roishin did as she was told. When the leather strip was set on the bed next to her and Enori began to brush her hair back, Roishin thought she got the idea. She held still, allowing Enori to pull her hair back into a single thick braid down her back.

"We have to be as contained as possible," she said, her fingers gentle in their task to bringing Roishin's mane to heel. "Can leave nothing behind."

Roishin swallowed nervously, as she could feel the intensity of Enori's energy in that moment. She had no idea what they were about to do, but she was getting the message quite clearly that it was serious business.

"Is that why you keep your hair short?"

"Partly, yes. The biggest part. Sorry," Enori said, giving Roishin's shoulder a little squeeze in apology as she tugged a bit too hard.

"Should I cut mine?"

"Something you can consider, yes. But if you are opposed, there are other ways, such as this." She tugged lightly on the braid she was creating. "You studied?" she asked casually.

"I did," Roishin said proudly. "Pretty sure I know that book backward and forward." She smiled at the little chuckle she heard.

"I want you to put a portrait together in your mind of who would be present in a stage crew," she said. "What type of person? What tasks would they perform, and what would they wear to do them?"

Roishin allowed her mind to wander back into the pages she'd read, paragraphs she'd studied, and images she'd drawn from the words.

"Do you see him?" Enori asked, her words not much more than a hum.

"Yes," Roishin murmured, the person in her mind taking shape.

"See him," Enori said. "Know his every detail." She reached for the leather strip and tied it tightly at the end of the braid. She leaned over Roishin, murmuring into her ear. "*Be* him."

The building was as imposing the second time as it had been the first. Roishin walked up to it with Enori, her blue cloak draped over her arm. Something told her not to put it on yet, and Enori had said nothing to the contrary. The Crystal Palace was a sight to behold. It was like looking at a massive diamond with endless facets.

"How does this even exist?" she said, looking up into that strange, swirling sky. "What is the red stuff?"

Enori stepped beside her and looked up. "Energy." She lightly tugged on Roishin's shirt. "Come. Livia is here."

That was all Enori had to say. Roishin hurried after the priestess to find Livia. The two women instantly shared a tight hug outside one of the archways. Livia's smile was large, her dark eyes bright. She was dressed simply, as she'd been the day before. Her midnight tresses were twisted up into a tight bun atop her head.

"Ready?" she asked.

"I have no idea." Roishin laughed, nervous and excited at the same time.

"I have a very serious question for you, Roishin," Livia said.

"All right." Roishin spared a glance at Enori before looking back to her aunt. "What?"

"Do I have your permission to haunt you?"

Roishin wanted to burst into laughter, thinking Livia was making a joke. But it was quite clear that both other women were serious as they looked at her expectantly.

"Um." Looking at Enori, she shrugged. "Am I supposed to say yes?"

"She's asking your permission to be able to follow you," Enori explained gently. "That allows her energy to merge with yours."

Eyebrows shooting up, Roishin looked back to Livia. "Um, well. Yes. I give you permission."

Livia grinned. "It'll make sense." She left a kiss on Roishin's cheek before she turned to Enori, eyes bright. "Ready?"

Enori nodded, then took the cloak from Roishin and moved to stand behind her. She eased the garment onto her shoulders. "This is a very special cloak, Roishin," she said as she moved around to face her and tied the garment in place. "It is unlike anything you have ever worn." She looked into Roishin's eyes, holding her gaze. "Intention. Hold on to your intention."

"Like when you told me to hold my intention with the rabbit?" she asked, never forgetting that traumatic yet profound moment so many years ago. A lifetime ago.

Enori's smile was beautiful. "Yes. You remember that?"

"I do."

Enori's gaze fell back to her fingers. "Second time we'd met."

"Second time?"

Enori gave Roishin a knowing smile before she brought her hands up like she was about to clasp them behind Roishin's neck. Instead, she raised the hood into place over Roishin's head. She looked deeply into Roishin's eyes as she placed her hands on her shoulders.

"Be him," she said before stepping back and pulling up her own hood.

"Be him," Roishin whispered, nodding as if to cement the words into her mind.

Again, she pictured the man she'd been seeing in her mind since the night before. She saw every detail of him. She heard his voice, saw his gait, even knew how short he kept his fingernails. She walked with the other two women toward one of the many archways that danced around the circumference of the Crystal Palace.

She took a deep breath. *Here we go.*

# Chapter Twelve

As they got closer to the archway, Roishin realized there were no doors, no windows, just a purity of blackness that she'd never seen outside of midnight itself. As they neared it, she felt every hair on her body lift a bit and the core of her gut seize for just a second. Then it was over, and they were inside.

There were no walls, no floor, no ceiling. There were no stairs to rise to higher levels of the large structure, no balconies to watch below, and no rooms. The red smoke-like energy that stretched down to electrify the outside floated around freely inside. There was no obvious light source, yet the red smokiness was easily seen as if *it* was the light source.

It reminded Roishin of the way dust particles seemed to dance and glow through a beam of light sent from an arrow slit back home. This red smoke danced around them, a cool breeze. Roishin watched, mouth open a bit in awe.

She looked to her left when she felt her hand taken. "Intention," Enori said.

Roishin shook herself out of her wonder and focused. She felt her other hand taken and knew it was Livia. She looked over to her right and, to her shock, she could see Livia in the red-tinted darkness. She had the slightest glow to her and looked as though she were made of glass—that same sort of smudged glass that appeared as the boundary between areas of Duras.

Livia released Roishin's hand and turned to her. "Ready?"

Roishin had no idea what she was being asked to do but nodded as she trusted Livia implicitly. She gasped when Livia stepped in front of her and then… inside of her. Her body went stock-still, spine straight and eyes wide. It felt like the coldest possible air had blown right through her. Roishin took a few breaths, trying to acclimate.

Feeling a squeeze to her left hand, she glanced over and just barely caught Enori's gaze as smokey red illuminated her eyes for just a second before she was gone in darkness again.

"Here we go," Enori said.

Before them, the red smoke began to gather, reminding Roishin of the gurgling water in a stream that bottlenecked at a narrow waterway. Slowly, it all came together to create the shimmering portal she'd come to recognize as a door.

"Stay close to me," Enori said, then the door she'd created was wide enough for them to step through.

Still holding Roishin's hand, Enori took a step, vanishing through the door, pulling Roishin to walk through behind her…

…into a room crammed with racks of dresses and trousers and hats and gloves, as well as many things Roishin wasn't familiar with. As she stepped up to one of the racks, she saw something flopped over the top of it. It was pink and looked like a bunch of peacock butts had been tied together.

Utterly confused for a moment, she then remembered a description in one of the books she'd read in the Underground that matched the item. It had been called a boa, and it was worn around a woman's shoulders or neck in adornment or as an accessory.

Moving on, she looked to a vanity that was

tucked into the corner of the room and saw little jars scattered across the wood top. Some were open, others closed, and the colors inside matched what she could see through the clear glass they were made of. There were also little brushes littering the top, some with their bristle tips stained white.

A mirror was mounted to two intricately carved posts protruding up from either side of the vanity. She nearly cried out when she saw the reflection, her heart racing. She jerked in protective reflex away from the man who stared back at her with his brown eyes, the heavy mustache that nearly covered his lips twitching as his mouth formed a surprised O that mirrored her own expression.

He wore a brown bowler hat atop his head. The slightly off-white button-down shirt was tucked into baggy brown trousers. As she struggled to keep her fear at bay, he began to fade. In his place stood a hooded figure, the deep shadows of the hood hiding her own face. This startled her all over again. She heard Enori's words in her mind: *Intention. Be him*

Taking a steadying breath, she focused. Her own cloaked image began to fade, the man slowly easing back into view. She released a slow breath as she studied this new reality. She had no idea how deep the ruse went, so she brought a hand up and was about to touch her face when she was nearly startled out of her trousers yet again. Livia's reflection appeared just behind her own.

"Don't touch," she said, though her voice was inside Roishin's head. "Projected intention. Focus."

Nodding, Roishin lowered her hand. "Okay." She glanced to her side, fully expecting to see Livia there. Nothing. When she looked back to the mirror, Livia still stood behind and to her left.

Livia grinned. "Come on."

Still just so struck by the unfolding events, Roishin forced herself to look away from the mirror. When she did, she found herself looking into the face of an older woman, her gray hair pulled up into a large bun atop her head. Her face was a roadmap of wrinkles that told stories of a hard life. Her dress was simple and drab, the downturn of thin lips telling.

Roishin was pretty sure she was about to be scolded for being there when she noticed the woman's eyes. Though a watery brown, it was the life behind them that made Roishin's own eyes widen.

"Let's go," the old woman said, her voice aged and filled with the irritation of a woman who had lived long enough to not tolerate much. Even still, there was no mistaking that Enori was in there.

It was dizzying, this reality, and would take time to get used to, if one ever did, Roishin thought. Either way, she gave one more glance to Livia's reflected gaze, then turned away from the mirror and followed.

They made their way out of the tight, dusty space, which Roishin now realized was the changing room for a stage production. The three—well, two— headed out of the room, Roishin making sure the door was securely closed behind her. They made their way down narrow wooden stairs.

Roishin's eyes were pulled everywhere once they reached the bottom of the stairs. The flurry of activity was overwhelming. From what she could see, she was in the middle of what she'd read was called "the house," where members of the audience sat to watch the performers on stage. She saw a row of gas lights all along the outer edge of the stage to light the production.

Incredible, she thought. Absolutely incredible.

She'd read about all of this! As there were not many people in the house and the people rushing to and fro across the stage didn't seem to be in costumes, Roishin figured that the players and stagehands were perhaps preparing for a rehearsal of their performance.

The sound of two men hurrying up the center aisle garnered her attention. One man had brown hair, worn in the style of the day, and his suit was impeccable. A smaller, squirrely man in a rumpled suit hurried after him, carrying papers.

"Mr. Ford," he exclaimed breathlessly, as though he'd been chasing the first man for blocks. "We have the playbills for tonight's performance."

The first man stopped so suddenly the smaller one nearly ran into him. "Let me see." He accepted a paper the smaller man handed him. "'Our American Cousin,'" he read aloud before opening the folded little booklet and scanning the contents.

"Follow Enori."

Livia's voice pulled Roishin's attention from the two men and she returned her focus to the older woman who had left her behind, walking down the side aisle of the theatre. Roishin hurried to catch up while doing her best to maintain calm and a relaxed I-belong-here demeanor. Up on the stage was a group of people standing together. Two women and one man were quiet while a second man was talking to them and gesticulating as he did so.

"Laura," the man was saying, Roishin able to hear him now as they began to climb the stairs at stage left. "You'll be here."

"Miss Keene!"

A young woman ran from the wings on the opposite side of the stage. Enori had already made her way into the wings on their side, but Roishin still stood at the top of the stairs, watching as the young woman ran up to the quartet already gathered on the stage.

"You asked for this," she said, handing something to the older of the two women in the group.

"Thank you, Ava," the woman said, taking whatever had been handed to her, the item blocked by the gesticulating man.

The young woman nodded, then was about to head back the way she'd come but stopped. She looked directly at Roishin. She was beautiful, perhaps in her early twenties. Her rich, dark brown hair was coifed back from her face in waves and into an intricate bun of braids at the back of her head.

She was a woman of her era, which was fascinating enough, but what compelled Roishin were her eyes. They were dark brown in color but penetrating and piercing. They spoke of a soul older than her couple of decades on earth, and as she looked at Roishin, it seemed she *saw* her. The woman's lips parted a bit, and those dark eyes widened.

The young woman seemed to be taking a step forward when Roishin heard, "Go! Leave her sight," in her head.

Heeding Livia's words, Roishin turned and hurried to follow Enori. She made her way backstage, noting Enori was waiting for her, still in disguise as the old woman and looking irritated. Roishin gave her a contrite nod before continuing on. They reached a back door to the theatre, which had trunks and crates stacked in front of it, some of them marked with "Ford's Theatre" on the side in wide letters.

Enori spoke to her quietly. "I need you to move all of this, make sure this door is clear." She looked deeply into Roishin's eyes. "Be the stagehand that you are."

Roishin nodded in understanding.

"Once you are done, there is a boarding house two blocks over. Livia knows where. Meet me there. Second floor, room three." Without even waiting for a response, Enori headed back the way they'd come, disappearing amidst the props and people who were moving into the wings to grab this or that for the rehearsal.

Taking a deep breath and feeling incredibly vulnerable, Roishin focused on the task she'd been given. She grunted slightly as she moved the first crate off the stack, setting it on the floor against the wall next to the door.

"Hey, son," a man's voice said. "Who told you to move them crates?"

Glancing over at the bespeckled man, Roishin deepened her voice, praying to the gods it worked. "Mr. Ford," she said, thinking of the man she saw earlier and presuming from what she overheard that he was the owner of the theatre.

The man nodded, then asked, "Why?"

Thinking fast, Roishin remembered a book she'd read about the Richmond Theatre fire of 1811, as well as those who battled the blaze. "Fire marshal's orders."

The man nodded and walked away.

"Good thinking," Livia murmured.

"Thanks," Roishin muttered.

She continued her task, mindful of who was around. Finally, she finished, dragging the final, largest trunk out of the way of the door. Taking one last look to make sure she wasn't being watched, she used the very door she'd just unblocked and headed outside.

She found herself in a bit of a tight alleyway. Livia gave her directions on which way to go, and Roishin followed them. She so badly wanted to take it all in, look at the crazy and unfamiliar surrounds with large builds lining the dirt avenue, made of brick or stone. She wanted to stop and watch the people, and the strange way they were dressed.

There wasn't a sword to be seen, though she had seen one man with what she'd learned was called a firearm holstered at his hip. She'd read about the rise of the Colt revolver and the Winchester rifle. To see the gun belt on display now, she was fascinated. Alas, she had to hurry.

She arrived at a tall, skinny house with windows that went all the way up to the attic window beneath the pitched roof. A front porch, like on Livia's house, was there also. She climbed the stairs and headed inside, then up to the second floor as Enori had told her. She was grateful that she hadn't seen anyone inside—and that no one had seen her.

Little metal numbers were nailed to the doors, and she went until she found number three. Glancing down the hall to the stairs to make sure she was still alone, Roishin turned the knob and pushed the door open, thankful to see Enori inside, the stunning blonde back in her own skin.

Quickly shutting the door, Roishin leaned back against it. So relieved that she'd gotten there safely, she felt suddenly exhausted. Enori, who still wore her cloak though the hood was down, walked over to Roishin. Reaching up, she brushed Roishin's own hood back.

Instantly, Roishin felt a weight lift from her shoulders. Her eyes closed and she took a deep breath. "Why did that make me feel better?"

Enori smiled. "Because the energy was basically turned off," she explained, then indicated herself and Roishin. "To hold our intended role takes a great deal of focus and energy, which the cloaks help to contain.

Plus," she added with a smile and soft tap to Roishin's chest. "You are not alone in there."

Roishin smirked. "True." She looked past the woman who stood before her. "Where are we?"

Enori turned to take in the very small room. It wasn't much larger than a servant's room back home. There was a bed with a brass headboard and footboard. There was a ceramic wash basin with ceramic water jug sitting inside it placed atop a narrow wooden stand. A single window looked to the brick wall of the building next door.

"This is the room of Ava Gentry," Enori said. "She must not be at the performance tonight."

"Why?"

"She will be killed if she is," Enori said simply. She reached inside her cloak and brought out a small leather pouch with a drawstring closure.

"And," Roishin said. "You don't want her dead?"

Enori shook her head. "No. She is necessary later." Enori walked over to the bed and reached into the pouch with a forefinger and thumb. She brought out the slightest bit of white powder, sprinkling it over the surface of the pillow.

Roishin watched, fascinated. "What will that do? And, why on her pillow when she won't go to bed until—"

"Like all the actors," Enori explained, never taking her gaze off her task. "She will come in and nap." She glanced at Roishin as she tugged the pouch closed again. "This will make her very ill. Too ill to attend."

Roishin hugged herself, not entirely comfortable with this. "But she'll be okay, right?"

Enori nodded, tucking the pouch away. "Oh yes. But most importantly, she will be alive." She walked back over to Roishin, pulling something else out from the inside of her cloak. "I brought this for you." She held up a narrow white thing that was a few inches long.

"What is this?" Roishin asked, taking it and looking it over.

"A rolled cigarette," Enori explained. "Put it between your lips or play with it with your fingers. Whatever you need to do to look casual and like you belong."

Roishin nodded in understanding, turning the little cigarette around to look at it from all sides. Again, something she'd read about. She knew they were lit on one end with a lighter or matches, neither of which she'd ever seen.

"I want you down on the street," Enori continued, pulling Roishin out of her musings. "Lean against the building next door. Livia, when you spot her coming, let me know."

"All right," Livia said.

"She said all right," Roishin repeated dutifully. She wasn't expecting the little grin from Enori that she got.

"I hear her, too. She has been haunting me for years."

Roishin chuckled, nodding. "Understood."

Enori reached out and brought Roishin's hood up into place. Looking deeply into Roishin's eyes, she said, "Focus."

Nodding, Roishin took several deep breaths and did just that. She focused on the man again, bringing him into her mind's eye. This time, she felt the transition begin. When it was complete, Enori took a step back from her, nodding toward the door of the small room.

Getting the all-clear from Livia that nobody was

coming, Roishin snuck out of the room, back down the stairs, and out of the boarding house. She felt better once on the streets, as it would not do for a man to be found where he wasn't supposed to be regarding a woman's private room. She saw the building Enori spoke of and found a good spot to lean on against the sun-warmed brick.

As she was told to do, she messed with the cigarette. Now that she understood what it was, she had a better understanding of how to try and look casual. She held the little white object between her lips, using her tongue to play with it, bobbing it this way and that.

Not five minutes later, she was stunned to see the brunette woman from the theatre walking down the sidewalk. She was hurrying along in her long skirts and pinned-up hair. As she neared the house, she spotted Roishin standing there. Her steps slowed, that dark gaze never leaving her. She stopped at the walkway up to the boarding but then seemed to change her mind. She continued on the sidewalk until there was no more than six feet between her and Roishin.

"Do I know you?" the brunette asked.

Roishin felt herself beginning to sweat. *Oh boy.* She shook her head, not sure if her voice would be convincing or not. It had worked with the man earlier while clearing the back door of the theatre, but…

"I do," the woman said, nodding. "I've seen you in my dreams before."

"Enori," Livia said. "We have a very large problem."

Roishin was vaguely aware of the chatter in her head, unable to hear anything Enori said in response. She tried to focus on the woman before her. "No, ma'am," she said, remembering a scene from the Louis L'Amour novel *Riders of the Dawn* and how the cowboy had spoken to the lady.

The young actress cocked her head slightly, a slight smile upon her lovely face. "Yes," she said, almost more to herself than to Roishin. "You're one of them."

"Roishin, get out of there now. We need to get you home!"

Roishin barely heard the frantic words from Livia but pushed away from the building and the young woman. "Ma'am," she said, nodding at her in deference, then turned and hurried down the sidewalk, heart racing.

# *Chapter Thirteen*

*The figure walked toward her, face hidden in the deep shadows of the hood and body covered by the deep blue of the cloak. She could just barely make out gold stitching. The figure sped up their pace, the cloak fanning out behind them as they began to run.*

*Fear gripped her as she turned and began to run away from it. She could feel the anger coming off the figure like heat. She felt her hand grabbed and was whipped around, the force slamming her into her pursuer.*

*No choice but to look up into murderous green eyes, she gasped. "I'm sorry."*

*"How could you?" the figure demanded. "How could you!"*

Elsie gasped, eyes popping open. Her heart was racing and she wanted to cry. Lying in her bed in her small bedchamber, she brought her hands up to cover her mouth. When she saw the glisten of the gold band she wore on her left ring finger, little doves carved into it, she did begin to cry.

After several minutes, the tears began to abate, and she sniffled as she used the sleeve of her sleep shirt to wipe at her eyes and cheeks. Sitting up, she ran her hands through her hair to push it back from her face and out of the tear streaks. She looked around the bedchamber and saw that she was alone.

Strangely, she'd almost expected to see Roishin

sitting at the end of her bed. She'd be watching her, condemning her, much as Elsie did every single day since the engagement had become official. Though it wasn't the heavy, bulky ring that would end up being the wedding ring of a princess, it still weighed her down.

She knew sleep would not be coming back anytime soon, so she opted to get up and start her day. From the position of the moon and stars, she'd be getting up in an hour or so anyway. As she made her bed, she considered her dream—well, nightmare, really—and the person who had been at the center of it.

The morning she'd awoken with Roishin gone after they'd made love was more than five months ago. Part of her had been really hurt, but another part had not been entirely surprised. Though she hadn't heard from Roishin since, somehow she knew she'd done that to make their parting the least painful as possible. It would never not be painful, but a bit less. She'd thought so many times about how it could have happened differently, if they'd woken up together, warm and naked.

Could her heart have handled watching Roishin dress and leave? No, it would have gutted her. So, she'd had a good cry that morning then forced herself to go on, no other choice in the matter. Even when Garratt had officially begun the engagement, Elsie had felt guilty on so many levels.

She didn't love him and knew she never would as he wanted her to and deserved to be. She'd already been unfaithful, considering she knew of his intentions the night she'd been with Roishin. She felt she was doing a horrible disservice to Fallon and Cateline to marry their son despite the previous two points.

But she'd watched Cateline over the years she'd served her, most spent as princess and not queen, and Elsie had seen all the good she'd been able to do for the people of Sursha. Elsie wanted to do that, too. Honestly, it was the main reason she'd accepted the proposal.

Roishin was lost to her, she knew that. It was further likely she'd never meet another woman of like attraction, so she decided she might as well stay in the family she loved and help the people of the country she loved. A bitter seed to plant, but hopefully it would bloom into beautiful flowers that would make it all worth it.

Bed made, Elsie changed from her sleep clothes to what she'd wear that day before she quickly brushed her hair out and put it up. Much like at the previous castle to the west, Fallon and Cateline opted to share the king's chambers as their chambers, so the queen's chambers had been converted into a similar family gathering place.

The lady-in-waiting's chamber was off of it, so she pulled that door open rather than the one that led to the hall. She started, shocked. A fire already danced in the large fireplace, sending warmth and shadows throughout the large space. A figure was seated in one of the two chairs before it.

Elsie's stomach roiled for a moment, first in surprise, then fear. She knew who it was, and her dream came back to her. How would she react to the news? Elsie couldn't keep it from her. She stood in the open doorway of her bedchamber, no idea what to do or say. Her hands fidgeted nervously and her heart raced.

"It's okay, Elsie," came the soft voice, somehow heard across the large space. "I don't bite."

Elsie squeezed her eyes shut for a moment before

releasing a nervous breath. She almost removed the ring, knowing Roishin likely wouldn't be there long, but she knew that was the coward's way out. She had to face this. Clearing her throat, she gently closed the door to her chamber, else she'd have a very energetic five-and-a-half-year-old Isabeau jumping on her bed.

As she walked toward the chairs, the seated figure stood. How was it that it had only been five months, yet Roishin looked even older than Elsie's twenty-two years? She was even more beautiful than she'd been last time. Her features had matured, somehow not looking like an   eighteen-year-old anymore. She looked more like a woman of twenty-five or older.

What surprised Elsie the most, however, was that her long dark mane of hair was gone. Much like Enori's, it was short, the dark wavy strands curling just over the tops of her ears and down onto her forehead. Ironically, it gave her the look of an innocent girl, though the deep green eyes read as anything but.

Her eyes were human in shape and detail, but that was where the familiar ended. Their depths were otherworldly. She'd noticed the same feature in Enori's eyes, and it had been riveting yet unsettling. As though her dream had bled into reality, Roishin was wearing a blue cloak with gold stitching, though the hood was pushed down. It was the same cloak Enori wore, and Elsie nearly gasped.

Roishin cocked her head slightly as she looked at her, the softest, most serene smile upon her lips. She said nothing, simply walked up to Elsie, who was trembling and filled with so much uncertainty, and opened her arms. Easily falling into them, Elsie let out a long, shaky breath as she was totally enveloped in all that was Roishin.

They held each other for long moments, neither

saying a word. Elsie buried her face in her soft neck, reveling in the familiar scent that was Roishin's skin. Her hands were up under the cloak to rest upon Roishin's back, clad in a thin garment. Her skin was warm through the material.

"When did you get in?" Elsie murmured into the hug.

"Just a bit ago," Roishin responded softly, her head resting against Elsie's. "I didn't want to wake you."

Elsie smiled. "You can always wake me, Roishin. I don't get to see you all that often."

"I know." Roishin left a kiss on her head and then lifted her own, as did Elsie. "I'm sorry."

Their gazes met and all sorts of winged things began to bat at Elsie's rib cage, making her feel nauseous. She so badly wanted to kiss her, but things had changed.

"I have to tell you something," Elsie said.

Without saying anything, Roishin gently took Elsie's left hand from where it rested on her back and brought it out into view. She looked down at the ring for a long, long time. A flurry of expressions and emotions washed across her face and through her eyes as she stared at it.

"When is it?" she finally whispered.

Elsie took yet another shaky breath, no idea what was going through Roishin's mind. "Four months hence."

Roishin brought the hand to her lips and left a lingering kiss on the engagement ring upon her finger. Releasing the hand, she cupped both sides of Elsie's head with the same gentleness. She kissed her forehead before resting her own there.

"Someday," she said softly, caressing the side

of Elsie's face with her fingertips. "You'll make a wonderful queen."

Elsie closed her eyes and placed her hands over Roishin's. "You don't hate me?"

Roishin didn't respond for a moment but then lifted her head. She looked into Elsie's eyes. There was tremendous sadness in them, but she managed a smile. "No." She left another kiss on Elsie's forehead, then took her in a second hug.

Elsie knew why Roishin wasn't kissing her on the lips, and she respected her for it, but she hated it. It brought back just how little control she felt she had over everything, anything, her own life. Why couldn't she just be a normal woman, grateful and blessed that a handsome prince wanted her to share his life? Wasn't that the dream?

"How long are you staying?"

"Couple days," Roishin said. "I really missed everyone, so stopped by for a short visit." She gave her a final squeeze. "Luckily," she said, grinning at Elsie. "I have a lot more freedom now. Lots to be done, but I have the freedom to come and go, overall."

"Can we…" Elsie felt shy. She looked down at her fingers, which lightly played with Roishin's cloak. "Can we spend some time together?" She looked up into Roishin's eyes. "You and I?"

Roishin's smile was beautiful. "I'd really love that." She gave her a devilish grin. *This* was the Roishin that Elsie had fallen in love with. "But first, I want to surprise the daylights out of my parents."

Elsie's smile was wide. "We can make that happen."

One of the biggest changes since the engagement became official was that Elsie had begun eating her meals with the king and queen in their private family chambers. She'd all but been removed from the servant class, save for her duties as lady-in-waiting, which would be taken over by a lovely young girl of eighteen she was training.

As she sat there, eating and joining in conversation with the king and queen and Isabeau, she was nearly vibrating in her seat. Earlier, she and Roishin had headed down to the kitchen where Millie had nearly pulled Roishin's head off her shoulders, she'd hugged her so tightly. The three of them had come up with a little ruse to surprise the family.

Now, she was drawn out of her thoughts of anticipation when there was a knock on the chamber doors. Fallon wiped her mouth with her napkin before setting it on the table and pushing her chair back. Elsie tried not to make it too obvious that she was watching intently.

The door opened, and sure enough there stood Millie, the most trusted family friend in the castle. Next to her stood a tall, hooded figure in a shambled brown cloak covering clothing that had certainly seen better days. Fallon looked from the figure to Millie, clearly confused.

"Needs a job," Millie said casually, nodding to the figure standing next to her.

The figure began to speak a language none of them at the table spoke, even though between Fallon and Cateline they spoke nearly ten languages. Fallon held up a hand.

"Wait," she said. "Slow down." She looked to Millie. "What on earth is he saying?"

Millie shrugged her shoulders and turned to walk

away. "How would I know? You're the king."

Elsie almost lost her composure at the stunned and baffled look upon Fallon's face as she turned to her wife. A look of *Do you believe this?* was written all over her expression. To Elsie's right, Isabeau's dark blue eyes grew wide as she gasped. She climbed down from the stacks of large blocks placed upon the chair she sat on in order to reach the table and ran over to the cloaked figure, who hadn't moved.

Looking up at the person, she smiled. "I know you!"

The figure bent down just enough to grab the little girl under her arms, then lifted the squealing child high over her head, the hood falling back. "You do!" she affirmed, bringing the girl down for a tight squeeze and loud kiss on her cheek.

Elsie glanced over to Roishin's parents to see they were completely stunned. Cateline was already crying as she jumped to her feet, Fallon only getting first dibs because she was already close by.

Roishin put Isabeau down before she was taken into a bone-crushing hug from Fallon. The two were silent for a long moment, just holding on. Finally, with tears in her eyes, Fallon cupped Roishin's cheek as she looked into her face. There was so much pride in the king's beautiful violet eyes. Neither said a word, though an entire conversation seemed to pass between them.

The moment Fallon stepped aside, Cateline was in Roishin's arms, the cloaked woman making the queen squeal in surprise when she was lifted off her feet in the enthusiastic hug. Elsie found herself with a lapful of snuggly Isabeau, clearly overwhelmed by her joy. Elsie kissed the little one's head to let her know she was there and she understood.

"My goodness," Cateline exclaimed, tears trailing

freely down her lovely face. She touched Roishin's clothes, touched her face and finally her hair. "Look at you!"

Roishin grinned. "Well," she said. "These are borrowed." She tugged lightly on the cloak. "But the rest is me."

Cateline held her again. "I love you, my Roishin," she said into the hug.

"I love you too, Mamaí."

Wiping her eyes, Fallon glanced over at Elsie, who continued to sit there calmly. "Did you know she was here?"

Elsie gave her a smile and a nod. "I saw her this morning." She smiled at the playful glare she got.

⚜ ⚜ ⚜ ⚜

True to her word, that afternoon, while the king and queen dealt with duties of the throne, Roishin took Elsie out for a ride. Elsie had never been taught to ride herself, so Roishin had pulled her up onto her horse with her. Now, they'd dismounted and were wandering through the forest.

Elsie was surprised to find Roishin so at ease as they strolled, considering the horrors that had happened not far from where they strolled. Needing to be connected, Elsie reached for Roishin's hand. When the taller woman looked over at her, she gave her a sheepish smile.

"Is this okay?" she asked, lightly squeezing the hand that held her own.

Roishin brought the hand up and left a kiss on her fingers. "It's very okay."

They shared a smile, then Elsie said, "I've never seen you so relaxed before, Roishin. You seem so at ease, at peace."

Roishin was silent for a moment, seeming to consider the observation. "Aye," she finally said, glancing over at her companion. "I think it's because I finally have a better idea of who I am, what I'm here to do."

"More reading?" Elsie teased.

Roishin groaned. "Gods, no. Though, at least now I know *why* I had to read all that."

"Why?"

"I needed the information." Roishin stopped walking when they came to a huge tree with a thick trunk. She leaned back against it, looking at Elsie who stood just a couple feet away. "So I'd recognize things, know where I was on our missions."

"Missions?" She stepped up to Roishin, fingers lightly trailing up the edges of the blue cloak Roishin wore, having changed back into her own clothing.

Roishin nodded. "We go where we're needed to make sure things aren't changed by colossal mistakes or really bad people."

Elsie's eyebrows drew. "What is colossal?" she asked of the word she'd never heard before.

Roishin grinned. "Big."

"Why do I have the feeling that you go to places that aren't even on the map, hmm?" she asked, losing herself as she looked up into beautiful green eyes which took on the lush growth all around them. She snaked her arms up until she clasped her hands behind Roishin's neck. With every fiber of her being she knew it was wrong, but she just couldn't help it.

Roishin's hands went to Elsie's waist, gently urging the lady-in-waiting a bit closer. She grinned. "Well, where we go is on the map, just maybe not yet."

"Roishin?" Elsie murmured.

"Hmm?"

"Would I be a terrible person if I told you I wanted you to kiss me?" she whispered, fingers threading themselves in the short strands at the nape of Roishin's neck.

Roishin gave her a ghost of a smile. "Would I be a terrible person if I told you *I* wanted to kiss you?"

Elsie smiled. "Maybe two terrible people equals one good person?"

Roishin lowered her head. "I like the way you do math," she murmured.

# *Chapter Fourteen*

Though it had only been five months technically, it felt as though it had been forever. Elsie couldn't help but sigh at the first touch of Roishin's lips. The kiss was soft, the two discovering the other again. She admittedly loved the feeling of short hair through her fingers and found it was a new favorite place for them.

She moaned as Roishin's tongue gently stroked against her own. She pushed deeper against the woman leaning back against the tree. She could feel soft breasts against her and eased Roishin's cloak open a bit more so there was nothing between them but the thin material of the tunic shirt and Elsie's own dress.

How she longed to be naked with her, to feel her body against hers once more, but she wasn't sure that would ever be able to happen again. Kissing was one thing—and a wonderful thing—but making love was very different. Both wrong, considering her circumstances, but somehow one didn't seem as wrong as the other.

She was startled out of her thoughts when she was lightly pushed away. For a moment she'd worried she'd done something wrong, but when Roishin lowered herself to sit at the base of the tree and reached for Elsie to straddle her hips, she grinned. She settled on her, relishing the closeness. She loved feeling Roishin's body beneath her and against her front. She loved the feel of Roishin's hands on her behind, holding her close.

"Better?" Roishin asked.

"Colossal better," Elsie said with a little smile.

Grinning, Roishin said, "In this case, it would be colossally better."

Elsie brought their lips close again. "I agree," she murmured before taking Roishin in another kiss.

She sighed when Roishin's hands found their way under her skirt, which was splayed out on the ground, nearly covering Roishin's outstretched leather-clad legs. They found her behind again, the warm skin nearly burning Elsie through her undergarments. Roishin moaned softly when one of Elsie's hands found one of her breasts, cupping it through the tunic shirt. The nipple almost immediately grew hard as her fingers coaxed it to life.

Their kiss became more passionate and heated. Elsie was aching, her hips beginning to rock a bit of their own accord. She broke the kiss as her head fell back when one of Roishin's hands left her behind and eased down into the front of her undergarments.

She could hardly breathe for a moment when those fingers found her need. She found Roishin's lips again and took her in an aggressive kiss as her hips rocked against those fingers, which found the most sensitive place on her body. She was panting now, the pleasure filling her entire lower half as Roishin stroked her.

Finally, her release crashed over her, her entire world narrowing down to those two fingers and that one tiny spot between her legs. Roishin continued to rub until another wave took her breath away. She clung to the woman beneath her, fingers like talons on her shoulders.

Relenting, Roishin pulled both hands out from beneath her dress as she held Elsie tightly to her. "I'm sorry," Roishin murmured into the hug. "I just couldn't help myself."

"Don't be sorry," Elsie managed after many moments of trying to calm herself from the intensity of the experience. Still breathing heavily, she cupped Roishin's flushed face with her hands. She left a long kiss on her lips. "I need your touch, Roishin," she said. "I know I'm getting married, I know that." She kissed her again, then looked Roishin on the eye. "I can't stuff who I am in a trunk and lock it." She shook her head. "I just can't."

Roishin studied her face for a long time, watching as her fingertips lightly ran along Elsie's jaw. "I think I can find a way for us to be together now and then." She looked into her eyes again. "But it won't be often. Certainly not as often as we'd like."

Elsie wanted to feel happy and hopeful, but the look on Roishin's face worried her. "You do want that, don't you?"

"I do," Roishin said with no hesitation. "But we have to be careful. We can't destroy the family in the process. You're not just getting married. You're marrying my brother."

That hit her like a blow to the gut. Literally unable to speak for a moment, Elsie climbed off Roishin's lap and turned away. She ran her hand over her hair and tried to calm down. She heard Roishin also get to her feet. Turning to look at her, she saw the question in her eyes.

"You're right," she finally said and hugged herself. "How unbelievably selfish of me." She looked away. "You must think me the most horrid of women, Roishin."

"No," Roishin said. She walked over to Elsie but didn't touch her. "Elsie. Please look at me." When

Elsie did, she continued. "I know the reasons you're marrying Garratt. My *parents* know the reasons you're marrying Garratt."

Elsie gave her a sad smile. "Aye. But, does he?"

❧❧❧❧

Their wonderful afternoon had ended with their brief but quite sobering conversation. Elsie felt terrible, and she felt like she truly didn't deserve the love and trust she'd been given by Fallon, Cateline, and even Garratt. He, away on military duty with the elite guard, and what was she doing back home?

As she made her way to the king and queen's bedchamber to change the linens on their bed, she was disgusted with herself. Yes, she loved Roishin. Yes, she *wanted* Roishin, but no, she could not have her. She could never, ever allow to happen again what had happened that day. She'd tuck it away inside her heart and let it warm her during the longest, coldest nights, but that was all.

She felt the tears come yet again. She'd actually managed to stop crying over the last couple months. Damn it! She stood in the middle of the huge chamber, face buried in her hands. She was startled when she heard someone enter. Halfway expecting it would be one of the residents of the room, or even Roishin, she wasn't expecting the woman who stood looking at her.

Turning away, Elsie quickly composed herself. "Can I help you?" she asked, wiping at her eyes and face. Getting no response, she turned to look at the woman again. She looked to be a few years older than Elsie, perhaps. She had chestnut brown hair and large brown eyes.

"Aye. Well, I hope so. Her Highness told me

I'd find Elsie up here. Are you Elsie?" she asked. Her voice, like Elsie's, was edged with a Scottish accent. "I sure hope so." She gave her a small smile. "I seem to be lost."

"I'm Elsie," she said. "You are?"

"Thank ya, milady," the young woman blew out with a small laugh. "Isla. I'm the dressmaker that will be making your wedding dress, milady." She held up an object Elsie hadn't even noticed she'd been holding. Elsie recognized the ell measure, a wooden rod of a fixed length that would be used to measure Elsie's body so the dress could be cut and constructed.

Though Elsie had been created a duchess a few months back, it still hit her as strange when she was referred to as *milady*. Pushing that aside, she nodded. "Oh."

"Is that all right, milady?" Isla asked, looking at Elsie with concerned eyes. "I can come back..."

"No." Elsie gave her the biggest smile she could. "No, it's fine." She headed toward the door. "Follow me." She didn't want to chance anyone walking in while the woman was trying to do her job with Elsie standing there in her chemise, so she led Isla to her own bedchamber. "Do you need me to light a candle?" The room was a bit dim with only the narrow arrow slit for light.

"Aye, milady, thank you."

Elsie lit several candles while the dressmaker got herself organized.

"Would you be so kind as to dress down to your chemise, milady?" She gave her an apologetic smile. "I can get the truest measurements that way."

Without a word, Elsie quickly removed the long tunic that covered her simple dress and laid it across the head of the bed. Isla used the space at the foot to lay out her ell measure, a small block of chalk, and parchment to jot down measurements.

Elsie felt incredibly raw. After her time spent with Roishin, her body was still very sensitive and she could feel Roishin's touch on her. And, most embarrassingly, she could still smell her own spent passion on herself. She felt the heated pricks of more tears behind her eyes.

"Milady?"

Elsie looked into the kind, compassionate brown eyes of the dressmaker who stood before her, and that was it. It was one kindness too many. The dam broke again, and she was once more sobbing into her hands.

Isla took her in a warm hug. "I know not if I'm allowed to hug a lady, but I think you need it."

Somehow Elsie managed to laugh through her tears as she hugged the perfect stranger in return. After a long moment, she managed to get herself under control. She got a squeeze from the dressmaker, who then pulled out of the hug but kept a hand on her arm.

Isla reached into a pocket in her dress and pulled out a scrap of material. She gently dabbed at Elsie's face and eyes. "Are you all right, milady?"

Taking a long, deep breath, Elsie nodded. "I'm so sorry. I feel so silly."

"No." Isla gave her the fabric scrap with a smile and light squeeze of her fingers around Elsie's. She turned to the bed, seeming to take far more time to study her tools than was necessary, almost as if to give Elsie a bit of privacy to get herself together. "I was married once," Isla said conversationally as she fingered the chalk.

Elsie tucked the cloth into her hand after she'd wiped her face dry. She met the slightly older woman's gaze.

"'Tis none of my business at all, milady. And,

please tell me to shut my trap should I be stepping over a line. But marriage is a serious business, and," she added with a little shrug as she walked over to Elsie with the long measuring rod. "Can be scary. Hold your arms out like so, milady," she said, demonstrating as her own arms lifted straight out from her body. She continued when Elsie complied. "As women, we don't always have all the choices."

Elsie nodded. "Aye." She stood still as the ell measure was placed on her upper back. The scratchy sound of chalk rubbing against it tickled her ears before it was moved a bit. "You're not married anymore, then?"

"No, milady. He died."

Elsie was surprised at the matter-of-fact response. "I'm sorry, Isla."

"Eh," the dressmaker hedged, again the chalk scratching against the wood. "Thank you, milady, for your kindness, but to be quite blunt, I was relieved."

Isla walked over to the bed and scratched a few things on her parchment before using the apron she had tied over her dress skirt to wipe the previous chalk marks off the wood.

"Not to sound cold," she said, looking at Elsie. "'Twas a blessing the day he fell into the river." She shook her head, retaking her place behind Elsie and moving her measurements to the center of her back. "You can put your arms down now, milady."

Elsie did as requested, very curious to hear what this woman had to say. It was so nice to hear from someone who understood, even if her circumstances were different.

"Martin was a mean man, milady. Though he drowned, the drink is what finally killed him. He was likely drunk when he fell in."

"He…hurt you?" Elsie asked carefully.

"Aye," Isla murmured, the ell rod now placed along Elsie's spine from the nape of her neck down to midback.

"I'm so sorry. I'm glad you're out from underneath him now. You never married again, then?"

"No, milady," Isla said, a note of pride in her voice as she etched a mark on the rod. "Didn't want it the first time, but alas, it's over and I can't be accused of not doing my duty." She made another mark, then went back to the bed and her parchment. "Unlike many women," she said, glancing over at Elsie before returning her attention to her writings. "I have a skill."

Isla set the ell measure down on the bed and produced a long strip of cloth from her dress pocket. She let one end fall with gravity to reveal a three-foot measuring length. She walked back over to Elsie and smiled as she stretched her arms to either side.

"Arms like this again, please. Forgive my reach, milady."

Elsie was all but hugged three different times as measurements were taken around her bust, her waist, and her hips. Isla worked quickly but efficiently.

"All done, milady," she said, walking back over to the bed to record the measurements.

Elsie redressed, feeling much better once her dress and tunic were     back in place. "Thank you so much, Isla. I truly appreciate your professionalism and your kindness."

Isla glanced over at her and gave her a genuine and lovely smile. "Of course, milady."

"Do you work for the queen, Isla?" Elsie asked, reaching up to straighten parts of her hair that had come loose during her undressing.

"No, milady." Isla was gathering up her material

strip, wrapping it around two fingers into a tight wad. "I was recommended to her, so one day she arrived at my door." Her smile was wide, dark eyes dancing. "Scared me to death!" She placed a hand to her chest in emphasis. "Thought I'd done something wrong."

Elsie chuckled. "Oh, I imagine so."

"Aye. I invited her in and showed her some of my work and a few projects I had underway for a customer." Her smile grew even more brilliant. "Hired me right then."

"That's truly wonderful. I hadn't seen you before, so I wasn't sure."

Isla looked around. "First time in a castle, milady," she said, her voice whispery, almost like a little kid telling a secret.

Elsie smiled. "Well, if you do a good job on this wedding dress I must wear, perhaps we can discuss further employment, hmm?"

"Oh!" Isla clapped her hands together. "Aye, milady. I'll do my very best for you."

Surprising herself, Elsie took the other woman into a quick hug. It felt good to meet a woman near her age who also seemed to be trying to find her way in this world. From what she'd been told of her story, which was similar to so many other women regardless of class and status, Isla had managed to persevere, and Elsie had a great deal of respect for that, for her.

Elsie needed somebody like that around her. Perhaps a friend, even. Yes, she thought. She needed a friend. Once she and Garratt were married and moved into Caisleán Thíar, she'd be completely alone. Cateline had been such a dear and close friend and mentor, and Elsie knew she was going to feel somewhat lost without her advice and counsel every day.

Cateline had mentioned Elsie would need staff of

her own at Caisleán Thíar. If all worked out with Isla, perhaps she could find a new closeness to help her get through her days.

# Chapter Fifteen

It was a beautiful August night, not a cloud in the sky. All the flowers were in bloom and the air was fragrant. It was amusing to Roishin as she strolled, however, because she now knew what real freshness smelled like. The purity of the air in Duras was unmatched. Once upon a time, a night like this would have seemed so fresh and clean to her, and though it was beautiful, she could still smell all the unsavory aromas of human and animal life floating on the light breeze.

As she headed out of the rose garden and toward the woodlands, she suddenly felt that she wasn't alone. Upon the moonlit ground, she saw a second shadow walking alongside her own. She smiled and shook her head, not needing to glance to her right.

"I'm beginning to think you stalk me," she muttered, teasing in her tone.

"Oh yes. Precisely what completes my life," Enori drawled. "Or," she added. "Perhaps it was just that the house felt empty so I came looking for trouble."

Roishin grinned outright. "I'm inclined to believe that one." She playfully nudged the other woman's shoulder with her own as they continued to stroll.

It wasn't lost on her that, for the first time since she'd arrived back home early that morning, she felt at peace. Though so unbelievably happy to see her parents, Isabeau, and certainly Elsie, she felt more like an outsider than she ever had. That was saying something, since she'd always felt that way to a degree.

The irony was thick in that one, considering she was the only child of the four that was actually biologically related to their parents. She understood more this trip than on any other that she truly was not understood at home. It was not lack of want by those she loved and who loved her, it just wasn't possible for them to do so.

No matter how guilty she felt about it, one of the reasons she'd allowed herself to give in with Elsie was that she'd been desperate to feel connected. It was all about connection, if even just for a moment.

Now, as Enori walked quietly beside her, she felt like she could breathe. They headed into the trees, the sounds of night critters scurrying about or sending out calls of warning to each other as the two women entered their nocturnal territory.

"I did something really stupid today, Enori," Roishin said, surprising herself for mentioning it. Enori said nothing, but she knew intrinsically that the other woman was listening. "I was with Elsie." She felt anger at herself bubble to the surface. Regardless of her reasons, they weren't good enough. "She's engaged to Garratt."

Finally, Enori spoke. "Young love, *first* love, is the purist, the most potent. It is not about parents, obligation, or politics." She waved her hand through the air dismissively. "None of that. It is about pure emotion and discovery of the heart, and often, the body." She sent Roishin an understanding smile. "Which is why it is also the hardest to let go of, if that must be what happens."

Roishin considered the words, mulled them around in her brain and her heart. It made sense. "Does it ever get easier?"

"To let them go?" Enori clarified. At Roishin's

nod, she shrugged her cloak-covered shoulders. "It does, but you will always carry her with you, Roishin," she explained gently. "And until the day Elsie dies, she will carry you with her, also. Over time, it will become beautiful memories."

They walked on in silence for a bit until Roishin asked. "Why are you here?"

"Fallon," Enori said simply. "She needed to talk to me about something."

Roishin felt a sudden heaviness in the air between them that hadn't been there before. She looked to her mentor. "Is everything okay?"

They emerged from the trees to a small stream, the water gurgling quietly. "Let us sit," Enori said, indicating two large boulders. "It involves you."

Roishin took the other boulder, pulling her legs up to sit cross-legged. She rested her hands on her knees and gave Enori her full attention.

"You are now very aware of your origins, how you came to be part of two women, their daughter."

Roishin nodded. "Aye."

"Fallon wanted to know if something similar could be done for this new generation."

Roishin looked down into the water, pure blackness with the very tips of the tiny waves painted silver with moonlight. She swallowed before saying, "You mean Elsie and Garratt's children." It literally made her nauseous to even think about that, and what it took for a pregnancy to happen.

"Clearly, they wouldn't have the same challenges Fallon and Cateline had in having children. But," Enori added, reaching over to take one of Roishin's hands in her soft one. "As I know it, the reason Ankou wanted you created with them wasn't just about continuing the royal line. It was to continue the Ankou line." She smiled. "It just so happens that it gave your mothers a wonderful little gem in the process."

Roishin smirked. "Oh yes, feisty little pain-in-the-arse apple of their eye."

Enori quirked an eyebrow as she released Roishin's hand. "You said it, not me."

Roishin grinned before she grew serious again. "So, this isn't about an heir for my parents, but to continue the Ankou line as well?"

Enori nodded. "Now that they have full understanding of things, I think they know how important the blood is." She grew quiet for a moment, her gaze boring into Roishin's to the point of making her incredibly uncomfortable. "I spoke with Ankou," Enori finally said. "There is a way."

"Like before? A woman who will die in childbirth anyway..."

She trailed off at the slow shake of Enori's head, her gaze never leaving Roishin's. Suddenly, realization hit her and the insatiable need to vomit hit her. She uncurled herself and hurried back into the trees, her dinner leaving her system at the base of a tree.

"I am *not* sleeping with Garratt!" She wiped her mouth with a handful of leaves she pulled from a branch. Throwing them aside, she turned and glared at Enori. "I don't care that we're not related, I'm not going to—"

"Stop!"

Roishin ceased talking, but tears were still sliding down her cheeks. She felt so violated, and nothing had even happened. Enori stepped up to her and, with her quiet way, used her fingertips to wipe at her tears before her hands gently cupped Roishin's heated face.

"That is not what we are asking of you, Roishin." She gave her the most beautiful smile. "A child should be created out of love, as you were." She shook her head. "Not obligation that borders on the enslavement of a woman's body."

Roishin relaxed, though still unsettled at what still may be coming. "All right…"

Enori stroked her cheek. "You, Roishin," she said softly, wonder in her eyes that had turned gray in the moonlight. "You are the bringer of life. You and Elsie love each other. Give her the ultimate gift of love."

*Dark blue eyes squinted in fierce concentration, long brown hair flew out behind her as she ran. Powerful thighs propelled her across the landscape. Leather armor covered the torso of a grown woman of perhaps twenty. Her forearms were covered in brown leather bracers darkened from blood, which also stained her hands.*

*Her mouth opened as a raging cry escaped her lips. Her hands held a large sword, the blade still covered in blood and gore, raised over her head by powerful arms. Following was another young woman, roughly the same age, perhaps a few years younger. Her mane of golden hair framed a tanned, beautiful face.*

*Dark green eyes penetrated the soul as she, too, carried a large blade. In fact, looking at her eyes, she saw they were her own. The second young woman was just as intent as the first on their target. They got closer and closer, and closer…*

Roishin gasped as the vision she'd had so many years ago while holding a three-month-old Isabeau slammed into her. She literally staggered backward until her back came into contact with a tree. She slid down to her butt as quiet tears slid down her cheeks. The second young woman was perhaps sixteen or so in that vision.

She felt overwhelmed by pride and love for her, something she'd never felt before to the intensity she did now. She felt the love of a mother. She looked over when she felt Enori squat down next to her.

"You can do this," Enori said softly.

"I don't know how," Roishin whispered.

Enori lightly brushed Roishin's cheek with the backs of her fingers. "I will show you."

❧ ❧ ❧ ❧

After they had gone their separate ways, Roishin back to the castle and Enori back home to Duras, Roishin found herself standing outside of Isabeau's bedroom. Chewing on her bottom lip, she turned the iron handle and entered the room. It was quiet, as she expected it would be. The child was sound asleep, lying on her side facing the wall.

Roishin closed the door behind her as quietly as she could. Shedding her cloak, she draped it over the back of a chair then sat on the edge of the bed. Looking down at that tiny figure all curled up into herself, she smiled. She now realized that she'd loved this little one from first sight on that horrible day when the accident took Isabeau's parents from her.

She'd literally given a little piece of her soul to bring the baby back. *The bringer of life.* She thought about those words and the implication behind them. She thought about what was being asked of her, trying to figure out how exactly this would work. Would it be a situation of a baby dead or near dead, then Roishin bringing it back to life and handing it off to Elsie?

Somehow, that didn't feel right. It also didn't feel right that Ankou would intercede as he had with Roishin's own creation and birth. So, how was it to be done? Did Elsie get pregnant the traditional way from her soon-to-be husband and then Roishin blessed the unborn baby somehow? Her train of thought was interrupted when Isabeau raised her little head and looked at her over her shoulder with sleepy eyes.

Roishin felt terrible, never intending to wake her. She just…needed to be near her, for some reason. Without a word, Isabeau turned over to face her, raising her covers in unspoken request. Charmed, Roishin removed her boots and slipped under the covers. The little girl scooted over to her and snuggled up to her, promptly falling back asleep.

Cradling the small body against her side, Roishin ran her fingers absently through long, wavy hair. Her mind went back to the vision that had crashed into her mind for a second time. She knew that the older of the two young women in the vision was the grown version of the little girl she now held. She knew it with everything in her.

Then her mind drifted to the other young woman, a teenager, really. She saw her face again, those fierce green eyes. Roishin's eyes. She'd been complimented her entire life on their unusually green color. She had seen Elsie in her too. The beautiful richness of her golden hair, the set of her jaw, and the intense look on the young woman's face.

But how? Roishin was a perfect mix of Fallon and Cateline—she saw both of her mothers in her reflection every single time she looked into a mirror. Was that this young woman's future as well? Would Garratt be in there somewhere? She hadn't seen him in the visions, but surely he'd be part of it. Right?

She held Isabeau tighter, resting her cheek against the dark head that lay upon her chest. The two girls were together, effectively aunt and niece. Were they close? Were they raised together? They looked to be only a handful of years apart. For that to happen, this baby needed to be born very soon. Perhaps a creation from Duras?

She could growl in frustration at the possibilities that cluttered her brain. Enori said she'd show her. So, she took a long, relaxing breath and allowed her body to settle and eyes to close. No reason to continue turning things over in her mind that would be explained eventually.

She needed "eventually" to be very soon.

❧ ❧ ❧ ❧

*They walked in a wheat field, the stalks nearly three feet tall. Roishin held out her left hand, smiling at the feel of the light touches that tickled her palm as she ran it along the feathery tops of the plants. She could feel him walking next to her, but every time she tried to look over at him, everything went black. So, she remained focused on what was before her.*

*"So beautiful, isn't it?" he asked, voice deep and somehow familiar.*

*"It is. It just goes and goes, as far as the eye can see."*

*Suddenly, the strangest sound met Roishin's ears. She gasped as she looked to her left.    In the distance, a beast of a machine was slowly plowing through the crop. Her eyes were huge as she watched it go, leaving a barren, flattened field behind it. She could see a man through the windows at the top of the machine. He wasn't paying them a lick of attention as he continued his destruction.*

*"What is he doing!" She felt anger rush through her and took a step forward. "He's killing all the wheat!"*

*The man beside her chuckled. "No, he's harvesting the wheat."*

*Roishin couldn't speak, stunned. She'd never seen anything like it. The only times she'd ever seen that done had been men with scythes doing the backbreaking work. "Wow," she breathed.*

*"Come," he said. "The Combine isn't why we're here."*

*"Combine?"*

*"That's what that farmer is using." He walked to the huge trail left behind the wide, so-called Combine. Following, Roishin stood next to the man she could feel but could not see. "See all this?" he said, the wide swath of naked field before them.*

*Nodding, Roishin took it all in. "Aye. Looks dead."*

*"So, bring it to life," he suggested.*

*She felt him move behind her, his presence immense against her back. It wasn't size, it was energy. "So, bring back the wheat?" she asked, unsure.*

*"Make life out of nothing, Roishin," he said softly, voice in her ear but also in her head.*

*She had no idea what prompted her, but she reached down and eased the dagger out of her boot. Looking down at the blade with the rose etched into it, she looked back to the harvested ground that stretched out before her. She tucked her bottom lip under her teeth as she considered.*

*With a small hiss, she used the deadly sharp blade to slice the tip of her pointer finger. A ruby red bead appeared. Looking at it, she felt a bit of understanding ease into her mind. His voice sounded again, this time fully in her mind.*

*"You hold the power of life inside you. That precious blood...in it is all that you are, all that you will be, and all that will grow."*

*Sheathing her dagger again, Roishin studied that blood, slowly rubbing her thumb and forefinger together, the blood creating a smudge upon both fingertips. In her mind, she visualized a row of brilliant red roses. Lowering herself to her knees, she lowered her upper body until her chin was nearly at ground level.*

*Taking a small fistful of dirt, she rubbed it around and around in her fingers, making sure the blood that oozed from her mixed in with the soil. Finally, she held her hand open, dirt resting upon her open palm. She blew over the surface gently until the dirt flew out over her hand and drifted back to the ground.*

*Raising her body until she sat back on her heels, she watched, astonished, as a dim white light began just in front of her then began to grow in brightness, as though somebody were turning a light up brighter and brighter. Finally, it was nearly blinding, Roishin squinting at the spectacle.*

*The ground began to rumble softly beneath her as the light began to expand from the size of a marble to the size of a tennis ball to the size of a dinner plate and then shot off like a rocket along the ground in a straight line away from her, leaving a trail of blood-red roses in its wake.*

❧❧❧❧

Roishin gasped as her eyes shot open. Her chest was heaving with her quick, heavy breaths. "The blood," she whispered. "It's in the blood."

# *Chapter Sixteen*

Admittedly, Roishin had never been more proud of her daidí. She stood in the king's solar behind the chair in which sat the queen. Behind the desk, surrounded by her advisers, Fallon signed one of the most important laws to hit the Surshan books since its conception, before Enori had even been born.

The youngest princess was held in Roishin's arms, per her insistent request. Garratt was also present, as was his intended. Roishin and Elsie had said little to the other during this historic meeting, as it just wouldn't do for either of them to broadcast what had happened the previous day. There was also one more guest that Roishin had personally invited.

Hitching Isabeau a bit higher up on her hip, Roishin glanced over toward the mirror mounted to the wall and got a beaming smile right back at her, the pride easily seen in her dark eyes. Roishin knew this had been something talked about extensively over the years between the then-prince and her closest adviser.

Fallon signed her name across the bottom of the document with a flourish, a round of applause afterward by those present. The king met the gaze of her wife, and so much passed between them in that moment. It was a victory for them that nobody would understand but the two of them and those in this inner circle.

Roishin smiled. Though she couldn't see her mother's face, she could so easily see the love in Fallon's, aimed at her wife of going on twenty years.

Fallon set the quill back into the inkwell and looked up at those gathered.

"It is now decreed law in Sursha that a female can take the throne as her legal and ordained ruler." Fallon looked to Elsie, beaming. "Long live the queen, should we have one."

"Here, here!" Roishin cried out, echoed by an excited Isabeau, who clearly had no idea what the fuss was about. Roishin grinned and left a noisy kiss on the girl's cheek. Another glance to the mirror showed Livia wiping tears from her eyes—happy tears. Once she was settled, she raised two fingers to Roishin. Nodding toward the sandglass, Roishin raised her eyebrows in question. Livia nodded, then was gone.

Knowing the advisers would stay and talk to their king about other pressing matters—mainly, how to inform the people of this new law—Roishin led the way out of the chamber. She was intending to head to the family chamber, but Garratt called her name. She stepped out of the way of her mother and Elsie, then waited for him.

"Can we talk?" he asked.

"Sure." Roishin gave Isabeau another kiss and set her down to scurry after the other two women. She faced the man who was still dressed in his military adornments. "What's up?" He looked at her strangely. Roishin cleared her throat, silently chastising herself. It was easy to forget that the people here had not been to many of the places—or times—she had visited, nor had they learned of the drastic changes in language over the centuries. "What would you like to talk to me about?"

"Let's take a walk," he offered, a hand to her lower back as he steered them into the hallway.

The two remained silent as they made their way

off the fourth floor of the king's residence and began to randomly wander the spacious castle. Finally, he began to speak.

"How are your studies going in France?"

Roishin bristled at the question. She knew that's what he and Laigen had been told, as there was no real way for their parents to tell them the truth when Fallon and Cateline themselves weren't entirely sure of all it entailed. At the time of her departure, neither was Roishin.

"My studies are going well," she said, not a lie. They just weren't in France.

"Great news. Learning much?"

She snorted. "More than I can even explain to you."

He nodded, hands clasped behind his back as they strolled, heavy boots thudding upon the stone they traversed. "Do you intend to return?"

"I'm talking to you here right now, brother."

"Indeed, you are," he agreed, sparing her a glance. "On a more permanent basis, I mean."

The answer was obviously a vehement *no*, but something told her to play coy. She loved her brother and believed he was a good person. He was a damn fine soldier and extremely loyal to the men he led and served. But she knew he could be extremely stubborn in his attitudes, holding his stance until the mountains crumbled regardless of evidence to the contrary. She'd learned long ago that arguing with him was not wise if one wished to remain sane.

Garratt had had such a difficult beginning in life, he and Laigen orphaned very young and tossed into an orphanage where he played protector to his terrified four-year-old sister. Roishin believed much of his black-and-white thinking had gotten him through the worst. If he stood firm in his principles, his strength and courage couldn't be shaken, either.

Unfortunately, as a grown man, his lack of nuance and flexibility made it difficult to deal with him at times. "I know not," she finally responded. "I suppose it depends on how my studies go."

He said nothing for a moment, simply nodded acknowledgment of her response. A handsome man, her brother stood tall, chin squared and jaw proud. In that moment, however, she felt more like she was walking next to a general than a brother.

"I must admit, I don't understand this transformation you've undergone, Roishin."

She groaned inwardly. "What would that be, Garratt? Growing up?"

He stopped her progress with a strong hand around her arm. "Don't be smart with me," he warned, eyebrows drawn. "I don't know what's really going on, little sister, but I don't believe for a moment that you're in some private tutorship or mentorship in France."

She yanked her arm from his grip and so badly wanted to pull Enori through a door and say, *Here's my mentor, fuckhead.* "Don't manhandle me again, Garratt."

He looked at her, stunned. "You're speaking to the prince of Sursha, Roishin. Heir apparent."

She quirked an eyebrow. "And you're speaking to Princess Roishin of Sursha, whose only allegiance is to the king and the queen. You're not one of those," she added, poking him in his leather-armored chest.

He looked away from her, jaw muscles working. "All right," he said after a moment. "I'll get down to it." He looked back at her. "I do not approve of what you're becoming."

"Oh?" She crossed her arms over her chest. "And

what's that?"

"Look at you." The disapproval of which he'd just spoken was evident in his voice and expression. "Your hair, cut off. These cloaks you wear." His hand reached out to touch the dark blue material, but she smacked it away before he made contact. Again, he looked stunned, but he pressed on. "You dishonor your family, Roishin. You abandoned your family to join gods only know what. Some sort of religious order?" he said, voice dropping. "I've seen you with that blonde woman, also with short hair and the same cloak."

Now Roishin felt her hackles rise. "Leave her out of this," she said, far more vehemence in her voice than she'd intended. She cleared her throat, forcing herself to calm a bit. "You have no idea what you're talking about, Garratt, so I strongly recommend you don't talk about it."

He eyed her as though weighing out an opponent on the training field. "I also heard you were out with Elsie yesterday," he said, almost as though she'd never spoken.

"Aye," she admitted, though her stomach was doing a slow roll into nausea.

"Why?"

"Garratt," she said, forcing irritation into her tone. "Elsie was my personal servant for more than two years, nearly three. Of course I'm going to spend some time with her when I'm home."

"I don't want that happening anymore." He raised a hand to silence her when she began to protest. "She is going to be my wife, Roishin, and someday queen. I do *not* want her associated with whatever nonsense you've gotten yourself into." Again, he indicated her hair and cloak. "End of discussion." With that, he turned and walked away, strides long and purposeful.

She watched him go, a part of her not entirely surprised by this. Regardless of what the world thought Fallon was, Roishin grew up in a household of women and had gotten spoiled with rational logic—not the emotion-based, testosterone-laced variety put on display by the one and only male in their family.

Garratt was often away on his military service, so she hadn't had to deal with it much growing up. So, when he was around and swung that little sword of his at a low-hanging target, she was reminded all over again of why she preferred the household to be comprised of just women. Rolling her eyes, she headed off to speak to her mother. She had plans for her parents in just over an hour.

⁂

She chuckled at the skeptical looks on her parents' faces. "Oh, come on!" She laughed. "You both have used a door before. How do you think I get around everywhere?"

"Uh," Fallon said, glancing at her wife then back to Roishin. "Why don't we just go to the stables and—"

"Because, Daidí," she said, exasperated. "We'd have to get the royal guard and all that to escort." She smirked. "You're not as easy to travel with these days with your promotion."

Fallon smirked. "Well." She looked to Cateline. "After you, my love."

Cateline gave her a look that made Roishin burst into laughter. "All right, Your Highness," Roishin said, amusement in her tone as she took her mother's hand. "You come with me." She nodded to Fallon. "The king is on her own."

They were in Roishin's bedchamber, and she led

her mother to the door that she'd arrived through the previous morning. She could tell Cateline was nervous, as the first and only time she'd experienced traveling this way had been on the worst day of her life—the day she'd had to rescue her wife from herself as the possession by Bahutha had taken full and deadly hold.

She turned to her now. "It's okay, Mamaí. I promise." She looked to Fallon, teasing finished. "It'll be worth it. Just follow us."

She stepped through the door, which for her was now an everyday occurrence. But for her parents, it was still quite new and quite breathtaking. When they ended up at the waterfall, she could tell they were confused. She'd told them they were going somewhere special to meet somebody special. All true.

Once all three out were out safely, Roishin closed the door. It wouldn't do to have somebody stumble upon it. "Clearly, you both know where we are," she said, almost unable to contain her excitement. "I thought this was the perfect place for me to explain a bit about where I live now."

Fallon stepped up to her flat rock, that wonderful peaceful smile crossing her lips that did every time she was there. She looked to Roishin, a look of serenity in her eyes. That made Roishin's very soul light up. She could see how her daidí had aged since the death of her father. Still beautiful and still a powerful force, but it was evident his death and transition to king had taken a toll.

"Both of you have mentioned that this place is unlike anything you've ever seen," Roishin continued. "Not like Sursha, not like France." She smiled at her mother, who rested against Fallon's side, a strong, protective arm around her shoulders. "You are both correct. This place," she said, indicating the eroded cave around them. "Is one of the few places on earth where a whole other realm and this one butt up against each other."

Fallon and Cateline met gazes for a moment before looking back to Roishin, curiosity and surprise in their expressions. "All right," Fallon said. "What realm?"

"It's a wonderful place called Duras," Roishin said, unable to keep the smile off her face. "It's a place where Enori and I and many others live, and where we work to fix things that have gone horribly wrong, or to intervene before it does."

"Using the doors?" Fallon asked slowly. At Roishin's nod, she seemed to consider this for a moment. Then, "And, why is it a different realm?"

"Because we live and work with a very, very special group of people," Roishin responded. "It's a place where boundaries don't mean what they do here." She indicated the country beyond where they stood. She was nearly buzzing now in excitement. "In fact, I work quite closely with someone you both know very well." She smirked. "And I don't mean Enori."

Out of the corner of her eye, she saw three figures making their way out of the jungle and toward the waterfall area. Right on time. She nodded in that direction.

"She can make introductions."

Fallon and Cateline looked in the direction Roishin indicated. The looks on their faces would have been comical if the moment weren't so moving. Cateline seemed to break from her stupor first. Hands to her mouth and eyes huge, she stepped away from Fallon and off the flat rock as the trio made their way fully into the eroded cave.

The man and boy stood back, the man's hand

on the boy's narrow shoulder. The woman, however, stepped forward, tears already in her dark eyes. She fell to one knee, head bowed in deference. "My queen," she said softly.

Cateline made her way over to her, hands never leaving her mouth. When Livia looked up at her, the dam broke. Both women dissolved into tears as Livia stood and they held each other tightly. Fallon shook herself out of her shock and walked over to them. She was wiping at her own eyes when Livia pulled back from the hug, her own tears starting all over again.

"Don't you dare bow," Fallon managed, her voice thick with emotion. "Come here."

Roishin stood back and watched, her smile impossibly big. She knew there was a lot of explaining to do for them to understand, but she knew Livia was up to the task. But at the moment, she watched as an excited Livia introduced her husband and son, both Cateline and Fallon overjoyed.

Though she was still learning and knew she had a long way to go, it made Roishin so proud to be able to do this for her parents. She knew Livia's loss had been a massive blow to all of them, but mostly to Fallon and Cateline. The sixteen-year-old orphan they'd literally taken in off the streets, they'd given her a home, a job, a family, and mostly, they'd given her love.

Cateline and Livia were talking nonstop, both seeming to try and get as many words in as possible. She glanced to Fallon and Gerald, chatting away like two old friends who'd known each other for years. Meanwhile, Mattia bounced from one pair to the next, finally ending up in Cateline's arms, hitched on her hip as she patiently answered every single question he could think to ask.

Feeling deeply satisfied, she nodded. For the first

time, so much of who she was and what she did came into focus. *This* is who she was. It wasn't about her, it wasn't even about Enori. It was about how they could change the world. Though they didn't stick around to see the results of what they did in their work, she knew that the tears and smiles she was witnessing right now *were* the results. Lives spared that would have been lost. Or, lives snatched that would have done irrevocable harm.

Yes, she thought. Being away from her family, away from her country and all that she'd known for the first thirteen years of her life, was worth it. She understood Enori and her endless drive and dedication a little bit more every day.

It was the same dedication and drive her own parents had toward Sursha and her people. Pride surged through her, and maybe just a little bit, she understood them better, too.

❧❧❧❧

Night had fallen, and it was time for Roishin to go. After spending the afternoon with Livia and her family, the two parties had said tearful goodbyes with promises to reconnect sooner rather than later. Roishin had spent the evening with her parents and Isabeau, soaking up as much time with them as possible before giving each one a bone-crushing hug and kiss.

Now, she stood outside of Elsie's bedchamber. What happened the previous day could not happen again, but she loved her and wanted to see her before she left. Taking a deep breath, she raised her fist and knocked quietly on her door. Knowing it was entirely possible Elsie was already asleep, she'd prepared a short note to push under the door just in case.

A second knock unanswered, Roishin was about to pull the parchment out from inside her cloak when the door was opened. Sure enough, a sleepy Elsie stood on the other side. Roishin gave her a sheepish smile.

"I'm sorry. I won't keep you up. Just wanted to say goodbye—"

"No." Elsie stepped back, indicating Roishin should enter, so she did.

They walked to Elsie's bed, the two sitting down. "I've made a really bad habit of leaving without saying goodbye, and I just don't want to do that anymore."

"I'm glad you stopped by," Elsie said. She looked down at her hands in her lap for a moment before looking at Roishin again. "I'm really sorry about yesterday. That was unfair and put you in a bad position."

Roishin shook her head. "No." She took one of Elsie's hands in her own. "I made the decision to do what I did. You have nothing to be sorry for." She looked into Elsie's eyes. "I love you, Elsie. I'm not going to be sorry for that. I know what we did was wrong, and I know that it can't happen again. Things have changed." She paused as a wave of sadness crashed over her. She swallowed it down and continued. "But I'll never be ashamed of loving you."

"I love you, too." Elsie scooted over and took her in a hug.

Roishin cradled the head that rested against her shoulder before running her fingers through soft, golden hair. "Please promise me something."

"All right."

"Please try and be happy," Roishin whispered. "Whatever that takes. Be your own person and follow your heart."

Elsie nodded. "I'll try." She pulled out of the hug

and cupped Roishin's face. She left a lingering kiss on her lips. "You, too."

Roishin nodded, giving her the bravest smile she could. "I will."

"Will I see you again?" Elsie asked, her hands dropping from Roishin's face.

"Oh yeah, I'll be back." She pushed to her feet and pulled Elsie back to her. Another tight, full-body hug and shared kiss, then she backed away toward the door. She took one last look at the beautiful woman who stood next to the bed. "I love you."

"And I love you."

# Chapter Seventeen

The carriage pulled up to an extremely small stone structure, which looked like many of those around it in the village. Smoke drifted from the chimney and onto the morning breeze. Elsie had been delighted to get the message that Isla had invited her to her home to look at sketches and material for the dress.

"Milady," one of the men said as he opened the carriage door and held out a hand. She allowed herself to be helped out of the carriage and thanked the member of the royal guard. "I should be about—"

"We have orders to check the premises, milady," he said.

"Oh. Uh, all right."

Two heavily armed men, one in front of her and one behind, escorted her to the door. The one in front pounded upon the wood plank surface, no doubt scaring the daylights out of the occupant inside.

"Open up!" he demanded. "Royal Guard!"

Elsie wanted to go hide in the village well, embarrassed by this completely unnecessary approach to a simple dressmaker. She squeezed her eyes shut for a second until she heard the door open. Isla stood on the other side, eyes wide. She looked from the large man standing in front of her to the very contrite woman just behind him.

"We need to search the premises on the order of Prince Garratt of Sursha," the first guard explained, his voice loud and intimidating.

"Aye." Immediately Isla stood aside to allow the

two men inside her home. Not a very large woman to start with, she hugged herself in the knitted shawl around her shoulders and became positively tiny.

A few moments later, the two men emerged. One walked right by Elsie, the other stopping just long enough to tell her it was clear. Elsie watched them head to the carriage where they'd wait for her to do her business. Turning back to the dressmaker, Elsie gave her an apologetic smile.

"I'm so sorry," she whispered.

Isla glanced over at the men at the carriage, then to the duchess, and nodded she should enter. "Am I allowed to close the door, milady?" she asked uncertainly.

Looking her in the eye, Elsie took the door and slammed it closed. "So unnecessary," she muttered. She saw a hint of a smile in the rich brown eyes of the woman standing before her. "Truly, my apologies."

"No, no, I understand," Isla assured. "I mean," she added with a nervous laugh and a little shrug. "You are about to become a princess, so…"

*Don't remind me.* "Well," Elsie said brightly, clapping her hands together. "What do you have to show me?"

Seeming to relax a bit, Isla nodded. "Much, milady."

She led Elsie through the small house, which was cluttered with fabric piled all over the floor and atop every flat surface. Rolled parchments were stacked in cubby-like shelves against the walls that stretched from floor to ceiling. A large swath of material was laid out on her kitchen table. Upon further inspection, Elsie realized it wasn't that the little house was messy or untidy, just that the dressmaker only had so much room to do her job. It took up most of her living space and even trickled onto the bed in the small adjacent bedroom.

"Now." Isla pulled out two rolled parchments from the shelves, then hurried to the plank wood kitchen table. She set one aside and rolled out the other atop the fabric. "Based upon your measurements and body type, milady, I drew these two ideas up." She glanced over at Elsie, dark eyes alive with the passion of her craft.

Elsie moved to stand next to her and looked at the revealed sketch. "My goodness," she said. "You are an exquisite artist." She looked over at the other woman, incredibly impressed.

Isla blushed, her eyes dropping to the parchment. "Thank you, milady."

"Why so shy?" Elsie asked, charmed. "This is what you do." She indicated what they were surrounded by in the small space.

"Aye," Isla said, looking around as if seeing it all for the first time. "But it's not often a client sees my sketches, milady." She shrugged, meeting Elsie's gaze. "They give me an idea of what they want, then we discuss it and I make it." She shrugged again. "This is very different, milady." She lightly tapped the parchment page with the dress design sketched upon it.

Elsie smiled. "I truly have so much respect for you, Isla." She waved a hand at the drawing. "This is exactly me in this beautiful dress. And all from memory." She shook her head in wonder. She could tell the poor woman was about to turn into a tomato, she was blushing so red, so she opted to get back to the reason she was there. "Tell me about this."

Clearing her throat, that sparkle returned to Isla's eyes as she began to go over every detail of her design. It was truly beautiful, Elsie thought.

"As you see," Isla said. "This one is wider at the neckline, milady. You have such a lovely bone structure, and this one shows that." She hovered her fingertip over the sketch at each mentioned body part. "Your shoulders and collarbones, milady. Your throat." She glanced over at her.

Elsie's hand came up to rest upon her upper chest and some of the areas mentioned. She'd never owned anything that revealed them in public. "Oh goodness," she murmured. "Do you think I'd look all right?"

"Aye! You're stunning, milady."

It was Elsie's turn to blush. Other than Roishin, no woman had ever called her such. Sure, handsy noblemen at parties had tossed the word "beautiful" at her as she served them, but that wasn't the same. And she hardly felt Garratt's flattering words counted, as he'd been trying to get her to accept his ring at the time. "Thank you."

Isla gave her a smile before she unrolled the other parchment. "This one is essentially the same dress with a few detail changes and a lace covering across your upper chest, in case you're not comfortable with that much flesh revealed."

"Oh," Elsie murmured. "Very clever." She leaned over the table and placed her hands on both parchments to keep them open. She looked from one to the other, trying to imagine which she'd feel most comfortable in.

Chewing on her bottom lip, she considered what the dress was for. It wasn't just any gala and dinner, or to wear around the castle. This was her wedding day, and certainly the only one she ever intended to have. Her gaze settled on the one with the upper chest and tops of her shoulders revealed. What would Cateline do?

Such an extraordinarily beautiful woman was their queen. When she'd finally married Fallon, she'd married for love and for passion. But when she'd first married Fallon's brother Fergus, it had been anything but. Elsie's marriage to Garratt was somewhere in between, she surmised. It wasn't about love or passion in her case, but she wasn't being sold off like oxen, either.

"You know," she said after deep consideration. "Let's do this one." She tapped the more revealing dress, which was still in the taste of the day. She smiled over at Isla, who seemed to be holding her breath as Elsie decided. "It's a once-in-a-lifetime event, so let's make it a once-in-a-lifetime dress."

Isla's smile was blinding. "I can do that, milady."

In a moment of camaraderie, Elsie took the dressmaker in a hug, enjoying her energy. She was hugged back before they parted, sharing a smile. "Thank you so much, Isla. I truly appreciate all you're doing."

"Oh no, milady. It's truly my honor."

In a moment of impulse, Elsie made a decision that she knew Cateline and Fallon would back her on. After all, they'd told her that whatever she needed for this was at her disposal. Turning to look at Isla, who was carefully re-rolling the parchments, she knew it was the right thing to do.

"I'd like to offer you a room in the castle to do your work on this," she said. "You'll have all the room you need, resources, whatever you need."

Isla's eyes grew huge. "Really?" she asked, almost sounding like a little kid.

Elsie smiled and nodded. "Aye."

❧ ❧ ❧ ❧

Cateline had been more than thrilled to host Isla as she worked on Elsie's gown. In fact, she'd suggested the dressmaker move in during the labor-intensive project. She'd also made the castle's seamstress available to help. Though Elsie was anything but excited for the event itself, it made her feel wonderful to be able to ensure the young dressmaker had a decent wage, comfortable workspaces, and one heck of a dress to show off her skill for further employment.

The best part was, Fallon and Cateline had backed her completely, as she suspected they would. From the look on Garratt's face when it had all been discussed at dinner, he seemed upset or unnerved. She had no idea why, and in truth she was beginning to feel a bit uncomfortable by his attitude.

If they weren't even married yet, what sort of control would he try to exert once they were?

A week into Isla's temporary residence at the castle to get the dress finished, Elsie was heading up the stairs to her own chambers. She'd been with the dressmaker much of the evening, helping her where she could, be it to cut fabric or stand still as her living model for further refinements and details.

She was tired and rolled her eyes in annoyance when she heard the telltale sound of Garratt's heavy, booted tread on the stairs not far behind her. She ignored it, hoping he was perhaps heading to his parents' bedchamber.

"Hold up, Elsie," he said. "I'd like to talk to you."

Closing her eyes for a moment, she groaned inwardly. Reaching the top of the stairs, she turned and waited for him, saying nothing. He gave her a small smile. With a little shrug, he nodded down the way toward her bedchamber door.

"May I go in and talk to you for a minute?"

She was quite surprised by the request, as unorthodox as it was, but after all, in just over three months he'd be her husband, so she nodded. "Aye."

Silently they walked to her bedchamber door, which he pushed open for her, indicating with a smile she should enter first. She felt a bit nervous, never being alone with him for any length of time, certainly not in a small room like this and certainly not since he'd made his intentions known.

He took a seat on the bed as she walked over to the small table and lit the candle there. She knew the servant boy would be by soon to get her fire started, so that made her feel better. She sat in the wooden chair where she usually folded her clothing once she'd stripped out of it and looked at him expectantly.

He looked at her and took a deep breath, hands resting on his spread knees. "What I'm going to say doesn't come easy to me," he began. "Never been much of a talker." He grinned. "I think Laigen did enough of that for us both our whole lives."

Elsie smiled at the truth of that but said nothing.

"First off, I heard that my men were a bit much when you went to that dressmaker's house. Yes, I ordered them to take you there and or make sure you were safe. But," he added, shaking his head. "I never asked them to harass that woman. So, for that I'm sorry. They've been spoken to."

She was stunned to hear that. "Thank you. I appreciate that."

He nodded, sparing a glance to her before he looked down at his hands, which now lightly tapped fingertips against each other in a nervous gesture. "You see, Elsie, I have one memory of my parents. Just one."

He held up a finger before going back to his previous nervous tick. "Thank the gods Laigen has no memories, but when I was about seven, I remember him beating our mother with his fists." He looked into the cold firebox for a moment. "Honestly, I think eventually he killed her. A bad temper, that one."

Elsie's heart went out to him. "I'm so sorry, Garratt."

There was a knock on the door. "Come in," he called out, voice loud and firm.

The door opened, revealing Patrick, the fireplace boy. He began to step inside but stopped when he saw Garratt sitting on the bed. He looked to Elsie, almost as if to make sure she was all right.

"Come in, boy," Garratt said with a smile. "Do your business."

"Aye, sir," he said in his soft, whispery way before he hurried in to build the fire.

Garratt kept quiet until Patrick was done and had bowed to each before he scurried out, slamming the door behind him. Elsie was amused. She looked back to Garratt, her expression urging him to continue with his story.

"Anyway, so Laigen and I ended up in the orphanage that was in the monastery. I'd already worried our whole lives how I'd keep her safe at home, and now I had to figure out how to keep her safe there." He shook his head, running a hand through long, light brown hair. "She was all I had in the world, and I all she had."

"What happened?" Elsie asked. Obviously, they ended up with Fallon and Cateline, but she'd never heard the full story.

He gave her a boyish grin. "One day, an angel walked into that orphanage. The monks used to talk about angels all the time, and the moment I saw her, I knew she was one. She walked right to where I was curled up with Laigen in a pile of other kids." He looked into the newly built flames. "She was so beautiful, and she wanted us." He looked back to her. "*Us.*"

Elsie couldn't help but smile, as she knew that feeling all too well. "So, she took you two home?"

He nodded. "But the moment I met Fallon, I knew sh-he…" He drew out the word to an exaggerated length, trying to cover his stumble. "He was somebody I wanted to be like."

"Garratt?" When he looked at her, she continued. "I know the truth."

He nodded, seemingly relieved. "Well, Fallon was everything I'd always wanted to be. She was big, she was strong, nobody could cut her down or beat her in battle." He shook his head, a little boy's wonder clear on his face. "She wore double blades on her back, and when she'd come into the room, you'd hear her first." He grinned over at her. "I used to get this little feeling in my gut, part excitement and part intimidation."

"So, you grew up to be just like her," Elsie said, a statement.

"Not as good," he admitted. "*Nobody* is that good. But yes, I did." He looked down at his hands again, now the fingers laced where they dangled between his knees. "The reason I'm telling you all this, Elsie, is because the military is in my blood, always has been. I haven't had to worry about anyone else in a long, long time. Not like how I used to, with Laigen. Do you understand?"

Elsie met his gaze and shook her head. "Not entirely, no."

He shrugged. "My men can take care of themselves. Now, Laigen has her husband. Before that, she had Fallon to protect her, which allowed me to breathe and try to figure out who I was without constantly worrying about my little sister. So now, with you in my life, about to be my wife, I'm having to figure this out all over again. Find the balance."

She took a moment, absorbing what he'd said. Though she understood it, and even sympathized with it, there was something he needed to understand, too.

"Garratt," she said at length. "Whereas Laigen had to depend on you because she was so young, and then Cateline and Fallon, and now Reinaldo, I have always taken care of myself." She placed her hand on her chest, fingers splayed. "My mother got very sick when I was a girl, and I had to take care of her and us, as my father was off at war. He was killed, and I was all my mother had."

He looked at her, not looking particularly pleased, but he nodded. She needed to make sure he truly did understand.

"I'm a survivor, Garratt. No matter what, I will survive."

"So," he finally said. "You don't need me?"

*Not really, no.* "I don't need you to worry about my every move," she said instead. "I mean, that's a burden you do not need to carry."

He looked away from her, jaw muscles pulsing. It wasn't so much that he seemed angry as disappointed. He looked down at his hands before they slapped on his thighs and he pushed to his feet. He walked to the door.

"Garratt?" When he turned at the door to look at her, she said, "Thank you for telling me that. Like Fallon, you are a natural protector, and that is something to be proud of."

He held her gaze for a long moment and then

nodded, exiting the room. Left alone, Elsie's eyes fell closed as she let out a sigh of relief. Truth was, she was glad he'd shared that with her. If she understood him better, it would help their situation much more than going in blind.

It made her sad to think that as long as they'd known each other, she'd never known his story, beyond his coming from an orphanage. No doubt they'd learn much about each other along the way. She just had to find ways to live her own life and live her own happiness, just as Roishin had made her promise she would.

# Chapter Eighteen

It was the weirdest thing, but slowly Roishin had gotten used to it. When a partner took on a disguise of the opposite sex from themselves, the voice came through as whatever gender was intended to those in the stratum they were in—stratum being the word they used to denote the world beyond the door they'd walked through.

But to those on the mission with said partner, they heard their normal voice underlying that of the disguise. It was creepy, for sure. Currently, Roishin was with Trudy, the fifth of their little training group that included John, Livia, Enori, and of course, herself, the trainee.

To anyone who looked at Trudy Weissner, they saw a cranky redhead somewhere in her fifties. She had the gruff, throaty voice of a woman who had smoked cigarettes since she was fifteen. She'd grown up in Newark, New Jersey, and Roishin often started at the gruff nature of her words and accent now that she'd become largely fluent in English.

Today, she was portraying essentially the male version of herself. She told Roishin she was "channeling" her father, whatever that meant. As for Roishin, she was a reed-thin man in his thirties who looked quite a bit like a local thief they'd yet to catch in this small town called Reading, Ohio. She knew this was where they'd eventually arrest the man, so she had been sure to look directly into every single security camera they came across to help the process.

Roishin was acting as the lookout in their target location, a small store that sold electronics. Back home in Duras, a man known as The Scientist had asked for a laptop of this era. He had told Trudy the specs he was looking for, so she was currently going through one of the machines on display to see if it satisfied his requirements.

The reason for all those years of endless reading was very clear to Roishin now. All she'd read had become part of the tapestry of her knowledge base.

So, when they landed in a stratum of a when or a where she'd never been, those endless pages were in her head, stored almost as memories to give her a basic understanding of what she was seeing or how to react to the culture. More often than not, they didn't interact with a local other than their target. But, on the few occasions that they did, she needed to understand the lingo, not just the language.

However, for treasure hunt missions—where they were sent to collect specific items from a specific time, thus how all the books had been collected over the millennia—at least one of them would be familiar with the era. Trudy was a computer wiz and was making quick progress on the laptop. Though Roishin's group had only five members, there were many, many other groups doing the same thing across the world and across time.

Roishin was pulled from her musings by Trudy's cackle, which sounded even creepier as man and woman cackled together. She glanced over to the older woman to see she was looking at something on the screen.

"Listen to this," Trudy said. "'Who needs crop circles?'" she read. "'Farmer, Joe Connelly found a row of red roses in his harvested wheat field that seemed to have bloomed overnight.'" She looked to Roishin. "Can you imagine?"

Roishin rubbed the back of her neck. "You about done?"

"Yup." Trudy slapped the computer closed and unplugged it. She wrapped the charging cord around the body of the machine and walked over to Roishin. "Ready to hit it? Oh!" she added, a little grin quirking her lips. "Nice job on the door today, kid. You actually got us not only the right room, but the right block."

"Hey," Roishin said with the same teasing tone as her trainer and friend. "I'll leave your ass behind."

Trudy cackled again as Roishin began to reopen the door for their next stop, which was a very short visit to Israel to drop something off. "You have it?"

Roishin produced the small object from her pocket that needed to be planted for someone named Dov Moran to find. She looked at it, turning it this way and that. "What is this?"

"Called a flash drive," Trudy explained, taking it from her. "Dude's own invention, but we'll give him a jump start." She grinned at Roishin. "All you put on this," she said, holding up the laptop, "can be stored on this." She held up the small object. "Pretty cool, huh?

Roishin nodded, though she had no idea what Trudy was talking about. She still had a whole lot to learn.

⁂

"Honey!" Roishin boomed as she entered the stone cottage. "I'm home!"

She trotted up the stairs to see Enori's bedroom door was open. Normally she slept with the door closed, so she knew it was a welcome message for

Roishin. Sure enough, Enori was sitting up in bed, book in hand. When she looked at Roishin, a look of *Oh, really?* was plastered on her beautiful face.

Roishin grinned as she plopped down to lay across the end of the bed on her side. She propped her head in an upturned palm. "You must think I'm such a kid," she said, eyeing the other woman. "I know we look in the ballpark of the same age, but I truly *am* eighteen, whereas you're nowhere near what, twenty-four? Twenty-five? In actuality, you're, like, four *thousand* years old?"

Enori's eyes softened and the most beautiful smile spread across her lips as she shook her head. "I don't think of you as a kid in a bad way," she said. "It has been truly wonderful to watch you grow. Not only literally come of age, but in here." She tapped the side of her own head with a finger. "To come into your own and understand who and what you are. And yes," she added. "That even means an inordinate amount of television while in stratums and taking language from it. How'd it go…*honey*?" A wicked little smile curved her lips.

Roishin chuckled. "Really good. We got everything he needs, according to Trudy. I'm super curious about this laptop thing. Can I get one?"

Enori slapped her book closed and set it aside. "Perhaps ask Santa for one for Christmas," she quipped, pushing the covers back. "Come." She got up and walked out of the room.

Roishin followed, the two heading into her own bedroom. There was something lying on her bed. Initially baffled, she then recognized it as something she'd seen once before—on the day she'd found the strange blanket made of the same material as the cloak she was currently wearing. She had no more of an idea now what it was than when she'd seen both it and the blanket in her daidí's trunk.

"Do you know what that's used for, Roishin?"

Shaking her head, Roishin met her gaze. "I saw one once back home, though that one was a lighter color than this. I thought maybe it was part of Daidí's weaponry."

Enori's smile sent a little shiver through Roishin. "Of sorts." She picked it up and held it in her hands as she explained. "This is a device used for sexual pleasure, Roishin."

She felt her eyes nearly pop out of her head. "Oh," was all she could manage. She still had no clue what it was used for, but in that one short sentence she had learned more about her parents than she'd ever wanted to.

Clearly very amused, Enori, never breaking eye contact with her, lowered the harness until it was at her own hips. The part of the contraption that protruded did so obscenely from her crotch, leather straps dangling down uselessly.

Roishin gasped. "Oh," she managed again, taking a step back. A thousand different shades of blush tinted her skin and heated her entire body as realization dawned. It took her a moment before she trusted herself to speak. "Um, why was that left in here, then?"

Enori set the device back on the bed and walked over to Roishin. Her manner was calm and conversational as she began to speak while untying Roishin's cloak.

"I spoke with Ankou today," she said, easing the ties loose. "We talked about the various ways this can be set into motion with Elsie."

Roishin swallowed. Hard. "The baby?"

Enori nodded. "You understand the basics

of human impregnation?" At Roishin's nod, she continued. "Your blood, Roishin, is very potent, along with your intention. Intention is everything, as you know. Together, you could demolish entire cities, or create a life."

The statement terrified Roishin.

Enori eased the cloak off Roishin's shoulders and tossed it to the bed. Roishin felt faint, no clue what Enori was going to do. She swallowed again, asking something she'd wondered about to distract herself. "When do I get to meet Ankou?"

Enori paused as she began to unlace Roishin's leather trousers. She met her gaze. "You have." She tugged lightly at the open flaps of the trousers. "Remove these and your boots."

Stepping away from her, Enori walked over to the bed and the phallus. Roishin took several deep breaths to center herself and did as she was asked. She thought she was beginning to get more of an idea of what was happening and, more importantly, *why* Enori was doing this. She followed instructions, feeling incredibly vulnerable standing there in her typical tunic shirt.

She'd wanted to start wearing the T-shirts and jeans she'd seen in other stratums, but Enori had warned her against getting too far away from the era she was from. It was far too easy to forget and bring something back with her that could reshape time, causing a lot of trauma to the fabric of history.

This, Enori had explained, was why she wore the flowing white gowns. They were comfortable, but they were also timeless. A variation existed in pretty much every era of time, and, as Roishin had quietly added, she looked quite stunning in them. Even the more casual frocks she wore in her own house were simpler versions    of the gown.

"Do I need to remove this, too?" Roishin asked, tugging lightly at her shirt.

Enori gave her a little smirk. "You certainly can, but it is not necessary for what I have to show you." She smiled at the brand-new infusion of blushing. "It will be okay," she assured.

Though she was doing something incredibly intimate—attaching the harness and phallus to Roishin's naked body—her touches and movements were light and almost clinical. Roishin could tell she was doing all she could to make it easier on her. Even still, Enori was an insanely gorgeous woman and it was impossible to not react to her in this situation.

"This is how you will put this on," Enori explained, tightening the straps against Roishin's hips. "You want this to be snug against you."

She took hold of the jutting phallus for emphasis, pushing the end resting against Roishin's body back into her, pressing it harder against an incredibly sensitive place. Roishin gasped. Enori met her gaze, very much in Roishin's personal space. For just a flicker of a moment, something passed through the cerulean depths of Enori's eyes that stole Roishin's breath. Just as quickly, it was gone.

Holding the base of the phallus where it was, Enori continued. Her voice was softer, losing a bit of its instructional tone. "You need to be able to feel what you are doing. This is about pleasure, yes, but also about getting a result."

Roishin nodded, her heart racing. She tried to speak, but the words failed her. She tried again. "That part goes…"

Enori tilted her head just a bit as she eased the tip of the phallus to rest lightly against her own sex covered by her gown, never breaking eye contact.

Roishin had to look away, her body pulsing. She was grateful when Enori released the phallus and took a step back. She had to take several deep breaths to steady her breathing and her heart. Finally, she managed to speak again.

"How do I not hurt her? She's never been with a man before."

"Touch her," Enori suggested. "Get her ready for you and go slow." She took one of Roishin's hands and tapped the tip of her index finger to Roishin's. "Lightly cut yourself before you enter her," she said. She moved their joined hands until Roishin's was covering just the tip of the phallus. "Place some of that blood here."

"How much?" Roishin asked, feeling a tiny bit better when her hand was released and Enori stepped a foot away.

"Not much. You see, your blood and intention together carries everything that will be needed to give Elsie's body what it needs to create a life. Ankou believes this is the best way," she said, indicating the apparatus strapped to Roishin's hips. "Because this will bring that nourishment deep inside her body. Deeper than your fingers could."

Again blushing at the mental image that created, she nodded. "I understand."

"You will need to go back to Sursha and talk to her, Roishin," Enori said softly. "Explain all this to her."

Grateful to get the subject off of the thing jutting from her body, she said, "What do I tell her?"

"The truth."

"When does this need to happen? And, what if it doesn't work?"

"You must do this as close to her wedding day as possible. Though not a normal conception, Roishin, this will be a normal pregnancy." She shook her head. "It doesn't matter how many children she and Garratt may have in their marriage after, but he *must* believe this one is his." Her gaze bored into Roishin's. "Elsie's life will depend on it."

Roishin nodded in understanding. No matter how progressive Sursha was in so many ways, especially toward women, there was still a heavy consequence for adultery. For a "virgin" princess, it would be quite impossible to explain how she was pregnant before the wedding night.

"As for the worry of failure, I told you," Enori murmured, quirking her eyebrow at Roishin. "Your blood is potent." With that, she left the room.

⁂

Sitting in the chair in the darkness, Roishin watched Elsie sleep. She looked so peaceful, so absolutely beautiful. Badly, she wanted to remove her boots and walk over to that narrow bed and slide in with her and share her dreams. But tonight, that wasn't why she was there.

After a moment, Elsie began to stir, her face drawing a bit as if her consciousness was becoming aware that she wasn't alone. Finally, sleepy blue eyes opened. They blinked a few times before they became focused and began to look around. Elsie gasped when she saw Roishin sitting there.

Pushing herself up into a sitting position, she looked at her with wide eyes. "Roishin," she breathed.

Smiling, Roishin pushed to her feet, walked the few feet to the bed, and sat down upon the edge of it. She reached out her hand and ran her fingertips down a soft cheek. "You're so adorable when you're all sleepy."

Elsie smiled before she tucked herself into Roishin's arms, the two holding each other tightly. "So good to see you," Elsie whispered into the hug.

"You, too." Roishin closed her eyes for a moment, allowing herself to absorb the familiarity and warmth. "I'm sorry if I startled you. I need to talk to you."

"No, it's fine," Elsie murmured into her neck. "Is everything okay?"

"It is," Roishin assured. "I just know you're a busy girl during the day, so I wanted to grab you for a bit alone tonight to talk to you about something very important." She brushed long, blond hair away from Elsie's lovely face once she lifted her head from Roishin's shoulder. She tucked those strands behind an ear as she looked into the depths of Elsie's eyes. "Do you mind if I take you somewhere for a little bit? I want to show you something."

"No, not at all." Elsie cupped Roishin's face and left a lingering kiss on her cheek, her fingers caressing the same spot before she pushed to her feet. "Let me get dressed—"

"No need." Roishin got to her feet. "Do you trust me?"

Elsie's eyebrows fell. "Of course!"

Nodding, Roishin focused and set her intent and destination. The air before her began its telltale shimmer as the door began to open. She could hear Elsie gasp from where she stood next to the bed, but she said nothing. Easing the door wider, it was finally large enough for them both to step through.

Turning to Elsie, who looked absolutely stunned, Roishin held her hand out to her. Elsie looked incredibly uncertain as her gaze went from the door to Roishin's hand and finally to her face.

Roishin grinned, hoping to set her at ease. "This

is how I travel these days." When the soft hand was placed into her own, she gently tugged until Elsie was standing next to her. "Don't worry," she said, bringing Elsie's hand up to her lips. "You'll be fine. Ready?"

"I have no idea."

Chuckling, Roishin turned to the door, ready to step through.

# *Chapter Nineteen*

Never in all her life could Elsie have imagined such a thing. She thought stories of Roishin bringing a dead baby back to life had been crazy, and then to see her bring *herself* back from a grave injury had been even crazier. But now this? How was it possible to go from her own bedchamber and into a strange shimmer in the air, only to step out into the night clear across the island nation?

Possible or not, that's exactly what had happened. She could see her first home on the island, and what would be her home again in a matter of months, not a mile away. They were just inside the tree line that bordered a large open field where outdoor events were held at Caisleán Thíar. She looked around the warm night, no idea why they were there.

"Why did you bring me here?" she asked.

"I want to tell you a story." Roishin leaned her shoulder against the tree they stood next to. "You see, there were two women who loved each other very deeply, very passionately. When they were married, they were given a rose and told to love deep and true." She smirked. "They did. But what they didn't know was that the rose wasn't just any rose, wasn't just a wedding gift for a beautiful bride. It was..." She looked off into the night as if to find the right word. "Magical."

Not entirely sure what to say, Elsie nodded, letting her know she was listening.

"After their night of marital passion, that rose was taken and given to the very god who had created it. You see, Elsie, he wanted to use the essence of these two passionate women and that of himself and create a new life."

"A new life? From a rose?" Elsie asked.

Roishin smiled. "No, from what that rose had captured. Remember," she added, raising a finger. "It was a *magic* rose."

"Aye. Right."

"So, from the essence of these three, a soul was created. A pregnant woman, already destined to die in childbirth along with her child, was chosen to nurture this soul into existence in her womb. Upon her and the child's death, that realized soul was inserted into the body of another baby, just born." She pushed away from the tree and faced Elsie. "She was swaddled in Ankou blue and left for a nine-year-old boy to find while he and his friends played during the Summer Solstice Festival's games." She indicated the open space. "Just over there."

She squatted down next to the base of the tree, right where she'd just been standing. Looking up at Elsie, she concluded with a smile.

"That little boy was destined to be that baby's older brother."

Elsie gasped as her eyes opened wide. "You're talking about you," she whispered. "Aren't you?"

Roishin nodded, fingers playing with a bit of the dirt before she pushed to her feet, wiping her hands on the thighs of her trousers. "I am."

Elsie could only stare at her. "And," she managed after a long moment. "This god…Ankou?"

Roishin nodded.

Elsie had no idea what to say, so she turned away to gather herself. She ran her hands through her hair, idly thinking for a moment that it felt utterly strange to be wearing it down while outside. Roishin said nothing, seemingly to let Elsie absorb what she'd just been told. Finally, Elsie turned back to her.

"I don't know how, but somehow this makes so much sense." She stared at Roishin for a long time, taking in her every feature. *Fallon's* features, *Cateline's* features. "And, all you can do," she managed. "The baby, us being here." She indicated the woods around them, and then an almost wild laugh from deep in her belly released with this incredible revelation.

"I told you all this for another reason, too, Elsie," Roishin said. "To help explain what else I need to tell you. To *ask* of you."

Mirth dying down, Elsie cleared her throat. "All right." She noted the intensity in Roishin's eyes, an intensity she'd never seen before. "All right," she said again, almost more to calm herself than to let Roishin know she was ready.

"When somebody comes from a line of mystics, it's in the soul, the blood," Roishin began. "Like you and your great-great-grandmother."

Elsie gasped. "You know about her?"

"Enori told me. Through her blood, she passed that down to you, giving you her gifts, even though you never met her. Her Druid blood." She gave her a little grin. "Turns out, both my mothers also carry the blood of Ankou. Clearly, I do."

Elsie smiled. "Aye."

"Now," Roishin said, growing serious again. "Obviously, everyone in Sursha knows that Garratt is not of Carthac's line, Fallon's line, the line of kings for hundreds of years. So, it's not an expectation that his heir would be, either."

Elsie swallowed hard. She hated the reminders of this but knew there was a reason Roishin was bringing it up now. She nodded, urging Roishin to continue.

"My mothers, and Ankou," Roishin added, "want to keep the blood in the line, however. In the family. If even with just one of    Garratt's    children."

Elsie eyed her, her brain spinning on this new bit of information. "So," she said slowly. "Are you saying you'll have to—"

"Oh, gods no!" Roishin exclaimed, waving off the very notion. "I literally threw up when I thought that was what I was being asked to do." She wrinkled her nose. "He's my *brother*."

Elsie looked sheepish. "Sorry. So, the rose thing?" she asked, truly trying to understand all this. "And another woman who will die in childbirth?"

Roishin slowly shook her head, her gaze never leaving Elsie. "You will be the birth mother of this child, milady," she said with a little smile. She brought her leg up and retrieved her dagger from its hidden sheath.

Elsie chuckled, noting the rose etched in the blade. "Well, I guess I'm getting my rose?"

"A rose you say?" Roishin's eyebrows shot up with the playfulness that was in her tone. "A rose the lady wants," she said, wincing as she used the blade to slice across the tip of her thumb. "So a rose the lady shall get."

"Roishin! You hurt yourself!"

Roishin held up a hand to forestall Elsie's advance to her. Staying put, she watched in utter confusion as Roishin turned to the tree she'd been leaning against not long before. On a low-hanging branch that was roughly at her eye level, she used the small amount of blood that had beaded up on her thumb to form a rudimentary drawing of a rose.

Not entirely sure how to feel about that, Elsie

said, "Roishin, that wasn't necessary…"

The words died on her lips when a strange sound reached her ears. She wasn't sure what it was. It almost sounded like the ship had when Fallon had sailed her from Scotland to Sursha so long ago. A creaking. Wood moving, bowing, expanding, and almost sighing in its relent to the forces.

Hands coming to her mouth, she gasped when the branch slowly eased itself away from the tree trunk from which it grew, groaning as it moved farther and farther away until finally it fell to the forest floor at their feet. Left in its place was a hole, perhaps half the circumference of a dinner plate and relatively shallow.

Roishin looked over at her. "There's something in there for you," she said softly, nodding toward the hole.

Eyes wide and hands covering her lower face, Elsie almost couldn't move. Finally, she took the couple steps to the tree and, with a shaking hand, reached inside the hole. She gasped and looked to Roishin when she felt it. Turning back to the tree, she brought it out, the deep red rose in perfect bloom.

Roishin walked over to her. "This rose will never die," she said softly. "As long as I love you…" She met Elsie's gaze, which welled with tears. "And as long as I love *our* daughter, it will never die."

❧❧❧❧

With a start and a little snort, Elsie burst into wakefulness from the warm embrace of sleep. Eyes blinking several times, she looked around to find herself in her bed in her bedchamber. Her internal clock told her it was morning, just before sunrise and her normal time to wake.

Rubbing her face with her hands, she had the strangest feeling that she shouldn't be alone, that she *hadn't* been alone that night. But, alas, she was. Raising her upper body to rest against her forearms pressed into the mattress beneath her, she got a better look around. Nothing remotely out of place or that didn't belong.

With everything exactly as it had been when she'd gone to bed, why did she feel that she should find Roishin's boots on the floor or her cloak hanging on the hook on the wall? Neither, of course, was there. That knowledge made her feel incredibly empty. And then she remembered the dream. Yes, that was it! That was why she felt so terribly alone and lonely.

She'd had that wonderful dream that Roishin had come to her, had taken her through her magical passageway to the forest. A yawn nearly splitting her jaw, Elsie sat up fully. She ran her hands through her hair. It wasn't the first time she'd had dreams of Roishin coming to her in the night. Sometimes they just held each other, while others they made love all night long.

Waking up alone after such dreams was awful. More than once she'd burst into tears at the loss of her heart's greatest need, played out in the land of her dreams. Blowing out a breath, she pushed the covers off her lower body and swung her legs until her feet touched the floor. It was then that something caught her eye.

Something *was* different and something *was* out of place. Pushing to stand, she walked over to the chair that her dream Roishin had occupied. A single rose rested on the seat. It was the most beautiful rose she'd ever seen, the bloom huge and impossibly fragrant. She smiled as she stroked the deep green of the leaves.

Strangely, not a single thorn lived upon the stem.

"You were here," she whispered.

Her smile grew when their conversation came back to her. They *had* gone to the forest. They *did* talk at the base of the tree, and Roishin *had* shared with her the unbelievable beginnings of the incredible woman that was Roishin. Moreover, Elsie was to have a baby. Somehow, that baby would also be part of Roishin. Their baby.

Elsie hugged the rose gently to her chest. "I love you, Roishin," she whispered.

❧ ❧ ❧ ❧

It had been a long couple days, largely because Elsie felt guilty leaving the young woman she was training to take over the duties of lady-in-waiting to the queen. But, with just over a month to go until the wedding, Caisleán Thíar had begun its transition into the new home for the heir apparent and his bride. Cateline had arrived to help Elsie learn her staff and how to run her new household. Isla had also accompanied her, Cateline insisting that Elsie have her dressmaker present for any last-minute adjustments to her wedding gown.

Elsie walked the empty room, once the family chamber and soon to be converted into the princess's chamber once more. There were endless good memories in the large space. She looked to where the table had been where the family had taken their meals. She'd never joined them at this table but had served them, and many a kind word had been sent her way when the family included her in their conversation.

It was within the mighty stone walls of this castle that she'd found security again. She'd found acceptance and friendship. She'd found a second chance at a family. And she'd found love. For not the first time, she wished that love had been Garratt. She wished she could be a normal girl with the normal inclination toward men. It would have made life so much easier.

She simply wasn't that girl, but she'd decided to make the best of it. And, she thought with a small smile as her hands subconsciously went to her belly, perhaps she'd have a piece of that love with her always. She'd been looking forward to becoming a mother, even before Roishin had stunned her with her announcement.

She wasn't looking forward to her martial duties, of course, but it was a small portion of her life and worth it for sweet fruit it would bear. Her children. She smiled. "Our daughter," she whispered, not even realizing she'd spoken it aloud until Garratt's voice pulled her from her reverie.

"What was that you said, my love?"

She turned to see him strolling into the room, hands clasped behind his back.

"Oh, nothing." She smiled at him. "I was just thinking about all the changes that will take place within these walls." It was not entirely a lie.

"I agree," he said, a bit of a twinkle in his eyes. He walked over to her and brought his left hand out from behind his back. Between his fingers he held a rose. "A token of my heart."

Elsie was left breathless, scared he'd found the rose Roishin had given her that she'd hidden in a trunk amongst her belongings for the journey to Caisleán Thíar. She was sure he was presenting it to let her know that he knew of their dalliances and that—

"Picked it myself in the rose garden." He gave her a sheepish grin. "Thought you'd like it."

So relieved she gave him a quick peck to the cheek, she took it from him. "Thank you, milord." Though certainly beautiful, she couldn't help but think that it didn't measure up to Roishin's rose. Even as she buried her nose within the fragrant petals, it smelled dull and uninspired comparatively. She feared Roishin's rose had ruined her for any other.

"Don't you think it's high time you called me Garratt?" he asked softly, hope in his eyes.

She nodded, twisting the stem of the rose in her fingers. She felt a little prick. Looking down, she saw a single sharp thorn still attached to the stem. The tiniest drop of blood beaded up on her fingertip. "Aye. Garratt."

His grin was large. "See now? Was that so bad?"

She gave him a shy smile and shook her head. "No."

He used a hand to gently urge her face upward so she was looking into his face. "You truly are the most beautiful woman I've ever seen, Elsie." His smile was filled with wonder as he shook his head. "I've been all over the world. Not one has come close."

She felt shy and a little uncomfortable but didn't move away from him. "Thank you, Garratt."

"Oh, how I look forward to making you mine," he said, backs of his fingers lightly trailing down her cheek and along her jaw. He grinned. "My *wife*, of course."

She gave him a tiny smile, knowing exactly what he'd meant.

"Have you ever kissed a man, Elsie?"

At least she could be honest here. "No, Garratt."

His grin widened. "Then I think it's time we change that."

Elsie braced herself as his lips lowered to hers. It

was impossible to not compare his kiss with that of his sister. Roishin was soft, gentle, and utterly sensuous in how she kissed. She made it clear with every caress of her lips or her tongue that Elsie was precious to her, that she loved her.

Garratt kissed like he was on the battlefield, trying to conquer his opponent into submission with aggression and demands. She was disgusted, and worried that if this was indicative of what having sex with him would be like, she'd vomit in the middle of it.

Finally, it was over. She wanted to grab his tunic and use it to wipe the slobber off her chin and cheeks. *Good gods! Aren't I supposed to be the inexperienced one?* She gave him a polite smile, grateful that he walked away even as he looked rather proud of himself. No doubt in his mind he'd introduced her to wonders of unimaginable proportions.

Turning away, she used her own tunic to wipe her face, unable to keep the disgust from her expression. How on earth was she going to survive this?

# Chapter Twenty

Colm, that goes over there, where Lewis is standing. Sean, no, not that one, the one with the upholstered seats, thank you. James, can you please help Colm? Thank you."

Elsie stood back watching, eyes wide as a flurry of activity flew all around her and Cateline, who retained calm control as she directed traffic. Currently, the two women were putting clean linens on the new mattress that had been created and stuffed for Elsie's chambers as the new princess. The furniture Cateline had used in her first marriage had been brought in for Elsie to use.

Elsie was amazed at how Cateline kept her focus on bedmaking perfection, all the while knowing exactly what was going on around them and the name of each person doing which task. It was as dizzying as it was impressive.

Cateline met her gaze across the expanse of the bed. "What?"

Elsie shook her head, amused. "I was just thinking I have no idea how you keep everything together, everyone going in the right direction."

Chuckling, the queen responded, "It's called nineteen years of herding cats named Laigen, Garratt, Roishin, Isabeau, and the biggest cat of them all, Fallon."

Elsie burst into laughter, knowing all too well the truth of the queen's words. "Aye," she managed. "What advice can you give me?" Elsie asked, growing serious. They were doing the final preparations on her new home, the two women and a small army of servants readying the bride-to-be's bedchamber.

Cateline was quiet as they finished up with the bed, seeming to contemplate the requested information. Finally, she looked around, noting the servants were finishing up their duties in the room. The last man hurried out, leaving the two women alone.

"Let's sit," Cateline said, giving her a warm smile.

She walked over to the chambers doors and pushed them closed. The two women sat in chairs before the fireplace. A cold December day, the fire was aglow, spreading its warmth. Curious what the queen would say, Elsie waited for her to speak.

"What I am going to tell you only four people ever knew about," Cateline said. "Of course, Fergus and Carthac are both dead now, so it's only Fallon and me who know…and now you. Like most young women of noble birth, I was sold off to the highest bidder." She smiled. "Or so I thought at the time. But Fergus was an awful, awful man. He had absolutely no interest in me, Elsie. None. He didn't even show up to consummate the marriage."

Elsie's eyebrows shot up. "What?"

Cateline nodded. "Yes. We were down to the wire of the marriage being ruled as not official, and myself and my lady-in-waiting at the time, Marie, would have had to go back home to France."

"Clearly he finally showed up," Elsie said, indicating the queen sitting in the chair next to hers. She was confused at the slow shake of Cateline's head, her beautiful gray-blue eyes never leaving Elsie's stunned gaze.

"Fallon was forced to step in."

Elsie's mouth fell open. "For proof of consummation? But…how?"

A saucy little smile spread across the queen's lips. "There are special things produced that allow a woman to make love to another woman like a man, Elsie." A little laugh burst from her lips at Elsie's expression. "You have to understand, Elsie, at the time, I had no idea Fallon was a woman, nor was I supposed to know."

She studied the younger woman's gaze for a long moment. She seemed to try to be telling Elsie something without saying the words, and Elsie wasn't entirely sure what it was. She decided to file that bit of information away. Perhaps it would make more sense later.

"So, once that was done and I knew my station here was safe," Cateline continued, "I understood that no matter how much it hurt that my husband wanted nothing to do with me and that my marriage was not going to be a fulfilling one, I needed to create my own life. That was when I began the food programs here. Fallon helped me. Millie helped me." Her smile made an absolutely stunning forty-year-old woman even more so. "I found my purpose. And that was when Laigen, Garratt, and Livia came into my life. Though they weren't officially my children yet, they were already so in my heart."

Elsie couldn't help but smile at that. "So, despite Fergus, you found your own happiness."

Cateline nodded. "Don't get me wrong, Elsie. It was a tough time, and Fergus was an evil, evil man. But Fallon was truly what got me through that the most." She turned somewhat in her seat and took Elsie's hands in her own. "My biggest advice to you, my sweet, is to do the things you love. Do not lose yourself in a man or in a marriage." She smiled sadly. "For you, and so many women, the marriage is simply the vehicle to get you where you want to go. You just need to be strong enough to take the reins of your own carriage."

Elsie thought about that, looking down at their joined hands. She was so grateful to have this incredible woman as her mother-in-law, whom she honestly saw as her second mother. "Do you think Garratt will be a good husband?" she asked finally, not sure if that was a fair question to pose to his mother.

"My son is a good man," Cateline said. "But, he *is* a man. That comes with its own complications, no matter how good a man he may be." She smiled, squeezing Elsie's hand before releasing it to lightly cup her cheek in a loving gesture. "Remember that. Have a best friend, Elsie. Someone you can talk to, laugh with. Someone you can trust and who can fill that emotional void that, I promise you, will be there. Garratt will not fill that. Fallon only has because of our unique circumstance."

"My father's purpose was to essentially be gone for prolonged periods of time," Elsie said. "Off to fight somewhere, then come home to boss us around and maybe deliver a slap now and then to my mam." She gave Cateline a shy shrug. "That's what I know of a husband. As you said, as much as I would love to have such a thing as you and Fallon have, well..."

Cateline's gaze bored into Elsie. "I want you to hear what I'm about to say and to never forget it. Am I understood?" Elsie nodded. "If Garratt *ever* lays a hand on you in anything other than affection, you leave immediately. Come directly to us. Never, ever accept that."

Elsie was somewhat taken aback by the message, let alone the vehemence behind it. "Aye, milady."

"No, no, no. Please call me Cateline. Or..." She gave her a shy shrug and look. "If you feel so inclined... Mamaí?"

Elsie tucked her lips in to try to tamp down the emotion that suddenly hit her. She blinked rapidly at the threatening tears. All she could manage was a nod. Cateline gathered her into her motherly embrace, leaving a kiss on the side of her head.

"It is our absolute honor to have you in our lives, Elsie," she said softly. "Fallon and I both love you very much."

In that moment, Elsie knew in her heart everything would be okay. Suddenly, she felt a strange warmth in her belly. It was quick and it was faint, but it was there. The moment she felt it, she knew it was the baby to come. It was *Roishin's* baby. She wanted to talk to Cateline about that, too.

But first she said, "I love you both as well." She smiled at the other woman when their hug ended. "I'm so grateful for you. When my mother died, I truly thought I'd be alone forever. Not to be."

Cateline shook her head. "Not to be."

"Roishin came to me," she said, eyeing Cateline to make sure she wouldn't think she was crazy for what she was about to say. Granted, Roishin had told her that Cateline and Fallon were in on it, but… "She told me about the baby."

Cateline nodded. "Yes."

"She told me about the rose on your wedding night to Fallon, Enori, Ankou, all of it."

Elsie swallowed, not sure whether she felt better or more nervous that Cateline was very much aware of everything she was saying. Either it was a collective case of insanity, or Roishin spoke the truth.

"How do you feel about all of this?" Cateline asked.

Elsie let out a slow breath as she considered. "From my family's history, I've been aware of my own gifts my whole life. So, I've always known the unthinkable is quite thinkable. But," she added with a small smile. "Roishin has taken that to a whole new level."

Cateline chuckled, nodding. "Oh yes!" Then she grew serious. "Elsie, this child will be something that you and Roishin will share forever," she said, lowering her voice to just above a whisper. Though they were alone, it was of the utmost importance that nobody ever knew of this except those who absolutely had to know.

"Roishin said I'll give birth to this child," Elsie added, her voice just as quiet. "How is that possible, Mamaí?"

"I'm not entirely certain. But I have to admit, I'm envious. I would have loved to carry Roishin. It doesn't make me love her any less, or see her as any less as our child, but I do wish that had been possible." She smiled. "Granted, at the time we had no idea that was happening."

"Do you think Roishin will do whatever she must do and then be gone?" She shrugged, looking around. "Once I'm married to Garratt, will she just disappear?"

"No." Cateline shook her head. "She will never abandon her child. Or you," she said pointedly. "No matter the state of your relationship with her, Elsie. No matter where in the world she is, all you'd have to do is ask, and she'll be there."

Elsie looked down at her hands in her lap. "I love her," she murmured.

"I know you do," Cateline responded. "And she loves you. That will never stop."

Elsie was nervous, but the look on Isla's face said she needn't be. The dressmaker had made her last-minute touches while the gown was upon Elsie's frame, then had taken an objective step back. Now, she looked on with her hands curled together at her own chest and brown eyes wide.

"You are so lovely, milady," she whispered, nodding at her own words. She walked slowly around the bride-to-be, lightly readjusting this or that as she finally made her way back to face Elsie again. "Would you like to see?"

Elsie took a deep breath and nodded.

She was guided over to the mirror encased in an elaborate frame. Elsie gasped, stunned at what she was looking at. They'd chosen a blue material that played beautifully with the sapphire of her eyes. White and cream material trimmed the oversized cuffs of the sleeves and along the neckline that, indeed, revealed her upper chest and tops of her shoulders.

The bodice was fitted, showing a lovely figure, flaring at the hips into the layered skirts accented in the white and cream. The girdle belt that hung at her hips and dangled down half the length of the skirts was a Celtic design of interwoven links of gold and silver.

Elsie looked at Isla's reflection, the woman standing a few feet behind her and visually feasting on her creation. This made Elsie smile. She was pleased that Isla was so happy with her dress. She turned away from the mirror to face the woman who had worked so hard on it.

"You did a wonderful job, Isla," she said, meaning it. "I am stunned."

The most beautiful smile spread across Isla's lips. "Thank you, milady," she whispered, seeming to be almost overcome by the moment. "I'm so pleased."

Elsie took her hands in her own. "In three days hence, I'll wear this and begin a new chapter in my life." She smiled at her, though she was nervous about what she was to say next. "Isla, I'd very much like to bring you on as my official dressmaker and seamstress in residence here."

Isla's eyes widened. "Do you mean it, milady?"

"Of course! You'll be guaranteed a wage, food, shelter and"—she raised her eyebrows for emphasis—"safety." She thought Isla's smile in response was beautiful. "After all," Elsie added. "If I'm to have these children I keep hearing about, I'll need dresses to fit my expanding belly, won't I?"

Isla laughed and nodded. "Aye."

"Plus, of course, those children will need clothes, and so on."

With a little girl-like squeal of excitement, Isla threw herself at Elsie, the two sharing a tight hug before Isla, seeming to remember her manners, stepped back from her. "Oh my," she murmured. "My apologies, milady."

Elsie laughed outright, happy to know this spunky young woman would be accompanying her into such an unknown future. At least it was someone to talk to, a friend. Just like Cateline had suggested.

"Do you accept?"

Isla's nod was vigorous. "Aye, milady. Very happily so." She let out a shaky breath. "My goodness. I never thought such a thing would happen."

"You're very talented, Isla," Elsie said. "Your eye for detail is incredible, let alone how quickly you work. Very impressive." She smiled. "In fact, I think the queen might just fight me for you."

Again, that girlish laughter that charmed Elsie. "Thank you, milady. I'm very excited to work for you and Prince Garratt."

"Well, you can start by going to get said queen. I know she was anxious to see this."

"Yes, of course!" Without another word, the little bundle of energy was gone.

Amused, Elsie turned back to the mirror. She studied herself this way and that. She took in her body in the gown, admitting that she did look beautiful. No one had ever made her feel beautiful until Roishin. She'd been told she was beautiful by boys in the fields or men in the corners at castle gatherings she'd served at.

But none of that mattered to her. From early on, the look in Roishin's deep green eyes had meant more than a hundred drunken noblemen's flattery at a party. She would give anything for this to be the dress she'd wear for her wedding to Roishin.

"What would you think of this dress, Roishin?" she whispered.

"I'd think you were absolutely stunning."

Elsie gasped, unable to believe her eyes as Roishin seemingly stepped out of the wall behind her. She was grinning as she brushed the hood of her cloak back. Elsie didn't turn around, so afraid that if she did, the mirage would disappear.

Roishin stepped up behind her, never taking her eyes off Elsie's reflection. Elsie nearly cried when very real arms slid around her waist and a warm body pressed up against her back. She leaned back into the solid body, Roishin's arms sliding tighter around her, holding her close.

"So beautiful," Roishin whispered into her neck, nuzzling it.

Elsie's eyes slid closed as Roishin began to sway, their bodies held tightly together. It felt like they were dancing. "What are you doing here?" she murmured, her head falling slightly to the side when she felt a soft kiss on her neck.

"I came to ask if it's all right that I take you tomorrow night," Roishin said. She inhaled Elsie's scent, the slow, warm breath she released making Elsie shiver and her body awaken.

"Take me where?"

Roishin smiled into the skin of her neck. "Somewhere where we can be alone." She lifted her head just enough to look into Elsie's eyes again in the mirror. She slid her hands from underneath Elsie's, placing them at her waist to urge her to turn and face her.

Elsie's arms immediately slid up around Roishin's neck, fingers going to play in her short, dark hair. "Is this when you'll do whatever you're going to do to..."

Roishin grinned, her hands running down to Elsie's hips, pulling them lightly into her own. "Make a baby," she murmured, a breath away from Elsie's lips.

Elsie felt herself becoming lost in the spell of all that was Roishin. She nodded. "Aye." Her eyes closed as Roishin initiated a kiss that was soft, slow, and deeply sensual. It took Elsie's breath away. "Will you kiss me like that?" she managed after the kiss came to a slow, natural end.

Roishin ran the backs of her fingers down Elsie's jaw, along her throat, and then across the smooth skin revealed by the dress. "Definitely."

"Can you take me there now?" Elsie murmured, making Roishin chuckle.

She shook her head. "No. I need to go, but I wanted to make sure with you." She left another soft kiss on her lips. "I'll come for you just after bedtime."

Elsie nodded, her heart wanting to panic as

Roishin loosened her grip on her hips and took a step back. Roishin studied her for a long moment, seeming to drink her in.

"You are so beautiful, Elsie," she said softly, so much love and affection in her eyes and her voice. She blew her a kiss. "Until tomorrow." Then she turned and disappeared, Elsie left alone.

# *Chapter Twenty-one*

Roishin stared into the flames, a mug of coffee cradled between her palms. She'd learned of the substance during one of their missions and had been curious to try it. Enori was willing to let her bring a percolator into the house, and ever since, it had become a comforting treat, like a hug from the inside out.

Now, she was in the simple cotton pants she slept in and lighter weight version of her tunic shirt. Normally always one to wear shoes, Enori had, in her quiet way, shown her the virtues of going barefoot, especially in a place where it was always pleasant. A fire was started simply for the joy of it, not because a body would freeze to death without it.

She was curled up on the couch, Enori preferring what Roishin had learned was called a loveseat . They often sat together and read, discussed upcoming missions, or just talked. Roishin enjoyed that time with her.

In her time with Enori, living in her home and working with her, she was finding the beautiful priestess was the ultimate onion. She was seeing beneath the layers of cool aloofness to the woman underneath. It was a fascinating journey. She forced her thoughts away from Enori and back to what had her staring into the flames in the first place.

Tomorrow night.

She'd considered going to Elsie the night before her wedding but decided the night before that would be better, giving Elsie a full day to focus on the wedding festivities. Love it or hate it, it was a big day and a big deal. Oh, how she'd looked in that dress. Roishin was pretty sure that image would be burned into her memory for eternity.

As she'd looked at her, it had been so easy to imagine slowly taking that dress off on *their* wedding night. She'd had to quickly shoo that thought away. There was just no reason to torment herself anymore, as that ending was not in the cards she was dealt. She was taking another sip when she heard soft footfalls down the stairs.

She saw Enori take the last few stairs before turning into the living area. She wore the gown she slept in, and Roishin had to make herself look away. Her body was already buzzing from her brief time with Elsie and the thoughts of what she had to do in twenty-four hours' time. Her imagination didn't need any more help.

"Did I wake you?" she asked.

Shaking her head, Enori said, "No. I felt your… dilemma."

Roishin stared at her. "Felt it?"

"I did." She smirked. "You share energy with someone long enough, you begin to feel them." She sat on the other end of the couch from Roishin. "Especially when that person's energy is enhanced by their reactions to strong emotions about a situation."

"Sorry," Roishin muttered sheepishly.

"Don't be." She leaned forward and gently tugged Roishin's legs from where they were curled up until they stretched out. She took her feet into her lap and began to gently rub one of them. "Tell me."

It was such a strange dynamic for Roishin. Enori could be one of the coldest people she'd ever encountered. Her beautiful eyes could instantly turn to chips of determined ice. But then, she could turn around and become the most gentle, affectionate person. Sometimes it was dizzying.

"I'm so torn, Enori." She tried not to groan, as the gentle massage felt so good.

"About?"

"I understand why I have to do this, I honestly do," Roishin said. "But my conscience is eating at me. I mean," she continued with a smirk. "I have no issue whatsoever being with Elsie."

"Obviously," Enori said with a little devilish grin.

"Obviously. But I think this is going to really hurt." She rested her mug on her thigh as she looked beyond Enori to the fireplace. "This is something deeply meaningful, Enori. Mostly for Elsie and her life, her *marriage*." She couldn't help the bitterness that entered her voice on the last word. "But also for me."

"And Garratt?" Enori gently asked.

She nodded and looked down into the dark depths of the liquid in the mug. "Garratt, too." She sighed and took a sip, allowing the warmth to swish in her mouth for a moment before swallowing it. "It's such a betrayal to him."

"Do you believe he loves Elsie?" Enori asked. "Or is capable of it?"

"You don't?"

Enori gave her a ghost of a smile. "This isn't about me, Roishin."

She growled deep in her throat. "Hate it when you get all logical on me."

Enori smiled, returning to her ministrations on Roishin's foot.

"Garratt is a tough nut to crack," Roishin finally said. "He has a good heart, I know that. A natural warrior, a natural protector. But I don't know that he has the heart of a husband or father. I mean, if Elsie gave birth to a bunch of boys, he'd be in heaven. He could take them out and show them how to hunt, play war games, all that. But to nurture, cuddle, be the safe place when a kid wakes up from a bad dream..."

"Like Fallon was?"

Instantly Roishin smiled. So many memories of just that. "Daidí gives *the* best hugs," she said quietly, reverently. "And, the way she is with Mamaí," she continued, looking back to Enori. "So loving, affectionate. Oh man, she can make her laugh!" She grinned at the thought.

Enori joined her in that smile. "Fallon came to Brittany when she found out we wanted to bring you with us." She gave Roishin a full-on smile, which nearly left Roishin speechless, almost unable to breathe. Seeming not to notice, she said, "She was like a tiger. Literally ready to do battle for you."

"Really?"

"Oh, yes!" The smile turned into a soft chuckle. "She was determined to keep her little girl at any cost." She met Roishin's gaze. "I'd never seen her so absolutely heartbroken as she was that night, Roishin. The love she has for you...I think that night she would have literally died for you."

Roishin had to look away from that gaze, hers dropping back to her coffee. "I miss them." She let out a heavy sigh. "I miss the me that I was with them before the me that I am now with them." She looked up again when she felt a light squeeze on her foot.

"When you're done with your training, Roishin," Enori said, so much understanding in her eyes. "You'll be free to move out from my house if you wish, but you'll be strong enough to bring them here to visit you."

Roishin was extremely confused by the order of her reactions. First, panic hit at the thought of no longer living in the little stone cottage with Enori, then the overwhelming happiness of being able to share Duras with her family replaced it. She decided to sort through that later and focus on her parents.

"Wait, really?"

Enori nodded. "Ankou runs strong in both your parents, Roishin. They cannot create doors like somebody I know, but they can walk through those you create for them. They cannot live here, as it would alter things in a way that would be irrevocable. But yes, they would be able to come see you." She smiled. "And Livia."

Roishin ran her hand through her hair. "Whoa," she blew out.

"So, Garratt," Enori said, getting them back on track. "Not Fallon. Of course, he is not a woman."

Roishin shook her head. "Nope. He is not."

"Would it make it easier on you if he were?" Enori asked.

Roishin met her gaze and held it. "For me, or for Elsie?"

"Yes."

Roishin honestly didn't know why it had never occurred to her that Elsie could be attracted to other women. That maybe, like her, Elsie was a lesbian. She pondered that as Enori switched to her other foot, fingers and hands magic in their strong massage.

"You know, I take no joy in Elsie being stuck with a man, even my brother," she finally said after considerable thought. "My heart hurts for her, Enori. If I'm truly honest and push my own feelings aside, I still don't want this jail sentence for her."

"Jail sentence of a bad husband or of a husband at all?"

Roishin grinned, using Enori's own response. "Yes."

Enori sent a little smile her way. "Then perhaps she will find herself a new love over time, Roishin. As you said, she deserves to be happy."

"She does." Roishin sighed as she took another sip of her coffee. Lowering her mug as she swallowed, she looked to Enori. "What about you?"

Enori tilted her head a bit. "What about me?"

"I know it's possible to be happy here, find love. Look at Livia. Why aren't you married, or at least with somebody?"

Enori met her gaze and held it for a very long time. "I told you," she said quietly, almost a whisper. "This isn't about me."

❧❧❧❧

It was her first mission alone, and she was stunned that she'd been sent to do it. It was a surveillance mission, a simple checkup on a former target, she was told. She was to go, observe, take notes, and return. She was to touch nothing, take nothing, and speak to no one. Check, check, and check.

She stepped through the door and right onto the grounds of the Crystal Palace. It looked as it always did, and took her breath away as it always did. She wondered if that ever went away. Today she was back in her brown cloak from her days in the Underground. It was where she'd mastered the ultimate trick: out of sight, out of mind.

Stepping into the Crystal Palace, she saw Livia waiting for her. She wasn't going with her, but she was going to be telling her where she was going. They exchanged a hearty hug before Livia spoke.

"You're going    back to Washington, DC," she said. "April 16, 1865. Two days after we were there the last time."

Stunned, Roishin said, "Ava Gentry? But she had that…weird reaction to me last time."

"Which is why you're going like this," Livia said, her tone like a mother explaining a simple solution to a child as she tugged at the brown cloak. She grinned at the glare she received.

"All right. How do I find her?"

Livia placed her hands on Roishin's shoulders, her dark eyes boring into Roishin's. "Focus on her energy, Roishin. Her soul. Find her soul."

Roishin nodded. "I can do that. I hope."

Livia gave her a loving smile, kissing both her cheeks before leaving. Roishin focused, the red smoke-like energy luminescing all around her, trailing its cold fingers over and through her. She brought the young woman's face to mind, dark hair and dark eyes. The pale skin and the shy nature she'd felt.

*Where are you, Ava? Show me.*

The image of the boarding house came to mind. And then, as if going into hyperdrive, her mind sped inside, up the stairs, down the hall to room three. There, everything slowed and came to a stop. Knowing that was where she was, Roishin focused her attention

.

The glowing red energy began to swirl in on itself and gather before her. It began to grow until it was large enough for her to step through…

…and into the hallway of the boarding house. There was no one around her, but she remained still for a moment anyway. She wanted to regain her focus now that she'd arrived. Loud voices outside garnered her attention. Walking to the window at the end of the hall opposite that of the stairs, she looked down into the street below.

A group of men were gathered, one hollering about how *that rat bastard coward Booth needs to be found and strung up!* The crowd around him made noise in agreement. Turning away from the window, as that wasn't why she was there, Roishin returned to the door. Listening, she heard soft weeping from the other side.

Knowing there was no way to remain unseen and open the room's door, she had no choice but to open her own door. She did so quickly, stepping through and into the small room beyond. She nearly held her breath once she stepped out, the door vanishing once she was through. Looking to the crying figure curled up in the bed, Roishin waited.

There was no reaction, no lift of the young actress's head to see who or what had entered her room. She simply remained lying there, crying. Looking around, Rishin saw that the doors to the armoire were standing open, the insides a jumble of clothing and accessories. Some were stuffed into a carpet bag while others littered the floor nearby.

It looked as though perhaps packing had been underway but interrupted or abruptly stopped. Looking at the young woman in the bed, Roishin had to wonder if Ava had been hurt in some way. Had someone come in here and done harm?

Moving closer to the bed, Roishin scanned what she could see of her, noting no bruises, cuts, nor rips or tears in her sleeping gown. Relieved, she looked away from the young woman and to the small bedside table.

There, she saw a small piece of paper, the deep creases keeping it still a bit folded.

Roishin looked down, reading as much as she could, as straightening the paper wasn't an option. She was able to see enough to discern that it was a cancellation of a contract. She saw what looked to be the title of the play, *Our American Cousin*, the production Ava had been performing in.

Roishin groaned inwardly. Her gaze moving away from the page, she also saw a Colt Sidehammer Pocket Revolver next to the paper on the bedside table. She wondered why on earth the woman had the small pistol. Protection, perhaps? Her mind went back to her initial concern of somebody doing her harm. Perhaps the tears weren't about apparently being fired after all.

"I know you're there."

Roishin gasped, head whipping to look at the young actress. She'd stopped crying and had lifted herself so her upper body rested on a forearm. She was looking around the room, her sweeping gaze moving through Roishin, clearly not seeing her.

"You're my angel, aren't you?" she asked, moving from her side to fully sit up. The bedsprings squeaked obnoxiously as she did. "Have you finally come to get me? I've been waiting my whole life." Fresh tears started again. She bowed her head into her hands, long, dark hair falling like a chocolate curtain. "I even bought the gun with the last of my money," she sobbed, her hand reaching out to cover the small gun. "I wanna go home."

Panic filling her, Roshin reached up and shoved her hood back and covered Ava's hand where it rested on the gun. Enori had been absolutely steadfast last time they were there: Ava Gentry must survive. Roishin was pretty sure the young woman taking her own life didn't quite fit into that category.

Rich brown eyes, huge with shock, looked at Roishin, following her progress as she sat on the edge of the bed. She gently gripped Ava's hand and moved it off the cold grip of the weapon.

Smiling, she said, "I don't think you should do that."

It took nearly a full minute for Ava to find her voice, but when she did, she whispered, "I've prayed for so long you'd come back and you'd finally take me home."

"What is home?" Roishin asked, removing her hand when she felt Ava's would remain in her own lap.

"It's a place I've dreamt of always. Rolling hills as far as the eye can see," she said, her eyes looking off into that dreamworld. "Blue skies above, never rain clouds    or storms." Her face crumbled, but she managed to keep the full force of her emotions under control. "You're never alone."

Roishin had the strangest feeling niggling at her that Ava was describing parts of Duras. Something about this young woman's energy just felt…familiar. She knew she didn't know Ava beyond these two encounters, but it felt like she was a kindred spirit, one of *them*, whatever that meant.

"My whole life," Ava continued, pulling Roishin from her thoughts. "I've felt like I don't belong here." She met Roishin's gaze. "Like, I'm a stranger in my own life." She looked away as her eyes began to well with tears again. She used a hand to wipe one away as it escaped. "It's only been my angels in my dreams that have kept me…I don't know." She shrugged, looking down at her hands in her lap. "*Here*, I guess."

"What do your angels look like?" Roishin asked, trying to get more of an idea of the situation. The irony was, that was exactly how she described Enori to her own young mind, unable to rationalize what or who she was.

"I don't see faces," she said. "Just the blue cloaks. Like you had on last time you were here. The day President Lincoln was shot." More tears.

Roishin reached out and covered one of Ava's hands with her own, the warm fingers curling around hers. "I'm so sorry," she said. No doubt it had been a horrifyingly traumatizing situation to experience, even though Enori had made sure Ava wasn't at the theatre that night.

"Please," Ava said. "Please take me home."

# *Chapter Twenty-two*

Roishin had been surprised to see Livia waiting for them when they'd come back through. She'd made the executive decision to bring Ava back with her, her gut telling her the young actress wouldn't live another day if she were left alone. By time they reached the Crystal Palace, the young woman was almost listless.

Livia had whisked them off down a darkened tunnel that had just appeared out of the shadows. It wasn't a door but an actual tunnel that seemed to grow as they proceeded and shrink behind them, so the "wall" was always at their backs. It was disorienting. But even more disorienting, once they reached the end, as it were, it looked as though they'd arrived in the Underground.

Looking over at Livia and seeing she was still quite solid blew that theory out of the water, as to her knowledge, that wasn't part of Duras. They found themselves in a medium-sized cave-like chamber made of stone. It was much smaller than the library, but certainly larger than Roishin's room of four and a half years had been. There was no exit, and the tunnel behind them had completely closed.

Looking to Livia, she shrugged. "Now what?"

"Now, we'll take over."

Roishin's head whipped to her left to see a very familiar figure walking toward them. Honestly, she wasn't sure whether to smile joyfully at the reunion or smack him. "Mystic."

He gave her a deferential nod before his focus returned to the woman braced by Roishin and Livia. He walked over to them and, using gentle touches, eased Ava's head up from where it drooped by two fingers under her chin. His heavy eyebrows were drawn in contemplation. Nodding, as if coming to some sort of decision in his own mind, he sent out a hand from the oversized sleeves of his brown garment.

The air before them began to shimmer and glow, growing brighter and brighter. Finally, a large expanse was glowing, about twice the size of a normal door. Silhouettes appeared, rolling something in through the blinding light. Roishin was squinting as she watched. The newcomers were dressed in strange garb: light blue matching baggy shirt and pants, the sleeves short and the neckline a V-shape.

They were hurrying in with a very narrow bed atop a metal frame with wheels. Roishin and Livia were shooed away as the team of three men picked Ava up and carefully placed her on the bed. Two of the men nearly ran back into the light, rolling Ava's jostled body atop the bed as they went. The third man and The Mystic stepped aside to talk quietly.

Roishin looked to Livia, utterly baffled. "Those who come in from the Earth stratum and are in need of medical care get them." She nodded toward the man in the strange clothing.

"Who are they? What will they do to her?"

"They're doctors, Roishin"

Confused, she glanced to the man, then back to Livia. "Then where's his white coat and stethoscope?"

Livia smiled, lightly squeezing Roishin's arm. "They wear scrubs."

"*That's* what scrubs are?" she asked, having seen that word described as clothing in more than one book.

At Livia's amused nod, she muttered, "Oh."

Livia gave her a tight squeeze. "You did good, my sweet." She kissed her cheek and turned to where they'd come in. The mouth of the tunnel reappeared. Roishin turned to follow.

"Roishin," the deep voice of The Mystic said. "A moment."

Roishin smiled at Livia, then turned back to the man who was walking over to her, the doctor and the glowing door gone. The two were left alone in the chamber which, like all the others she'd gotten used to, seemed to have its own unseen source of light.

Arms crossing over his chest, he met her gaze with a drawn brow. "What made you take this target out of her environment?"

*Uh-oh. Here we go.* Clearing her throat, Roishin said, "My gut told me she would not be alive much longer, Mystic. I believe she was suicidal. And, Enori had made it clear to me that Ava was to remain alive, which was why she was put out of commission to return the night of the shooting."

He quirked one bushy eyebrow. "And, how do you know she wasn't to remain alive that night so that she could take her own life two days later?" He studied her. "Wouldn't they have two very different impacts?"

*Good point.* Even so, it didn't feel right to her. Shaking her head, she decided to be honest about what she'd felt in the moment. "I don't believe that was her destiny, Mystic. Saving her from one death only to leave her to another didn't feel right. She just..." She chewed on her lip as she tried to decide what exactly it was she'd felt. "This may sound crazy, but I feel she's one of us." She smirked. "I don't even fully know what that means, but it's my gut feeling."

He studied her for so long, she began to feel like a

bug beneath the microscopes she'd read about but had yet to see. After what felt like an hour, she was stunned that his face didn't split in two when he actually… smiled! She blew out a relieved breath. Placing a meaty hand on her opposite shoulder, he turned her around.

Livia was gone, but the tunnel once again appeared. They strolled, his hand never leaving her shoulder. "Congratulations, Roishin," he said, his voice softer than she'd ever heard it. There was actual affection in it, almost like a parent would have toward a child. "You've passed the test."

She glanced over at him, his features just barely seen as the tunnel behind them swallowed the light as it closed in on itself, the tunnel before them growing foot by foot. "You mean, that was a test the whole time? Was Ava in on it, too?" She felt betrayed, as she'd felt genuine concern for the actress.

"A test, yes. One that Enori felt, correctly, you were ready for." The tunnel opened up into the Crystal Palace, the familiar luminescent red energy billowing around. "As for Ava…"

Roishin gasped. Every time the swirl of the smoke-like energy crossed over The Mystic, it revealed another feature of not the pudgy man she'd come to know with graying light brown hair, but a figure in a dark cloak. One brief revelation would be of a jagged cheekbone. Another, bared teeth, lips long ago pulled back. This time, a cavity where once the cartilage of a nose had been.

"She was a young woman in grave danger," he said, his voice that same soft, paternal timbre. "It was time to bring her home before *I* had to bring her home." With a squeeze to her shoulder, he vanished.

❧ ❧ ❧ ❧

Roishin arrived back at the house to find Enori gone. She wasn't entirely surprised, as the two were constantly busy, and often separately. She climbed the stairs and went to her bedroom.

Her bed was made to perfection, as always, a well-learned habit from the Underground. The phallus contraption that Enori had given her was waiting on her bed where she'd left it. She hadn't been sure how long her mission would take today, so she had set out the most important component so she could grab and go if necessary. She'd practiced putting it on a few times, and the process made her giggle every time.

It was a strange thing, and she just hoped she'd be able to do what was necessary without hurting either Elsie or herself in the process. She pulled open the bottom drawer of her dresser and removed an empty bag she kept in there. Loading the phallus and some candles into it, she stared down at the open bag that lay upon her bed. Anything else?

Enori had told her where she could take Elsie to have complete privacy. It was no longer a good idea to do anything like this in Elsie's world, Roishin thought. They couldn't be seen together so close to the wedding, especially with Garratt's warning words to her.

Did she have any intention of listening to him down the road? Not really. But this mission was too dire, too important to not play it safe. Once the pregnancy, marriage, and perceptions were in place... Well, that would be a different story.

It wasn't that she thought Garratt suspected anything untoward was happening or had happened between the two women. Honestly, she didn't even think it would occur to him, which was a good thing for them, though mainly for Elsie.

The funny thing was, though all the children—except Isabeau—knew the truth about Fallon, Roishin was beginning to believe that Garratt and Laigen just figured it was a onetime thing and isolated to their parents. Fallon had been forced to live a certain way for the sake of the kingdom, and Cateline, also forced into a situation like many of her station, had just gone along with it.

Somehow, miraculously, the two had found love anyway. Roishin grabbed the clothing she planned to change into and headed to the shower. She continued her ponderings as something else occurred to her. Fallon, Cateline, Elsie, and herself all seemed to have the lesbian leanings. Further, all four of them had either Ankou or Druid blood.

Livia and Laigen both seemed to be very happy in the world of men, Garratt in the world of women, and none of them carried any such blood to her knowledge. There could, of course, be absolutely no connection, but she found it interesting. Perhaps a higher level of consciousness? Or, she mused, perhaps she was overthinking the entire thing and should just shower.

She decided to take her thinking cap off and focus on what was about to happen. Any thoughts of her siblings and their non-lesbianism, Livia, The Mystic, Ava, and Enori would have to wait.

❧❧❧❧

When she arrived at Elsie's bedchamber, she found her standing before the small fireplace. She was dressed, though her hair was down. She was staring into the flames, a look of contemplation on her lovely face. She looked very serious, and Roishin hoped she hadn't changed her mind.

"Hi."

Elsie's head whipped up, surprise in her eyes. Hand to her chest, she blew out a little nervous laugh. "Sorry. I was so lost in thought, I didn't even hear you come in."

"Sneaky, sneaky," Roishin said with a small smile. "Are you okay?" She walked over to her but didn't touch her. "Has something happened?"

"No." Elsie turned to her, though kept the distance between them. "I was just thinking about all of this." She indicated the two of them and the door Roishin had just stepped out of that still shimmered in the air.

"Have you changed your mind?" Roishin asked gently. "I will not make you do anything you don't want to do, Elsie."

The blonde studied her for a long moment before she walked over to her, taking her in a tight hug, which Roishin returned. "I don't understand all this," Elsie murmured. "And I have no idea what will happen tonight, what I need to do, or what you'll have to do, but if it gives me some part of you to keep with me..." She caressed her face before kissing her lips. "I'll do it."

Nodding, Roishin took her hand as she stepped away from her. "All right. Ready?"

"Should I douse the fire?" Elsie asked. "I didn't want to cause any suspicion by asking Patrick not to light one, so..."

Roishin gave her a winning smile. "Where I'm taking you we have all night, but when I bring you back here, no time will have passed at all." She nodded toward the fireplace. "Including your fire."

She held to Elsie's hand as she led them to the door, stepping through and into...

...a small cave. It was about the size of Elsie's current bedchamber, as there was no need for anything larger. The space was warmed by the many candles she'd lit, the heat bouncing off the stone walls, floor, and curved ceiling, making it incredibly cozy. She'd also brought in many quilts before she'd left for Ava's mission, creating a soft nest for them, replete with pillows.

The phallus and her knife sat atop the quilts. Elsie looked around, eyes wide and a smile growing on her lips. "It's so warm and wonderful in here."

Roishin smiled, reaching up to tug the tie of her cloak loose. "I'm so glad you like it." She shrugged the garment off and tossed it aside, away from their makeshift bed and the strategically placed candles—close enough to give them light and warmth, but plenty far enough to not accidentally get knocked over.

Elsie glanced at the bed and then at Roishin, looking a bit baffled. "Is this some sort of sacrifice?"

Roishin chuckled, shaking her head. "No." She walked over to Elsie and, hands on her hips, lightly pulled their bodies together. "With a few alterations," she murmured, her lips mere inches from those of the woman pressed lightly against her. "Tonight, you and I are going to make a baby the traditional way."

Elsie looked at her, stunned. "Really?"

Roishin nodded. "I know I came to you with this, Elsie," she said softly, looking into the beautiful blue eyes turned goldish gray in the candlelight. "Just as Enori came to me. But I need to know that you absolutely want this." She gave her a sweet smile. "It can't be undone. It's a real pregnancy."

"And," Elsie said, her hand sliding from Roishin's face into her hair. "It would be yours? Yours and mine?"

"Aye."

Elsie brought her lips to Roishin's. "Then that's all I need to know."

The kiss was fiery, the knowledge and understanding of what it all meant seeming to ignite Elsie. Roishin returned her passion, certainly for what they were about to create, but it was also a second chance for them to truly make love, to both be naked and free to enjoy each other. This time, she wasn't going to allow herself to worry or feel guilty. This *needed* to happen, Garratt or no Garratt.

The thought of having all night with Elsie nearly made Roishin orgasm right there from anticipation. But, she knew she wanted to slow things down. She had no idea if she'd ever make love to Elsie again after this, so she wanted to take her time and remember every moment.

Slowing the kiss, she pulled away and rested their foreheads together. Both were breathing hard, the energy between them thick and heavy. She eased the sleeveless tunic up and over Elsie's head, revealing the simple dress beneath. She resumed their kiss, though slow, exploratory. She wanted to gradually build their fire and not be consumed by it before they'd even undressed.

Seeming to understand, Elsie's fingers played absently through the strands of Roishin's hair as they kissed. The little moans that escaped Elsie's lips into their kiss were throwing more logs onto that fire. Bringing her fingers up, Roishin began to work the buttons on Elsie's dress, so badly wanting to see her again, touch her again.

Once the buttons were all undone, Elsie eased her arms out of the sleeves and the top half of the dress flopped down to her hips. Even through the material of her chemise, Roishin could see her nipples were hard, the firelight licking a shadow across the rigid flesh. She brushed her fingernails over the tips, making Elsie gasp.

Her mouth watering for them, Roishin couldn't wait any longer. She took a step back from her, quickly undressing herself while Elsie removed the remainder of her own clothing. Roishin moved the phallus and dagger aside—there would be plenty of time for that—and lowered herself to the quilt. Elsie joined her, though she stopped when she spied the phallus.

She stared at it for a long moment before she gasped. Eyes wide and hand over her mouth, she looked to Roishin. "That's what Cateline was talking about!" Her hand fell away. "Isn't it?" Roishin just stared at her. Elsie chuckled, seeming to realize the question was ridiculous considering Roishin hadn't been present for that chat. "She said there is something made for a woman to make love to another woman like a man."

Roishin felt a wee bit uncomfortable in that moment, knowing her parents had more than likely used this very type of thing in their own lovemaking. She gave her a sheepish grin. "Aye."

"So," Elsie said, her voice nearly a purr as she lay down and pulled Roishin on top of her. A sexy little smile crossed her lips as her fingertips trailed down along Roishin's spine. "Does this mean you'll be my first then?"

"Aye. Is that okay?"

Elsie leaned her head up and left a kiss on her lips. "I wouldn't want it any other way," she whispered. "Garratt may have my hand, but he'll never have my heart."

# Chapter Twenty-three

Their kiss was soft, Roishin's hand running down along Elsie's side, urging her leg to bend when she cupped the underside of her thigh. The feel of Elsie's mouth, her breasts pressed to her own, and her fingers roaming over Roishin's back, her shoulders, and into her hair felt so good.

She could feel how aroused Elsie was, and that made her feel a lot better, knowing she was far less likely to hurt her when it came time to use the phallus. She remembered overhearing a couple of servants talking years back, no idea a curious little Roishin was around. One had mentioned the reason it had hurt was, in her words, "He hadn't bothered to get me ready."

At the time, she'd had no idea what that meant. But now, feeling so much wetness building against her thigh that was pressed between Elsie's legs, she fully understood. She groaned at the amount of wetness. She left soft lips and moved to an even softer neck. Elsie sighed as her head fell to the side, giving Roishin as much access as she wanted.

"Did you ever think, all those years ago watching my behind as I picked up your trail of clothing, that we'd be here?"

Roishin chuckled deep in her throat. "That is a mighty big no," she murmured into the softness she was sampling.

"Colossal, no?" Elsie teased, words breathy as she arched her back, pressing her breast farther into Roishin's hand.

"Nicely done," Roishin murmured right before she took a nipple into her mouth. She moaned right along with Elsie, loving the feel of her fingers in her hair.

She absolutely loved how responsive Elsie was to her, how sensitive her body seemed to be. She loved how excited she got, how wet. As she moved to the other breast, she had the strangest feeling. She literally *ached* to be inside of her. She felt a burn deep in her belly, and it was almost as if something was telling her the time was now.

Releasing the breast, she moved up to Elsie's lips. "Are you ready?" She looked into Elsie's flushed face, her eyes hooded. At her nod, Roishin left a kiss on her lips before climbing off her.

She walked over to the phallus and began to strap it on. She was so aroused that her hands were trembling. Glancing over when she heard Elsie get up, she watched as the absolutely beautiful woman walked over to her.

"Can I help?" she asked, her gaze falling to the phallus portion of the contraption before meeting Roishin's eyes.

Swallowing hard, Roishin instructed her what strap went where to get buckled in. The feel of her touch, soft on her body, was making Roishin's heart race in her chest. She was so sensitized.

"Too tight?" Elsie asked softly.

"No."

The contraption buckled into place, Elsie looked down at it again, wonder and curiosity in her eyes. "Can I touch it?" At Roishin's nod, she lightly brushed the soft leather with her fingertips, running them down the length of it, lightly tapping it. She giggled when it bobbed obscenely from Roishin's body. "Sorry. Is this like the real thing?"

"I don't know," Roishin said. No doubt, neither of them wanted to even put thought into the fact that, soon enough, Elsie would very much know.

Wrapping her hand around it, Elsie stepped up to Roishin and initiated a sweet kiss, so tender and full of love. Roishin felt like it was her way of letting her know that, regardless of how unorthodox the situation was, she accepted it.

Pulling out of the kiss, she murmured against Roishin's lips, "Let's make a baby."

Elsie took her by the hand and led the way back to the little quilt nest. She lowered herself to lie on her back, watching as Roishin did the same, though she stayed on her knees.

"What do you need me to do?" Elsie asked.

Roishin nudged her to lift her knees and spread her legs, Roishin positioning herself between them. She could see how wet Elsie was, her sex flushed and swollen. She remembered the last time they were together in the woods and how much Elsie had loved for that special place to be stroked with her fingers.

Looking up the length of Elsie's gorgeous body, she met her eyes. She saw so much love, so much trust in their depths as she watched her. Roishin took hold of the phallus and turned her attention back to what was before her. She decided to use the tip to rub on that same spot, making sure she was ready for this.

Placing the length of the phallus against her sex, she used her hips to ease the slightly enlarged tip on that special spot. Elsie's eyes closed and her lips fell open. Roishin glided her hands down along the softness of her spread thighs, loving the feel of the skin. This was also helping her get a feel for the rhythm her hips would need to set. She remembered Enori telling her to go slow.

Reaching over, Roishin grabbed her dagger and held it in her hand as she got settled back into place. "Are you ready?" she asked, her words breathy as her body vibrated with need.

Elsie nodded. "Aye."

Roishin winced as she sliced the tip of her finger with the blade, setting it aside as she focused on the blood beading up. She began her intention, focusing on the purpose for tonight, what was to come of this union. A warmth began to spread through her as the words marinated over and over again in her mind and into her soul.

Stopping her movements, she took the phallus, now covered in Elsie's need, in her hand and brought her cut finger to the tip. She lightly coated it with her precious life force before guiding the phallus to Elsie's entrance. She eased it through the swollen folds until the blood-tipped head disappeared inside of her.

Roishin's gaze went up to Elsie's when she heard a little gasp. She kept her eyes on her face, looking for any hint of pain or that she should stop. Getting none, she continued to ease herself inside. When her hips were fully flush with Elsie's, she let out a slow, shaky breath.

"Are you all right?" she whispered. Elsie nodded, her eyes remaining closed, and Roishin remained kneeling between her legs as she slowly eased her hips back, not fully pulling out before gently pushing back in.

The smallest whimper escaped Elsie's lips, and though it didn't seem like pain, Roishin wasn't sure if she'd quite call it pleasure. She caressed her thighs as she began a very slow rhythm, in and out.

Her hands roamed up over her belly, thinking

that in a matter of months, what they planted there would begin to grow. Up over her belly and to her breasts, her hands massaged both of them, thumbs lightly running over hard nipples. A quiet sigh of pleasure left Elsie's lips, her own hips ever so slightly beginning to move. Roishin used her fingers to pinch and tug the rigid flesh, earning her more soft sighs and moans, and more movement of Elsie's hips.

"Does it feel good?" Roishin whispered.

Elsie's nod was vigorous, her eyes never opening. "It's beginning to, yes."

Needing to be close to her, Roishin lowered herself until she was resting over Eslie's body. She braced her upper body on her forearms as she continued her slow thrusting.

Elsie immediately wrapped her hands around the backs of Roishin's shoulders. Her legs spread wider and knees raised closer toward her body. Roishin lowered her lips to Elsie's, needing to feel as connected to her as possible. Elsie responded, one of her hands moving into short, dark hair.

Their kiss was slow and lazy, much like the rhythm of Roishin's hips. It was the most amazing feeling in the world to be inside of Elsie, to hear the immense wetness with each gentle thrust. The sounds Elsie was making were driving her wild. Their kisses were punctuated by little sighs and whimpers of pleasure, pleasure which Roishin could feel, too. Each thrust inside put pressure against her own swollen wetness.

Soon, Elsie was breathing entirely too hard to kiss. Roishin lifted her head, her own breathing deeper and more rapid. Elsie's hips had also increased their movement against her own, seeming to be asking her to quicken her rhythm.

Raising herself to her hands, Roishin moved her

hips faster, the phallus easily sliding in and out, Elsie was so wet. As her thrusts picked up, so did Elsie's moans. Her hands gripped Roishin's forearms in a viselike grip as she seemed to be hanging on for dear life. Roishin's eyes slid closed, the pleasure nonstop.

She remembered back to their first time, in this very position, and how she thought it felt so much like she was inside of Elsie. Now, she actually *was*, and she felt her very soul was making love to Elsie's. In her heart, she knew it would work. She knew Elsie's body was in the process of accepting all that Roishin was giving it and would soon begin a life.

That thought pulled her orgasm out of her, her cry loud and long as it seemed to pull her very soul from her body with its intensity. Within a few thrusts, Elsie gasped loudly beneath her, her entire body arching up into Roishin's. Her nails dug into the flesh of Roishin's arms as her eyes squeezed shut and teeth bared as her release exploded out of her.

Roishin didn't stop thrusting until Elsie's cries died down to little mewls. Panting from the experience and the exertion, she stilled her hips and was pulled down into a bone-crushing hug. Elsie wrapped her legs around her hips and arms around her back. Roishin held her just as tightly, their bodies essentially one.

The tears came, hard and fast, for them both. Roishin was surprised at her own, but she was just so overwhelmed by the experience. She had to imagine the same was true for Elsie. The tears still flowing, she kissed her deeply, their lips salty as they met.

"I love you, Roishin," Elsie whispered.

"I love you, too." Roishin lifted her head, resting on her forearms as she used her hands to brush back golden hair from Elsie's beautiful face. "Are you okay?"

Elsie nodded. "Aye. Honestly, I think that's

the most beautiful thing I've ever experienced." She smiled. "I feel it, Roishin. It worked."

Roishin nodded. "I do, too." She grinned. "Maybe we'll have twins."

Elsie quirked an eyebrow. "Will you be carrying one, then?"

Roishin initiated a slow, deep kiss to connect. It ended sweetly before Roishin was released, Elsie's legs falling free. Roishin eased out of her, noting the blood was completely gone. Not a huge surprise considering the amount of wetness, but she was glad. She unbuckled herself and tossed the contraption over by the dagger at the end of the quilt, then lay back down.

Elsie cuddled up to her, resting her head on her shoulder. "Are you warm enough?" Roishin asked.

Without a word, Elsie sat up and grabbed the folded quilt that sat atop a large rock nearby. She gave it a shake and covered their bodies with it once she lay back down against Roishin.

After a bit of contented silence, Roishin's fingers playing absently in Elsie's hair while Elsie's fingers traced random patterns over Roishin's stomach, Elsie spoke. "You've said a few times that we'll have a girl. How do you know that? Did Enori tell you?"

"No." She smiled. "Believe it or not, I had a vision of her when I was just shy of thirteen. Isabeau had just come to us. Obviously, I had no idea who I was seeing at the time, but she was with Isabeau."

"In the vision, you mean?"

"Aye." She was silent for a moment as she saw the two young women again from her vision in her mind's eye. "Both young women, Isabeau perhaps just a bit younger than you are now. Our daughter just a bit younger than me."

"And you think that was her?" Elsie asked softly,

fingertip trailing along the rounded underside of Roishin's breast.

"I know it was."

"What did she look like?" Elsie asked, her voice soft, almost reverent.

"You." Roishin smiled at the small slap to her stomach. "No, I'm serious. She looked a lot like you, your beautiful golden hair. Your gorgeous mouth. But she had my eyes."

Elsie raised her head, resting it in her palm as she planted her elbow into the quilt next to the pillow Roishin's head rested on. "What is her name?"

"I don't know," Roshin said, looking up into that beautiful face. "What is it?"

"She's not just mine, Roishin."

"No, she'll be Garratt's, too." Roishin was just barely able to keep the bitterness out of her voice. Elsie didn't need that. "He'll be the one there for that conversation."

Elsie let out a heavy sigh. "Aye," she finally muttered. "But I think we should come up with one that I can offer as a suggestion."

"How about after your mother?" Roishin suggested with a shrug. "To honor her, bring in some of your heritage."

"Then, how about my great-great-grandmother?" Elsie suggested. "Mariota?"

"The Druid?" At Elsie's nod, Roishin smiled. "I think it's incredibly fitting. Don't you?"

"Aye," Elsie murmured.

Roishin sighed into the kiss that Elsie initiated, somehow her body responding to Elsie's touch already. She would have thought that after the experience they'd had, she'd be sated for weeks. But, as Elsie's tongue teased her own, soft fingers teased her nipple, lightly tugging it erect before rolling it with the pads of her fingers, she felt her own desire rise.

"Roishin," Elsie murmured against her lips. "I want to be inside of you."

Roishin nodded, easing her legs open as she took the hand on her breast and guided it down to the volcanic wetness between her thighs. She sighed at the first contact of Elsie's fingers. She'd never before been touched like that. She had no idea what to expect, but she knew she wanted to feel her inside.

Elsie moaned as her fingers easily slid within Roishin's depths. "So soft," she whispered against Roishin's lips.

Roishin's eyes closed as she fell out of the kiss, concentrating on the feeling of Elsie's fingers easing back out before gently moving back in. She moved her hips in sync with Elsie's hand. A long, languid groan fell from her lips when Elsie's mouth found her breast, a hot tongue gliding over her nipple.

She opened her thighs wider as sensations oozed through her like hot molasses. Her breasts were heaving as the pleasure grew, between the mouth on her breast and fingers inside her. Her body was on sensation overload. Elsie began to bat her nipple with her tongue in time with her thrusts inside of her.

The pleasure built with each thrust, each lick and suck. Finally, it crashed over her. Her back arched and her thighs slapped shut around Elsie's hand, imprisoning it as she rode out her orgasm. She was gasping for breath as her legs fell open and then limply back to the quilt.

The mouth disappeared from her breast and was at her face, raining kisses down along with murmured words of love. Finally, Roishin wrapped her arms around Elsie, pulling her to lie atop her. Still panting, she held on, desperate for her warmth against her.

"I love you," she managed.

"And I you," Elsie said softly. "With all my heart."

⁂

The water rained down upon her bowed head, her falling tears mixing with the diamond-like droplets. It was all actually quite beautiful, if she could see beyond the devastation. They'd made love a few more times before it was over, because they both knew that was it. They'd gotten dressed in silence, each lost in her own sorrow and regret.

Candles blown out, Roishin had taken Elsie back to her bedchamber. Again, in silence, they'd held each other. There was nothing left to say. Finally, with a kiss, Roishin had let go of her and backed away to the door with one last look.

Now, her eyes hurt, her throat hurt, and her heart hurt. Perhaps it had been a mistake to give herself like that. She'd already given Elsie her heart, and now she'd given her part of her very soul. Blowing out a breath, she raised her face to the spray and pushed her hair back. It was time to clean herself up, time to accept what she had no choice *but* to accept.

To her surprise and gratitude, sleep came quickly, drawing her beneath its dark blanket of peace.

# *Chapter Twenty-four*

Roishin absolutely could not remember ever feeling as dark as she did when she woke up. She'd slept straight through the night and wasn't even sure she'd changed sleeping positions. But, her eyes burned and her face felt tight from the waterfall of tears. It certainly didn't help in the "forget about it" department when her body was so sore.

With a groan she sat up in bed, running a hand through her hair, which stuck up in crazy directions as she'd gone to bed with wet hair. "Brilliant," she muttered, shoving the covers off her.

She quickly cleaned up her bedroom to military specs, then headed downstairs. Enori sat at the kitchen table eating her ever-present fruit for breakfast. She'd gotten Roishin into it as well. Roishin could feel her entire bodily energy makeup changing since living in Duras.

It didn't take as much sustenance, nor as heavy. She had no cravings for meat or some of the so-called "meat packing" suppers she'd lived on all her life in Sursha. There, it was about staying healthy and warm. No need for that in Duras, as things just seemed simpler, somehow.

"Good morrow," Enori said, just before popping a cube of pineapple into her mouth. "Coffee is made for you."

Roishin nodded acknowledgment as she made her way to the percolator. The look Enori gave her every time she drank it was amusing, the priestess very much not a fan of the beverage. The silence stretched out as Roishin readied her mug, which Enori had also left out for her. Very kind. Sadly, on this morning very little registered in her mind but the terrible turmoil she was feeling.

Glancing to the table, Roishin studied Enori for a moment. She continued to eat in the quiet way she did just about everything. Over the months, Roishin had learned what to listen for and now pretty much knew where Enori was in the house at any time. It was a strange hearing-sensing combo.

It had been nice to finally get that tuned, as Enori had scared the living crap out of her more often than she cared to count in her early days. She'd turn around and… *Bam*! There she was. Carrying her mug to the table, she took her seat. She eyed her mentor, who was reading over a stack of parchments set on the table just to the side of the small plate she had before her. The fruit was in a large bowl at the center of the table, enough for them both.

Not hungry, Roishin focused on her coffee. She hoped that it gave her some semblance of feeling human. She just felt…empty. And, looking across the table to Enori, who looked so relaxed, so calm, and so goddamn beautiful, it just made her angry. She felt almost like she'd been set up. Again.

"Do you have any questions?" she muttered, mug of coffee to her lips. "Since it was at *your* request I do this."

Enori lifted her gaze from her reading to Roishin. "Do you have any answers?"

Roishin smirked. Setting the mug down, she tilted her head as she studied Enori. "No." She snorted. "In fact, all I got is more questions. Like, why didn't you tell me the truth about The Mystic?"

Enori placed her elbows on the table on either side of her plate and laced her fingers as she rested her chin on them. Clearly, she was settling in for whatever Roishin had to say. "It was not my truth to tell," she said simply.

Roishin smirked. "Right." She took another sip. "And what was last night, Enori? Just another of your *tests*?" She slammed the mug down on the table. "To see how much I can endure? How much more you can fuck with me?" She brought up her hands, using her fingers as air quotes. "Go on a surveillance mission for Ava Gentry." She glared at her. "A test! A goddamn test!"

She shoved back from the table, needing some space from the person she had decided was the perfect target for her rage.

"Would Ailfred have sent young Fallon out onto the battlefield without testing her strengths, Roishin?" Enori asked in that infernal soft voice of hers. How could she remain so calm during a time like this?

Running her hands through her crazy hair from where she stood in the living space, Roishin looked at her. "How would I know?" she sneered. "He's dead."

"And so would Ava Gentry be if you had not followed the strong instinct that I knew you had inside you."

Roishin opened her mouth for another tart remark, but nothing came out. All she could do was stand there dumbly. She didn't know what to say or what to do.

"Today," Enori continued softly. "I am organizing a cleanup crew to—"

"I want to be part of it," Roishin interrupted.

"—clean up Ava's life," Enori finished, as though Roishin hadn't said a word. "They will take everything, and it will be as if Ava was never even there."

"I want to be part of it," Roishin said again, her voice louder, more demanding.

Enori pushed back from the table and made her way over to her. Standing a couple feet away, she tilted her head slightly, looking into Roishin's face. No, it was more like she was looking into her damn soul. Finally, the softest smile touched full lips.

"All right," she murmured. "You will go."

⚜ ⚜ ⚜ ⚜

They stood inside the Crystal Palace, the familiar red energy swirling around them. Even in the pitch darkness, Roishin could feel Enori's eyes on her. She looked her way, just barely catching a small bit of that beautiful face as luminescent red caressed it before it was gone.

"I'm sending you ahead to the saloon," Enori said. "You can do what you need to do there while we work on her room at the boarding house and the theatre."

Roishin's eyebrows drew. "Okay." She didn't remember any saloons in Ava Gentry's biography. She was about to voice that when Enori began creating a door.

"This is for you, Roishin," she said. "Go. I will meet you there later."

Nodding, Roishin dutifully stepped through and…

…into a saloon, sure enough. Her boots thudded dully on the wide-plank boards of the floor. Some were knotted and buckled a bit from time and settling of the building. There was a bar that ran the entire length of the wall to her right, stocked with glassware and corked bottles filled with gods only knew what. No doubt the content was strong enough to burn away Roishin's nose hairs.

Round wooden tables peppered the area, wooden chairs to match stacked atop them as if the saloon was closed. An upright piano was tucked into the corner, the lid closed over the keys and bench seat stowed beneath the keyboard, its legs straddling the player pedals.

Everything was present that made a saloon a saloon. Everything, that is, except an ounce of life, an ounce of feeling that there ever *was* life. Confused, she walked over to the swinging doors. From a distance, it looked like there was a world beyond. But, upon closer inspection, Roishin saw that it was a mirage. There was nothing beyond the doors, which stood stock-still. She poked one, expecting it to swing outward, but it didn't move.

Turning back to look at the room at large, she felt a sinking suspicion creep inside. Though she'd never been on such a thing, she felt like she was on what she'd learned from her readings was called a soundstage. This location, as authentic as it seemed, was totally a setup.

The rage began to build anew. "You fucking lied!" she yelled at the top of her voice.

She tried desperately to focus in order to create a door, but nothing happened. Her mind wouldn't settle, and she felt absolutely impotent to do anything. She wanted to cry, she wanted to tear the place apart with her bare hands, and she wanted to go home. But then, where was that?

It was then that she noticed something at the beautiful bar. The bar itself had ornate designs carved into the front, and a brass pole that ran horizontally along the lower front. There, a cowboy could rest his boot while he drank his whiskey. But that hadn't been what caught her eye.

A sledgehammer leaned against that bar. Its ten-pound steel head rested against the wood floor while the thirty-six-inch wooden handle leaned against the front of the bar. Her chest heaving with her outburst and building rage, Roishin stared at the tool whose sole purpose was to destroy.

Teeth clamping together and jaw muscles bulging, she walked over to it and picked it up. She studied the demolishing end of the tool, fingers taking a good, tight grip around the handle. Looking over toward the closest table to her, she walked over, stopping just a foot away.

With an unearthly roar, Roishin unleashed. The head of the sledgehammer crashed through the spindles that helped stabilize the legs. Next, the seat, which she chopped at until it gave and split in two. Chest heaving, she used a hand to grab what was left of the chair and threw it behind her, listening with satisfaction as it crashed against the bar.

She was about to start on the next chair but then caught sight of     all the glassware behind the bar. Far less work and far more mess and noise, she thought. With a mighty shove from her booted foot, the table slid into another table, sending stacked chairs toppling. Sledgehammer in hand, she made her way behind the bar.

First, she made quick work of the cash register. The elegant metal machine was built to withstand an attack to secure what was inside, but that didn't stop the keys from being smashed to smithereens, nor the entire heavy machine being toppled to the floor on the other side of the bar. The racket was horrible, the sound ringing in Roishin's ears.

She didn't care. She had more rage to get out. So much more.

Her intended target came back into view and, with gritted teeth, she smashed every single glass, shards exploding into the air and catching in her hair, on the front of her tunic shirt, and even a larger one cutting into her chin. Panting heavily, she caught sight of herself in the mirror that spanned the entire back wall behind the bar.

She did not recognize the woman staring back at her. The deep green of her eyes was nearly black. Her teeth were bared, the snarl animalistic. With an unholy growl, she sent the head of the sledgehammer into that image, the glass shattering, splintering that one demon of fury into a thousand pieces. Next went the bottles as she rammed that sledgehammer into the first one baseball bat style, and she didn't stop until all of them had been shattered, broken, or knocked to the ground only to break.

It was only then, as the putrid smells of strong alcohol, sweat, and blood hit her nose, that her rage began to lower from a boil to a simmer. As she dropped the sledgehammer with a loud *bang* on the wood floor near her feet, the burner was turned off altogether. She was breathing hard, her shirt had become a second skin, and hair stuck to her scalp from sweat, bangs in her eyes.

She turned and faced the expanse of the room, and that's when she saw Enori standing there, in the area between the tables and the bar. She said nothing, just stood there. Roishin met her gaze for a long moment before, almost as if in a daze, she walked over to her, her entire being seeming to deflate.

Her head fell in shame of her rageful behavior that morning. Enori simply wrapped her in her arms. She cradled Roishin's head against her shoulder, her hand feeling cool as it cupped the back of Roishin's heated neck. Roishin returned the embrace, the two standing there, Roishin allowing herself to be held. There were no words, no need.

After long moments, Enori left a kiss on the side of her head. "Let's go home," she whispered.

⁂

The ceremony was well underway, crowds gathered for the momentous event. Needing to see it, needing that permission to finally let go, Roishin watched.

Garratt looked handsome as ever, dressed in his military attire, of course. He beamed as he faced the woman before him, their hands entwined. Elsie had never looked more beautiful, her gown of blue, white, and cream. She spoke, words unheard.

Roishin didn't need to hear the words, as they meant nothing to her. She needed to see it, and seeing it she was. She'd done her part, and soon enough Elsie would have proof she was with child. Bells would toll across the country in great joy of the new life. No doubt, the prince of Sursha would be slapped on the back by his comrades for a job well done.

She smirked at the thought. The one tiny glint of light in this otherwise dark situation. A secret, one that only Roishin and the bride knew. A bride who, for just a split second, glanced her way. From across the expanse, Roishin met her gaze. With a nod of acknowledgment, she turned and headed to the double doors at the back of the cathedral.

Taking a steadying breath, she pulled one open and stepped through, the door slowly closing behind her.

# *Epilogue*

Modern day – Somewhere in the Mediterranean Sea

Stretching his arms high overhead, Professor of Marine Archaeology Dr. Darby Hollis stepped out onto the deck of the *Endeavor*. It was the vessel he and his team from East Carolina University had commissioned for their research. It had already been a grueling, and somewhat disappointing, two weeks of their three-week expedition.

"Beautiful morning," he said to research assistant, Laura Fielding. She was a grad student in the program, and certainly a little hottie to look at. He gave her what he'd always thought was his winning smile. She simply nodded in acknowledgment.

"We may have found something, Dr. Hollis," she said, the dark lenses of her sunglasses shielding gray eyes.

Instantly, any thoughts of flirting flew out of the fifty-one-year-old's mind. He hurried over to her, running a hand through a full head of sandy blond hair. "What's up?"

Laura was standing near the monitors that showed the live feed from the cameras their divers had on their person. Her brown hair was pulled back into a ponytail, which blew slightly on the sea breeze. She said nothing, simply stepped aside for him.

It took a moment for him to get oriented, as there was a lot of silt covering much of the image for a moment as the divers used gloved hands and brushes to try to remove the layers from whatever they'd found. It was clearly not a shipwreck, which was why they were there in the first place.

Though disappointment initially coursed through him, Darby pushed that aside. He'd done enough of these in his career, both inside and outside of academia, to know that this could be part of a debris field. He certainly hoped, anyway.

"What is that?" he murmured, leaning in a bit closer to the screen. He felt Laura leaning in next to him.

"It looks like…" Laura grew silent as more was revealed on screen. "A chest?"

"Definitely metal. Look at those chains around it," he said, marveling at the image as the object came into better focus.

"I think that's a trunk," she said. "Look at the shape." She used a finger to lightly outline what seemed to be edges of a rectangular object, despite the patina that distorted the shape a bit.

He nodded. "Yes, I agree." He grinned, thrilled. Clapping his hands together once, he called out. "Let's bring it up!"


The journey continues in book 4, She Who Dreams.

# *About the Author*

Kim has spent her life in Colorado and can't imagine living anywhere else. She's been writing since she was 9 and stumbled into her first book being published in her mid-20s. She's worked in the film industry as a writer, director and producer, but now enjoys the quiet, happy life of a professional author. She can be reached on Facebook and on her website at, www. kimpritekel.com

# *If you liked this book...*

Share a review with your friends or post a review on your favorite site like Amazon, Goodreads, Barnes and Noble, or anywhere you purchased the book. Or perhaps share a posting on your social media sites and help spread the word.

Join the Sapphire Newsletter and keep up with all your favorite authors.

Did we mention you get a free book for joining our team?

sign-up at - www.sapphirebooks.com

## *Check out Kim's other books.*

*1049 Club* - ISBN - 978-1-939062-97-0

Almost two hundred souls, one plane, six survivors, endless heartbreak.

When flight 1049, headed from Buffalo, NY to Italy falls from the sky, a firestorm of drama, pain, angst and sorrow ensues. Can an author, a business owner, a teenager, good ol' boy, veterinarian and ruthless lawyer survive? Better yet, can those left behind?

1049 Club is a story of survival, love, deep regret and miracles. Can the living make peace with the presumed dead? Can the presumed dead make peace with the lives and loves they thought they had before?

*Blinded* – ISBN – 978-1-943353-53-8

After a horrible explosion sends local television news reporter, Burton Blinde reeling both physically and emotionally, she walks away from her life and the dream job she was about to start at a major news network.

For six long years she hides out in a small mountain town, working at the local library, though is haunted by the life she had, including mysterious messages and gifts she was receiving before her life was turned upside down, a veritable bread crumb trail leading to the unknown.

Unable to resist, Burton begins to follow the clues,

which will lead her into the darkest places of human nature that she may not be able to return from.

*Damaged* - ISBN - 978-1-939062-45-1

Family. A group of people you are related to by blood or love.

Nora Schaeffer has come home to her family after twenty years working around the world as a photographer for National Geographic. She's welcomed into the open arms of her father and siblings.

Family. A group of people who support you, lift you up when you fall.

Shannon, the youngest of the four Schaeffer siblings, has vanished, leaving her five-year-old daughter, Bella, terrified and alone. To help find Shannon, Nora has no choice but to turn to the dark-haired specter who has haunted her for twenty years. Along the way, she finds her own long-dead heart and uncovers chilling family secrets beyond imagination.

Family. A group of people who will stick together to hide the rotten soul at its core at any cost.

Who will live? Who will die? Who will be the most damaged? And who will learn to love again?

*The Gift* - ISBN - 978-1-948232-47-0

The dead do speak. You just have to listen. Homicide Detective Catania "Nia" d'Giovanni is the only daughter in a large Italian family of six children. The backbone—a position not applied for nor wanted—she continues to create new glue to hold the dysfunctional group together. For Nia, family time feels more like herding cats than spending time with her brothers and feisty, aging parents.

Her heart has always been in her career with the Pueblo Police Department, especially since it will never be okay with her very Catholic mother to openly give her heart to any woman, until she meets a secretive waitress who has her at, Can I take your order?

And then it begins…

Three murders that are so gruesome, so horrible, they rock the small town to its core. Nia and her partner Oscar are left to piece together a deadly puzzle to find the key to unlock the monster they hunt.

Or, are they the hunted?

As they dissect the murder scenes where not one shred of evidence is left behind, more bodies begin to show up, each cleaner than the last, the shadowy specter that is the killer vanishing without a trace, making the woman Nia loves disappear right along with it.

When there is no evidence to follow, Nia must trust her instincts…or, is she being guided?

*The Plan* – ISBN – 978-1-948232-43-2

As the dark days of the Dust Bowl came to an end, the

midsection of the United States tried to rebuild and revitalize. In the small, dusty farming town of, Brooke View, Colorado, teenager, Eleanor Landry and her mother were dealing with her father, a self-appointment fire and brimstone preacher to his congregation of two. A plan to survive.

As the dark era of the robber baron comes to an end, giants of industry and innovation emerged with fabulous fortunes manifested in the mansions that dotted the landscape across the country. Lysette Landon, the teen daughter of the wealthiest family in Brooke View, was everything a good, proper girl of privilege should be. Only problem was, she wasn't dreaming of finding a young man to raise a family with. A plan to be free.

One look, one touch, all plans are off.

Secrets deeper and darker than the grave would bring Eleanor and Lysette together, their families connected by a web of lies and broken promises. A plan to escape.

Be careful because, life has other plans…

*The Traveler Book One: The Hunted* - ISBN - 978-1-948232-91-3

A story so epic one book can't contain it. BOOK ONE:

1977: In the era between flower power and the yuppie, Sonia Lucas is a young wife and mother, just starting out in life. Without warning, a strange presence and dark force enters her life, clouds building…

1917: ...and a storm brewing as the world reeled from the horrific events of World War I just before it was ravaged by a Spanish flu epidemic that would kill millions. Sephora Lloyd is a 16 year old girl lost in the responsibilities of an adult world helping to support herself and her mother. A beautiful young nun-in-training enters her life, bringing love and hope with her. That is, until a force bigger than either of them threatens everything Sephora holds dear.

Four women - three deaths - two words - one house
THE HUNTED

*The Traveler Book Two: The Hunter* - ISBN - 978-1-948232-93-7

A story so epic one book can't contain it. BOOK TWO:

1890: In the dying days of the Old West, Sally Little runs her booming brothel with the passion and tenacity the business of sex requires. Savvy and indulgent, there's one itch Sally can't let herself scratch. Afraid of hurting the woman she loves, she instead unleashes...

Present Day: ...her renovation crew and fixer upper TV show on a dilapidated mansion that has known nothing but death since a murder there in 1977. Samantha Leyton sees ratings gold in bringing the sagging old house to life, but instead she discovers only she has the power to unlock the mystery that hunted four women across time, leaving death and destruction in its wake. Can she release her sisters who came before her and finally be granted the gift of love that is stronger than any evil?

Four women - Three deaths - two words - one house
THE HUNTER

*Finding Faith* (Wynter Series Book 1) - ISBN - 978-1-952270-16-1

Faith Fitzgerald thought that if she got an education and became a high-powered attorney in Manhattan, maybe—just maybe—she'd gain the attention and respect of her absentee father. Considering he was the only parent she had left after her mother's suicide when Faith was just a child, she thought that's what it would take.

She was wrong.

What she dreamed would be glamorous and satisfying turned out to be grueling and thankless. Since she wasn't willing to play the game between the sheets, she was forced to stay in the cubicle jungle doing all the heavy lifting while the men got the credit and the rewards.

Deciding she is done, Faith packs up and, with the flip of the bird to the rearview mirror, leaves New York and heads home to Colorado. She has nothing there: no job, nowhere to live, no relationship with her father. Truth is, she barely has a relationship with herself.

On the drive home, she finds herself in Wynter, a tiny mountain town at the foot of the Rockies. Looking more like it belongs in a made-for-TV Christmas movie than on the map, Faith is utterly enchanted. When she tries her luck and buys a raffle ticket at Pop's, Wynter's charming café, her prize is far more than meets the eye—or the heart.

Enter Wyatt, a feisty, sexy southerner and waitress at Pop's, who just happens to be married to a local sheriff's deputy. All is not as it appears with the All-American boy and his Georgia peach.

A colorful cast of unforgettable and charming characters will teach the jaded attorney that sometimes to find yourself all you have to do is go back to the basics…and have a little Faith.

*Taking Liberty* (Wynter Series Book 2) - ISBN- 978-1-952270-24-6

A victim of a massive corporate downsize, Liberty Faulkner suddenly finds herself without a job, without a home, and without a plan. Though certainly not part of her vision, Libby decides that the familiar is the safest path back to her life goals. In this case, the devil she knows is home: the tiny mountain town of Wynter, Colorado, a close-knit place where everybody knows everybody and everybody's business. Seems like the perfect place for the twenty-five-year-old to start over and figure out who she is without being noticed…not.

Sergeant Grace Montez escaped her dead-end job and toxic relationship in New Mexico and moved to Wynter to help build their police department from scratch. Now an established figurehead in the community, she's got her professional life dialed in and even mentors new recruits on the force. After a challenging childhood and lifetime of abandonment and disappointment, Grace hasn't been interested in another relationship—especially because no one has caught her eye since a certain quirky college student who used to make her caramel macchiato at the local coffee shop moved away three years ago.

Now that quirky college student has returned as the beautiful, mature woman Libby has become. Can Grace keep her distance, or will she finally take liberties with what is being offered?

*Justice Won (Wynter Series Book 3)* - ISBN - 978-1-952270-36-9

In 1890, seventeen-year-old Justice Kilkoyne and her mother, Ninny, are one bad decision away from living on the streets of Azrael, Pennsylvania. Ninny's propensity for the bottle has left Justice to play the adult, her androgynous good looks helping her pass as a young man to gain employment and keep them—if just barely—above water.

Determined to find a better life for them, Justice saves every penny to get them on a train headed west to the sunshine of California. Before they can leave, the bigotry of one shopkeeper sends Justice on the run, chased by the police for a crime she didn't commit and straight into the unwitting arms of a stunning young prostitute, who, after an unexpected connection, becomes Justice's Angel.

The day arrives to leave Pennsylvania for good. As

Justice and Ninny get settled, they're surprised by the appearance of Angel, also wanting to start anew. When the trip is violently interrupted in Colorado, Angel just may be lost to Justice forever.

Can Justice find a new life when she makes her way to the fledgling mining town of Wynter, Colorado? Can her heart ever be whole again?

*Curtain Call* - ISBN - 978-1-952270-42-0

What do you do when you come from a long line of dancers that spans the globe and generations, yet you can't tell your right foot from your left? You fall in love with a dancer, of course!

Gray Rickman is an awkward seventeen-year-old when she first sets eyes on Christian Scott at the dance studio/theater Gray's parents own and run in Denver, Colorado.

Though only a handful of years older than Gray, Christian carries herself with poise and wisdom far beyond her years. A woman of few words, she speaks volumes with her body.

Before Gray even really knows what her type is, Christian stars in endless daydreams and even fulfills a couple of her fantasies before vanishing out of thin air, leaving Gray in an empty bed with nothing but bittersweet memories and broken dreams.

With no choice but to move on, Gray attempts love, even moving with her college girlfriend to New York

City to pursue a career in journalism. But her standard has been set, the bar way too high for any other woman to reach or clear. It's an unexpected encounter in an obvious place when Gray sets eyes on her dancer again. Will the bright lights of Broadway illuminate the way back to the woman of her dreams? Or will they blind her to any other possibility of happiness?

Break a leg, Gray. The Great White Way calls.

*Encore Performance* - ISBN - 978-1-952270-52-9

Grey Rickman, a journalist for The New York Times, is offered the opportunity of a lifetime and a huge boost to her career—ghostwriting a memoir for one of the world's most beloved actors. She is deeply in love with her girlfriend, dancer Christian Scott, and her world couldn't be better.

Christian, though proud of Grey and all that she's accomplished, is facing her own career dilemma. All she's ever wanted to do is perform and create, her body her kinetic canvas. But, in one of the few industries where youth matters above all else, her time is coming to make decisions that no woman in her mid-thirties should have to make: is it time to retire?

As the career of one begins to explode into the stratosphere and the other's implodes after a career-ending injury that makes any retirement discussion irrelevant, Grey and Christian begin to drift apart. Changing priorities and newly built walls lead to fears and accusations, further tearing at the fabric of the love they've worked years to create.

Will cooler heads prevail to warm up the hearts of the deeply passionate couple in time to create a new dream for their second act?

*Swann Song* - ISBN - 978-1-952270-63-5

Christine Swann is a world-famous singer/songwriter and lesbian icon, known for her edgy style and heart-pounding songs. Gorgeous, rich and miserable. Her music has always been her life, her escape from an unimaginable childhood, and choices no thirteen-year-old should have to make.

Now, pushing thirty, she wants out. From all of it.

Willow Bowman lives in the farmhouse her beloved grandmother left her, with her husband. A pediatric nurse and small-town girl, she relishes in the safety of her marriage that keeps difficult questions at bay and keeps her life quiet and peaceful, because that makes sense to her.

Until one night when Willow is driving home and is about to cross the old, rickety Dittman Bridge not far from the farmhouse, and she sees a figure jump off into the cold waters below.

The moment she jumps in and pulls the woman dressed in leather pants out, both their lives change forever.

*Keeping Hope (Wynter Series Book 4)* - ISBN - 978-1-952270-78-9

Twenty-four-year-old Hope DeSilva has been released from a three-year stint in a Georgia prison. After returning to her family property in a tiny Georgia town, she decides she's had enough of the poverty, violence, and progound family dysfunction. It's time to get out on her own. She buys a $400 car and heads to find work out west.

After the car breaks down in Colorado, she's given a ride into a mountain town called Wynter where she runs into brash, aggressive police officer Samantha Gains, who has not one ounce of patience or sympathy for a felon in her black-and-white world of right or wrong, good or bad.

But, running from her own family trauma and inexplicably bewitched by the young newcomer Hope, Samantha begins to realize that maybe her strict worldview isn't as simple as it seems. When a freak accident brings the two women together, it will take both of them letting go of their pasts to truly move on.

Take another trip to Wynter and revisit old friends as they work their magic to help Hope and Samantha find their footing—and ultimately bring them home.

*She Who Would be King* - ISBN - 978-1-952270-89-5

Cateline is the seventeen-year-old daughter of a nobleman in fourteenth-century France. It's a time when children aren't seen as those to be loved and cherished, but instead are used as pawns and bargaining chips on the chessboard of control and privilege.

She is married off to a prince in the country of Sursha, a Gaelic-speaking island nation near Ireland. Fergus, her betrothed, is next in line to take over once beloved King Carthac dies. Or is he?

Fallon, the youngest royal child and only girl, has been raised as one of the king's sons her entire life, for reasons she has never fully understood. A natural fighter, she was raised to be a warrior and head the Crown's Elite Guard assigned to protect her boorish brother Fergus.

Forced to fill in for her brother in an unexpected way, an instant attraction between Fallon and Cateline forms. In a game of thrones filled with deception and betrayal, even the most secret love can mean death.

*Control* - ISBN - 978-1-959929-01-7

Keller Mitchum has already lived a lifetime in eighteen years. Fully responsible for her five-year-old sister Parker, Keller has seen and experienced things in life that should exist in the most intense fictional plot. Wise beyond her years, she will do absolutely anything to keep Parker safe.

Garrison Davies is a twenty-three-year-old pilot in Massachusetts, working with her father in a small, family-owned cargo business. Independent, feisty, and brilliant at what she does, she makes little time for anything outside of her beloved planes and dogs. Her simple and structured world is turned on its head when a difficult situation lands two unexpected guests into her life and her house.

Garrison tries to make a safe space for Keller and Parker, only partially aware of the horrors they come from. As time passes, it becomes clear that it's not only the past that keeps the two sisters at arm's length. Can Garrison break through Keller's defenses and help her regain control?

www.ingramcontent.com/pod-product-compliance
Lightning Source LLC
Chambersburg PA
CBHW032340310726
48973CB00007B/1785